Voices from the Susquehanna: Volume II

A Collection of Diverse Fiction and Non-Fiction Writers, Poets, and Photographers

Edited by Ted M. Zurinsky

Cover illustration by Joanne Galantino

Published by Rocky Waters Publishing Group

Copyright 2011

Dedication

To Charlotte R. Wrublewski, contributor to our first anthology, whose love of family, honor, and heritage will live forever in her printed words and in our hearts.

4

TABLE OF CONTENTS

WELCOME TO AMERICA, David A. Stelzig, story 9

DEADLANDS, Joel Furches, photo 17

HOURGLASS, Joyce M. Shepherd, poem 18

HEAVENLY CREATURES, Leslie Picker, essay 19

HIS WAY, Nancy Heath, poem 21

AH, DOMINICA!, Ted M. Zurinsky, photo 22

ONE LAST TIME, Lee Bruce, essay 23

JUST LIKE GIGI, Joanne Galantino, story 26

THAT BUBBLE OF MINE, Joyce M. Shepherd, poem 36

HOPE, Joyce M. Shepherd, photo 37

THE HOMECOMING, David A. Stelzig, story 38

UNTAMED, Ann Cook, poem 58

THE PAST AS PRESENT, Joanne Galantino, story 59

BALTIMORE'S CITY HALL DOME, Marie E. Edmeades, essay 78

CITY HALL OCULUS, Marie E. Edmeades, photo 83

KUME AND THE VOLCANO, Marie E. Edmeades, story 84

BEAUTY OF THE STORM, Carla J Wiederholt, poem 92

CAFÉ SEABREEZE, Karin Harrison, story..93

VINEYARD, Joel Furches, photo..103

SYMPHONY OF A WOMAN, Joyce M. Shepherd..................................104

DIGGING WITH A PURPOSE, Leslie B. Picker, story........................105

MY SEVEN DECADES WITH POLIO, Peter Raimondi, essay..............106

MOSS ON THE RIVER, Dianna J. Zurinsky, photo............................116

STARDATE, JoAnn M. Macdonald, essay..117

CLOUD DANCER, Susan C. Buttimer, poem....................................124

RETURNING, Lee Bruce, essay..125

AUDREY GETS DRAWN IN, Joanne Galantino, story.......................129

MOVING DAY, David A. Stelzig, story..138

PRIE DIEU, Leslie Picker, photo...140

GRAVE POTENTIAL, Sarah Shilko-Mohr, story................................141

IMAGINATION, Joyce M. Shepherd, poem..153

NIGHTS OF TERROR, Karin Harrison, story....................................154

ODE TO SUMMER, Ann Cook, poem...163

ARCHITECTURE II, Ryan Twentey, photo..164

TURNABOUT, Mary Beth Creighton, story.......................................165

AT THE END OF HIS ROPE, Ann M. Cook, story.............................168

SO MUCH, SO LITTLE, Carla J. Wiederholt, poem...........................186

STOP, Joel Furches, story..187

GHOST SHIP, Ted M. Zurinsky, photo.....................................188

THE WOODEN PONY AND AN OLD MAN, Ann Cook, poem..............189

IRIE AND ME, Lois Gilbert, essay...190

LOVE, LUCK, AND LUCIANO, Sarah Shilko-Mohr, story...................193

SKIPJACK ON THE BAY, Susan C. Buttimer, photo.........................197

A BIG LIE, Lee Bruce, essay...198

A DRAGONFLY, Joyce M. Shepherd, poem/story...........................199

TWISTED FATE, Karin Harrison, story...211

ON THE EDGE OF THE INFINITE, Dianna J. Zurinsky, photo..............224

SHOOTING MARBLES, Frank Soul, essay...................................225

GRAY AND THREADBARE, Leslie B. Picker, story..........................227

MYSTICAL HANDS, Joyce M. Shepherd, poem..............................232

WINDMILL, Joel Furches, photo..233

PAYMENT, David A. Stelzig, story...234

BUTTERFLIES AND CHILDREN, Peter Raimondi, essay..................235

TAKING A NAP, Frank Soul, essay..237

ABSOLUTION, Joyce M. Shepherd, story...................................239

WINTER FROSTING, Ted M. Zurinsky, photo.................................243

Authors, Artists, Poets, and Photographers: Backgrounds..................245

9
WELCOME TO AMERICA

by David A. Stelzig

Southern Arizona. Near the Mexican border. Dry sand. Dry air above. Low bushes and scrub cacti contain a little water, but it is barricaded behind thick coats of surface wax. And so, with no buffer to prevent it, the sun will bake this desolate land. By noon, the temperature will reach ninety degrees. Mid-afternoon might even see the hundreds. But now it is night, half an hour before sunrise. The low humidity, which allows the daytime to become an oven, is also no defense to the loss of heat. The temperature has plummeted.

Jack Powers, JP to his friends and comrades, Jack to his second wife, has lived his entire 58 years—except for his marine tour in Nam—on this land. He knew it would be chilly. He is dressed in thermal underwear, insulated boots, and a heavy black leather jacket. A black woolen watch cap covers his shaved head and his ears. His face is a little chilled. So are the fingertips of his left hand, protruding from the thick plaster cast that extends to his shoulder.

Jack rubs the thumb and fingertips of his left hand with his right, and then retrieves his thermos through the open driver's side window of the Ford Explorer against which he has been leaning. Ella Mae, slouched in the passenger seat snores quietly, her round face turtled into a heavy sheepskin coat so that only her blonde curly hair is showing. Jack stares at her for a moment, and then holds the thermos between his knees, unscrews the cap, and downs the last of the liquid directly from the container. It has chilled to just lukewarm, but it is mostly brandy and feels satisfyingly warm in his throat and gut. He reseals the thermos and drops it back onto the seat, next to his holstered Colt 45 pistol. Jack owns this land. And he is its protector.

    *   *   *

Manuel Salvador Gomez pushes his backpack up onto the desert floor, then raises his head and listens intently for a few seconds before placing his hands onto the cool sand and lifting himself out of the tunnel. Quietly, he moves his pack a few feet from the opening. When he hears sand crumble into the hole, he reaches down and touches the top of his sister-in-law's head. She grabs his hand. He deftly pulls her to the surface, hugs her, whispers in her ear.

"Recepción a América." Welcome to America.

Juanita squeezes his hand. Smiles. Together they move to the edge of the tunnel and lift the tiny body of his five-year old niece as she is hoisted up to them. Juanita kneels, hugs her daughter, gently brushes sand from her long black hair. Manuel helps his older brother climb out of the tunnel. They embrace. Together they tug at the rope tied to Carlos' ankle. Two more backpacks and half a dozen gallon milk containers of water snake to the surface. Each adult slips on a pack. The brothers divide the water between them. Then, silently, they walk to the north. Manuel, having been here before, leads the way.

As they begin their journey, Manuel recalls his first trip north of the border. He had walked thirty miles from his home because Carlos, who worked for the Americans making washing machines, told him the factory was expanding. It was. But many hundreds of his countrymen had also heard this news and they had taken the jobs before Manuel arrived. With the unemployed crowding the town, finding work of any kind had been impossible. Carlos had opened his home, but it was a gift he could ill-afford. And Manuel bolted for the border.

La migra, the border patrol, had found him unconscious and near death three days later. They hospitalized him overnight, and then returned him to Mexico.

That was almost a year ago. In all that time, Manuel had been unable to find a job. Then, a week ago, the Americans laid off one quarter of their employees, including Carlos. With no money coming in and food running out, flight to the United States seemed the logical choice.

And so, Manuel is again trying to cross the desert. This time his companions, especially his young niece, add a responsibility that is like an extra ten pounds in his pack. But their presence also provides incentive. Manuel shifts the rope holding the water jugs so that it cuts less into his shoulder, slightly picks up the pace, and softly whispers, "tendré éxito." I will succeed.

*   *   *

Jack is ready to call it quits. He and Ella Mae had talked in low whispers for the first hour or so, but she has been sleeping for the last three and he is bored. Jack isn't surprised at the quiet. Even the beanheads should be smart enough not to try crossing the desert this time of year. He reaches for the truck door. Pauses. He removes his cap, cups his hand behind his ear. Yes. Something, somebody, is out there. He leans through the open window and whispers, "Ella Mae." When she doesn't respond, he tries again, just a little louder.

Ella Mae stirs, lifts her head from the coat, opens her eyes, and turns toward Jack.

"Jeez, JP, it's freezing in here."

"Quiet. Gimme the glasses."

Ella Mae sits up, alert now. She picks up the night binoculars and hands them to Jack.

"We got action, JP?" she asks, excitedly.

"Yeah. Maybe. Keep it quiet."

Jack leans on the cab of his Explorer, training the glasses toward the south. At first, there is only the electronically-enhanced image of sand and cacti on the light-green phosphor screen inside the binoculars. But when he sweeps the field a bit to the west, he sees them. A short spic in front, maybe a coyote. A few steps behind, a taller Mexican, then another shorty, this one carrying a bundle. No. The one in back leans over and the bundle becomes a child.

Damn, Jack thinks, one thing to walk across the desert, but to drag your kid with you? Clearly, family values carry little weight south of the border.

"Lemme look, JP." Ella Mae has slid into the driver's seat.

Jack hands her the glasses. She accepts them, passes his pistol to him.

"If the assholes got guns again, you take care you're not the one getting shot this time."

Jack rolls his eyes in the dark, but slips the gun into his coat pocket.

"Jeez," Ella Mae breathes, "They're gonna walk right up to us."

Even though she whispers, Jack hears her voice break with excitement. He wants to slap her, make her realize this is no goddamn game. Sure, he has an adrenaline rush too, but he didn't join the Minutemen for sport. America's borders are porous and nobody else seems to give a damn.

Jack shakes his head in disgust and reaches for the glasses. The four Mexicans are just fifty yards away, walking slowly, looking around. Must have heard us whispering, Jack thinks. He waits until they're nearly in front of the car, a mere twenty feet away, and then gives the glasses back to Ella Mae. He whispers for her to hand him the flashlight and then to turn on the headlights.

Caught in the glare of the light, the Mexicans freeze for an instant and then run. As Jack takes up the chase, he hears Ella Mae squeal with delight, "Oh boy, look at 'em run. Get 'em, JP, get 'em."

The two Mexicans in front are already nearly out of range of his powerful flash and Jack has no chance of catching them. The other two are another story. The one turns out to be a woman, the child a small girl, probably her daughter. Jack catches them easily, pushes them to the ground. He has just managed to use plastic tie-downs to cuff their wrists, a task made difficult because he has the use of only one hand, when the taller of the two men walks up, hands held high in the air. The shorter one, the one who may have been a coyote, has gotten away, but three out of four ain't bad for a night's work.

* * *

Manuel lies behind a creosote bush and watches as the gringo and his woman march the only family he knows back to their truck. He continues lying there until the headlights are out of sight. Then he stands, picks up his pack, and, crying quietly, continues his trek. It is slower going now, because he has all the water bottles and because, to a large extent, the trip is already a failure.

* * *

Five weeks pass. Manuel's luck turned markedly better. With ample water, the desert crossing was relatively easy and upon emerging he almost immediately came upon an old Mexican delivering vegetables and canned goods to a small roadside market. In exchange for helping unload the truck, the old man gave Manuel a ride to Tucson.

Manuel spent the next day and a half on the streets, but then landed a job washing cars several mornings during the week as well as all day Sunday. Better still, the owner of the carwash, maybe because Manuel proved to be an industrious worker, sent him, along with a letter of introduction, to his cousin, the owner of a small Mexican restaurant. Soon, Manuel was clearing tables and washing dishes late afternoons and early evenings, Monday through Saturday. He was excused on Sundays because he retained his job at the carwash.

13

Manuel received no salary for his duties at the restaurant, but was given a small percentage of the tips, allowed two generous meals of reasonably good food each day, and was assigned an area to sleep on the second floor. That space, which Manuel shared with twelve other young illegals, nine men and three women, was just that, an open space. Twenty feet wide by forty long, the only internal walls enclosed a small bathroom containing a toilet, washbasin with cracked mirror, and shower with lukewarm water. Small animals chewed and ran above the ceiling throughout the night, but they were no real bother. The room was air conditioned and dry and kept scrupulously clean by Manuel and his new band of brothers and sisters.

Soon Manuel was wiring nearly fifty dollars a week to his brother in Mexico.

*   *   *

Jack is in foul temper. Ella Mae started it, bitching three nights running that he didn't spend enough time with her. Then, this morning, over runny eggs and burnt toast, his cow of a wife made the same complaint, adding for good measure that he should get a job and that he spent too much time and money on his car collection.

Hell with them. Both of them. All of them, Jack thinks as he eases his classic 1933 Buick Victoria into the South Tucson Car Wash. The manager, who'd been watching a short Mexican vacuum the inside of a late model Caddy, walks over to him. Jack lowers his window.

"Senor Powers. You come for the car show. But you run late, no?"

"Hey, Hector. Still plenty of time."

"And I think you have a new automobile."

Jack grins, nods his head. "You got something new too," he says, pointing to the short Mexican. "Haven't seen that wetback before."

"No, senor! No, no! He has card. I saw." Hector raises his hands, palms toward Jack and twists them wildly, as if to erase any thought that he might hire an illegal alien.

Jack snorts his disbelief. He reaches his right hand across his body, opens the door, and steps out of the car.

"Oh, senor. Your arm. It is broke?"

"Yeah. I fell." It's a lie of course, but he is not about to admit that he'd been shot by one of this guy's countrymen.

"I'll be inside, Hector. Getting coffee. Just wash the road dust off."

"And a nice wax?"

"Nah. But chamois it dry. And don't run it through that damn machine."

"No, senor. Yours we wash by hand. Always."

Jack sips his coffee, watches through the window as the Mexican finishes vacuuming the caddy and then uncoils a hose and starts rinsing his Buick.

"Jesus!" Jack shouts and drops his coffee in the wastebasket by the door as he rushes outside.

"Hey, kid. Stop. The window's open."

Hector runs over. "Open?" he asks. Then, understanding the situation, shouts, "Manuel, parade! Parada! La ventana!"

The Mexican turns off the water, looks confused for a moment, but then hurriedly opens the car door and rolls up the window. Jack decides to forego coffee. He'll stay outside and make sure this stupid spic doesn't screw up again.

*   *   *

Eight hours later, Jack's spirits have improved considerably. He didn't win an award, but his Buick created a sensation at the car show. Afterward, he visited a flea market and bought a small oak chest of drawers, exactly what he'd been seeking for more than a year. It was painted an ugly brown, but he could take care of that. Best of all, the attractive senorita he'd bought the dresser from joined him for a couple beers at a nearby tavern. He'd gotten her phone number, but she'd laughingly rebuffed his attempts to get her to a motel, and so he decided not to spend the night in Tucson. He has just purchased a gallon of paint remover and a pack of four-aught steel wool from Wal-Mart and is on his way to the interstate to start the trip home. He is driving a little fast because it looks like rain and he doesn't want his new dresser, which is tied in the open trunk, to get wet.

*   *   *

15

Manuel is humming a happy tune. He has over a hundred dollars in his pocket and is on his way to Wal-Mart to wire it to Carlos. Furthermore, he has heard they are looking for people to stock shelves after hours. If he can get such work, a couple hours each night, he'll be making more money than he'd ever dreamed possible. He might even be able to purchase Wal-Mart clothes and other necessities at a discount. Manuel starts to cross the street, planning to cut diagonally through the corner lot and enter the parking area from the rear.

*   *   *

As Jack rounds a curve, he sees a Mexican walking down the middle of the damn street. He swerves automatically. He lifts his foot to apply the brakes, but well before it reaches the pedal the right front tire leaves the roadway and digs into the sand. The car rolls. A full three hundred and sixty degrees. Another ninety, then comes to rest, the roof leaning against a twenty-foot saguaro cactus.

Since the car is equipped with nothing that wasn't standard factory issue, there are no seatbelts. Jack is tossed like a cork in a whirlpool. He ends up on the passenger door, now the bottommost part of the car. His right arm, his only good arm, is pinned beneath him, caught on something, and he cannot move.

Just then, Jack sees the Mexican walk to the front of the car and peer through the windshield. "God, it looks like the kid from the carwash."

At about the same time, Jack hears a gurgling noise and smells solvent. The paint remover had been thrown around too and it had apparently popped open or burst a seam. In either case, it is leaking and he is now in serious trouble.

Jack yells to the Mexican. "Hey, kid. The door! Open the door!"

The Mexican stares at him, shakes his head.

"The door!" Jack shouts. "Open the goddamn door!"

The Mexican looks confused for another moment, but then smiles and climbs onto the side of the car.

Jack sees the driver's door open and feels the warm, lifesaving air wash over his face.

*   *   *

Manuel leaves the accident scene at a fast trot in the direction from which he had come. The restaurant is less than a mile away. His boss, Senor Diego, speaks English. He'll know how to call for help. But, as he nears the restaurant, Manuel slows, then stops. An Arizona highway patrol car is standing next to the curb with two police officers in the front seat. Manuel melts into the shadows and cowers there for half an hour or so, until the policemen finally drive away. Then Manuel rushes into the restaurant in search of Senor Diego.

*   *   *

It is night by the time Manuel returns, but a nearby streetlamp gives a little light. Enough that he can see the old car and even the lone occupant lying on the bottom side of the overturned vehicle.

Manuel thinks he should try to tell the gringo that help is on the way, but his eyes are closed and he seems to be sleeping peacefully. And so, rather than wake him, Manuel squats next to the car and waits for the emergency vehicle, the siren of which can be heard in the distance.

A gentle, cooling rain begins and Manuel is pleased that he was able to understand the gringo and to have climbed onto the overturned car to shut the window.

17
Joel Furches, "Deadland"

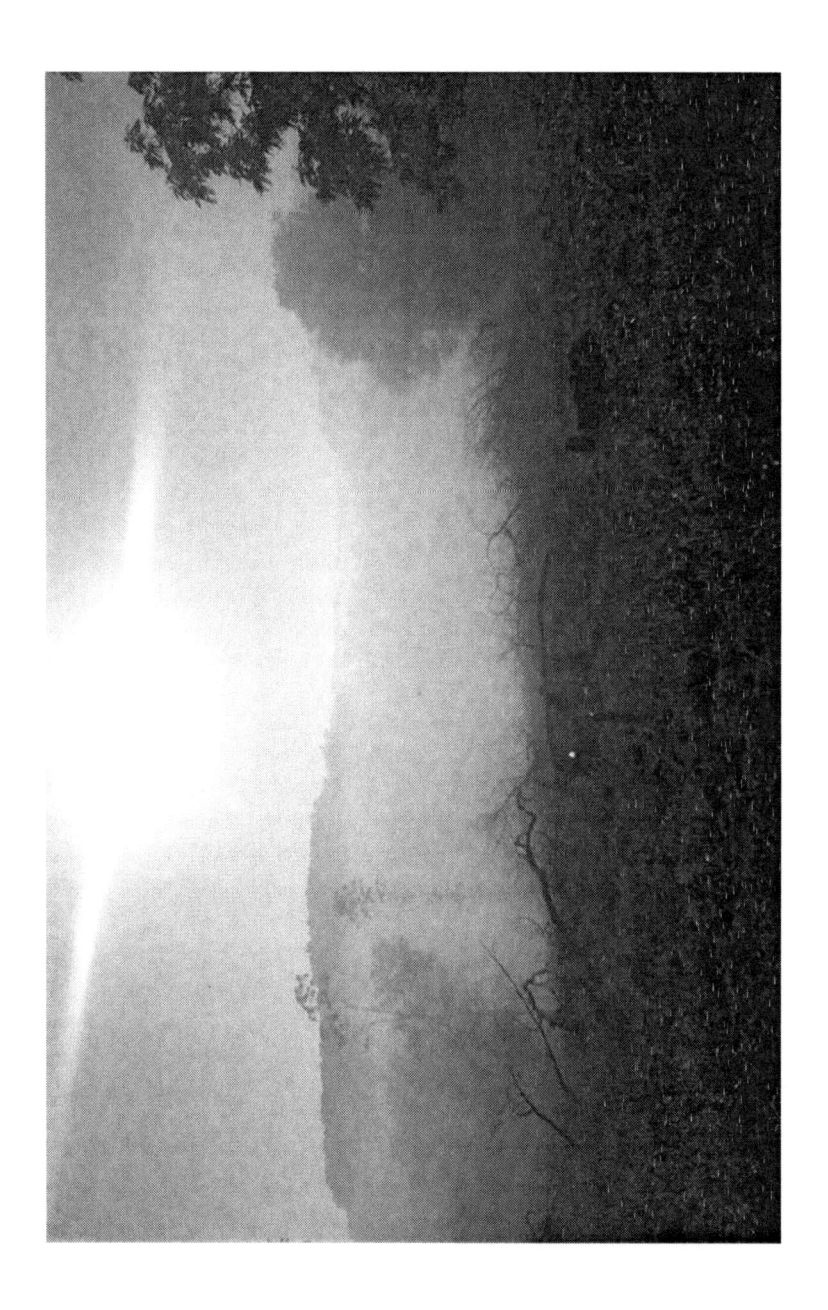

18
HOURGLASS

by Joyce Shepherd

Like the wind,
it flutters among the leaves,
whirling like a tornado, then slipping
into stillness. There is too much or, barely
enough of it. It marches on. It flies.
It stands still. As children
we think, it will
go on forever.
Grown, we
wish
there
were
more
of it.
With gray
hair we ask,
where has it gone?
Then realize it has just
ticked away. It has been
cherished, sometimes cursed.
Taken advantage of, often wasted.
We know not how much of it
we have, but how we use it
is what matters.

19
HEAVENLY CREATURES

by Leslie Picker

Barely 8:00 am on Saturday morning. I helped my six-year-old twin granddaughters, Simone and Morgan, zip up their jackets and pull on their boots, hats, and mittens. I was already tired and was thinking it would be nice to sit by the window and look out at the first snowfall with a hot cup of tea. But seeing them jump and skip around the kitchen with so much excitement changed my mind. I, too, bundled up.

Although it was supposed to be a dusting, we ended up with five and a half inches, quite a lot of snow for a skip and jump below the Mason Dixon Line. I opened the door to a blast of cold air and led the girls outside. Brrr! I pulled up the collar of my jacket. The three of us crunched up the alley adding to the footsteps that already marked someone else's progress.

The girls tasted the flakes, squealed, cavorted and giggled as we trekked through town, the joyful sounds muffled by their winter wear. The weak sun made the ground glisten and sparkle: "It looks like *diamonds!*" they shouted. The girls tried to make snowballs in their mitten-covered hands, but the dry snow didn't hold together. The flakes stuck to the wool; it smelled like lanolin.

We crossed the street, our boots starting mini-blizzards, and saw an empty lot, the virgin snow begging me to show off.

"Watch this!" I said to the girls.

I took a giant step backwards and carefully lowered myself into a sitting position. I lay down, the cold snow touching my bare neck. Sweeping my arms up over my head, I looked at the girls' puzzled expressions as they watched their "old" grandmother lying in the snow. I sat up—not as easy a task as it had been three decades earlier, and put out my hands as the girls helped me stand. I turned around to show them the snow angel.

"Wow!" they exclaimed, their eyes widening in wonder and awe. They exchanged looks and then each took a giant step backwards, one on each side of my impression.

They repeated my angel exercise, then got up, balanced on one foot in the head area, and took another step backwards into virgin snow and then stepped rearward again. Carefully, they made their way back to my side, smiling. Quite pleased with themselves, they proudly announced, "Grandma, now you're surrounded by angels!"

21
HIS WAY

by Nancy Heath

You try so hard,
You work so fast,
To meet the bills
And life's demands,
Yet stop and see
That all you do,
Your toil and pain
And efforts too
Are all for naught
For He provides, for in His world
His Love abides.

22

Ted M. Zurinsky, "Ah, Dominica!"

23
ONE LAST TIME

by Lee Bruce

The dog and I were entering the house from our early morning walk in the woods behind the house. It was not quite 7:00 am. The church bells had not pealed Morning Song. The dog fussed. I realized my phone was ringing and thought that my son, Tom, was calling to say his car wouldn't start again. I'd have to drive him from his dorm to work.

"Hello." I was expecting to hear a male voice. It was a familiar female voice, not that of my son. All sorts of images flashed through my mind. Why was my friend, Loats, calling at this hour? It was not 6 am in Iowa. This was the person with whom I had shared a dorm room for so many years. No one could speak to her in the morning until she had at least two cups of coffee and a cigarette. She must have been up all night.

How long had we been like sisters? Two slender blue eyed girls who always seemed to be exactly the same height. Both families referred to us as "the girls." We had matching certificates announcing "You Are Two. You Have Completed the Cradle Roll Class of The First Presbyterian Church." We hung the certificates side by side in our dorm room the first year of college. Now we were about to receive Social Security benefits. How time had flown by.

I thought about how she came to have such a silly name. We had had to introduce ourselves to the members of our seventh grade English class. Her given name was Leota Faye. George, our class "funster," suggested that her mother must have come up with that name in a barnyard. He said it sounded like "oats and hay". Had she been expecting a colt? We all laughed together as good friends do. She was from that day Loats to all of her friends.

"Hi."

"Hi yourself, Roomy. How are you doing?"

"How about you? How's work?" She was asking questions, not giving answers.

"The usual. No one has blamed any deaths on the diet kitchen. One VP from a local business thinks he should have his own chef. We have had a few pointed discussions." She had never been able to fathom my choice of vocation as a therapeutic dietitian and often called me Mrs. Pots and Pans.

"I'm still working on some writing, mostly sonnets. I fear Elizabeth Barrett Browning I am not."

"I hear you are supposed to write about what you have experienced. How about "Ode to the Wayward Husband"? We could both write about that.

"My next attempt should be "Milltown Girls Go Wild." Do you remember how my to-be-mother-in-law called us mill-town girls when she had never seen our quiet residential community nor met either set of parents? She thought all people from Pittsburgh lived in shacks below a smokestack.

I could not stand this banter any longer. I took a deep breath and asked what was really on her mind.

"It's back."

The awful "It." I could visualize the pain in her blue eyes. A twenty-year battle with only a year and a half respite from the worry. Now the realization that after all of everyone's efforts she was likely to lose the battle.

"I'm coming to see you in four days. I have to stop to see my brother. He isn't well. I want to go and sit in the old apple orchard behind the house." My mind flashed back to that orchard. How our mothers complained about wood slivers in our socks after we climbed those trees. Her father had made a ring of stones so that our group could cook hot dogs on wood fires, then walk up the hill to the football stadium. We all had the sweet apple-flavored smoke on our clothes. She continued, "Remember how we would sit in a tree on the bluff over the river and wonder why the Monongahela flows north? I liked to see the bridges to the south and look north to the Allenport Mill where our fathers worked, one in Building Three and one in Building Four."

So many visions of little girls: Easter dresses in our favorite colors, hers always pink and my choice of yellow or blue. I wondered if she recalled our learning to ride a bike, first dates, shared clothes, Rainbow Girls, school plays, church choir, packing for college, the sorority. Even after I said she should not marry the man she chose, she let me plan her wedding and reception.

And now this! I knew exactly what the doctor had said. Thank goodness she could not see my tears. As she would have expected, I asked if she wanted anything special to eat.

"Bob said if you should happen to ask I should casually mention meatball subs and apple pie with lots of vanilla ice cream. Is that casual enough?"

We both laughed. Neither of our voices sounded quite normal. Still I could hear the sound of shared memories wrapped in her beautiful, true soprano.

There was nothing to do but bake the pies and wait. She died ten days after our very special visit. Her ashes were scattered in the apple orchard she loved so dearly.

JUST LIKE GIGI

by Joanne Galantino

    Daisy Lanham walked home from the bus, turned on the path that led to her small townhouse, pulled out her key to unlock the door, and stood in the narrow hallway to remove her coat. Mom wouldn't be home for a while, but Daisy knew it was no time to fool around. Homework was the first thing on the agenda. Actually, it was the only thing on the agenda, because it always took her forever to get it done. She studied and slaved, and no matter how hard she tried, Daisy could never do better than a B-. It wasn't fair that Sloane Stevenson, who was always giggling and whispering during class, could get A's in everything. And Sloane always made sure everyone knew what her grades were. Plus, Daisy felt her teacher, Mrs. Delancey, didn't like her. Her voice always sounded mean when she talked to her, whereas with Sloane and the other so-called smart kids, she was always sweetie-sweetie. It didn't help that Mrs. Delancey had big, owl-like glasses, either. Those huge, horrible lenses magnified that stern look she always gave Daisy, even when she only asked to go to the bathroom. Oh well, I'll just slave away and get my big red C+. Or B-. Woo-hoo! So what if I'm not in Honor Society?
    Daisy sat down at the kitchen table and opened her English book. She had to write a rough draft of a persuasive essay. The only time she ever tried to persuade anyone to do anything was when she wanted red-glitter Dorothy shoes from Target. Daisy got down on her knees and told Mom, while holding onto her hands, that she really, really, needed them.
    "You need those like you need a hole in the head," was the answer. Daisy was five at the time, and Daddy had just left. That was six years ago, and she hadn't seen him since. Daisy was glad he was gone. And no wonder! Daddy yelled at her mom so much, calling her stupid, and telling her what she could and couldn't do and making her cry all the time. Why would he do that? Well, at least Mom wasn't crying anymore, but she was always tired and often crabby. Daisy worried about her so much. Maybe she could write a persuasive essay to Mom's boss, asking for a raise. "No, I gotta pick something else," Daisy said to herself. Just as she wrote her name and date on her paper, the phone rang. Daisy ran to it so the machine wouldn't pick it up.

"Hello?"

"Hello, Daisy? It's Aunt Patricia. Is your mom home yet?"

"No, she's still at work. She won't be home until six."

"Oh, that's right. I lost track of time; I'm at Katie's field hockey game."

Daisy wished Mom didn't have to work and had all the time in the world like Aunt Patricia did. "Do you want me to take a message?"

"Sure, Hon. Could you tell Mom that Uncle Jack and I have a golf tournament Friday and Saturday, and I'm not going to be able to do the dinner for Gigi? Grammy already said she'd watch Sophia and Kate at our house, so she can't do it, either. Tell her I'll do it twice next month."

Gigi was Daisy's 90-year-old great-grandmother. Great-Grandmother Gladys was hard for three-year-old Daisy to say, so she started calling her Gigi. Gigi loved it, and now everyone called her that, even her neighbors. Her mind was sharp and she could get around; it just took longer. Two years ago, Grammy thought it would be nice if she, Aunt Patricia, and Mom took turns preparing dinners for Gigi and delivering them on Saturdays. Gigi and Daisy were best friends, so Daisy looked forward to when it was Mom's turn.

Daisy couldn't conceal her delight. "Sure!"

"Allriiiiight, Katie!" Obviously, Katie just scored a goal. Then, the phone clicked. "I guess she heard me," Daisy shrugged and went back to her homework, smiling. Now, instead of hanging around the house on Saturday, she was going to get to see Gigi. "I can't wait to tell Mom."

*   *   *

Daisy was studying for her Social Studies quiz when Mom got home. "Hey, Mom, guess what?"

Mom put down the Chinese take-out, and went to the closet to hang up her coat. "What? What's going on?"

"Aunt Patricia just called. She and Uncle Jack have a golf tournament Friday and Saturday and—"

"What?!"

"Well, she and Grammy can't do dinner for Gigi for this weekend, so that means we get to do it."

Her mom was angry. This was the third time this happened. And, of course, because Sophia and Katie couldn't be left alone all day, Grammy would have to babysit. But she said none of this to Daisy, especially because Daisy enjoyed doing it so much. Of course Patricia wouldn't call her at work. She didn't want her to say no. She obviously thinks she doesn't have a life. She said to herself, "I guess I don't: all I do is sleep, work, and survive." She can't keep doing this, she thought. She started to dial her sister's number when Daisy spoke up.

"What can we make for Gigi? Can I help you plan?"

"We'll worry about that later. How far along are you on your homework?"

"Almost done, believe it or not. I was hoping you could help me go over my Social Studies stuff for my quiz tomorrow. We're learning about the Great Depression. It's pretty interesting."

Ms. Lanham sighed, and hung up the phone. "Story of my life."

"What, the Depression part, or the interesting part?"

"Never mind. Let's eat."

"Did you remember to get two fortune cookies this time? You have to ask for an extra one whenever we split a meal."

"No, you can have mine. That fortune stuff is bogus, anyway."

*   *   *

"Daisy, come in here and have your lunch," called Mom from the kitchen. Daisy was waiting by the door, holding the paper bouquet she made for Gigi. She made one for Mom, too, and left it by her bed, but her mother must not have seen it, because she hadn't said anything.

"When are we leaving to see Gigi?" Daisy dragged her feet.

"As soon as we've had lunch. We had Chinese take-out on Wednesday, pizza on Thursday, and Friday's dinner was Ben & Jerry's to celebrate your A+ on that Depression quiz. You've got to have real food at some point."

"At least ice cream is a dairy product; it's part of that pyramid thingy," Daisy offered.

"Yeah, and the fat and sugar put it at the tippy-top. Good thing we're both skinny-minnies," Mom laughed.

"Probably because we have to do everything ourselves. You know, like housecleaning, yard work. Aunt Patricia hires people to do all that menial stuff. That's why she has such a big..."

"Respect, Daisy."

"It's true, though. At least you can still wear two-piece bathing suits, and I don't mean those tankini ones, either."

As soon as they finished eating, they boxed up all of the food and took it to the car. The last thing Daisy carried out was the paper bouquet. She worked for hours on it, and didn't want it crushed.

Finally, they were on the road. Daisy could smell the food she and her mom prepared: roast beef with gravy, potatoes, onions, and carrots, and banana cupcakes with cream cheese frosting for dessert. Mmmmmmmmm. She always had so much fun planning and cooking those meals with her mom. She never understood why her cousins never liked visiting their great-grandmother. Being there was the best part. It was like stepping back in time, because Gigi had such cool old furniture and appliances at her house. Sophia and Katie got creeped out by the tables and chairs that had animal claws on the bottom. Didn't they watch *Animal Planet*? There was also a spare bedroom full of awesome old clothes and accessories. Sophia and Katie always said they smelled funny—so what? Daisy learned something new and exciting about Gigi every time she went to visit. Sophia and Katie always stuck close to their mother, looking at her as if to say, "Is it time to go now?"

Ms. Lanham was exhausted. There was so much to be done this weekend, and she still needed to pick up a birthday gift for Sophia's birthday party tomorrow. What do you get an eight-year-old who has her own laptop, three pairs of UGG boots, and a cell phone?

"Mom, look at the bouquet I'm giving to Gigi. Isn't it beautiful?"

"Where'd you get that?"

"Get it? I made it! Anybody can buy one from a store."

"Okay. We're here. Let's get this stuff unloaded."

"I want to give Gigi her bouquet first. I don't want it to get squooshed." She ran up the stairs onto the wooden porch where Daisy and Gigi often sat on the wicker furniture and had tea parties, surrounded by flowers she and her great-grandmother had picked. Daisy rang the doorbell and waited, because she knew it took time for Gigi to answer.

In a short moment, the door opened.

"Daisy!" cried Gigi.

"Gigi!" The two warmly embraced. Daisy held up the bouquet. "Look, I made this for you. They're roses, your favorite flower."

Tears formed in Gigi's eyes. "Daisy, this is the most beautiful gift I've gotten in a long time."

"I'm so glad you love it. I got the idea from Martha Stewart's magazine."

"Daisy! Come down here and help me with this food!"

"Oops. I forgot. We made dinner, too." Daisy ran toward the car, and helped her mother carry up the food. Gigi gave a smile to her granddaughter, but it wasn't like the one she gave Daisy when she received the bouquet.

"Hello."

"How are you, Gigi?" Mom asked, giving her a hug.

"I'm doing all right, Debra, but I thought it was Patricia's turn this week."

"No, she's doing golf with Jack." Ms. Lanham frowned. "Daisy. Why did you put that box down? We need to carry it into the house."

"Sorry, Mom." Mom was really being a grouch. "Gigi, I'm glad Aunt Patricia couldn't do it, or I would've had to wait to give you your present. You know, maybe one day I can take turns with Mom, Aunt Patricia, and Grammy and make dinner for you."

Gigi laughed. "Well, when I'm one hundred, you'll be on the list."

As Daisy carried in the food, she noticed a large, well-worn book on the coffee table. "What's that book over there?"

"Into the kitchen, please, Daisy," Mom ordered. "Then you can look at it."

Daisy put the cupcakes into the refrigerator and went back into the living room, where Gigi was sitting with the book in her lap. Daisy nestled next to her, and Gigi slid her one half of the book.

On the first page, was a beautiful, blonde-haired woman wearing a slim, satin gown.

Daisy gasped. "Who's this lady? Do you know her?"

"That is a picture of me, my dear. I was modeling this gown for a local department store, Blondell's. It's not around anymore."

"Gigi, that's really you? Omigosh, this is the coolest thing ever! Mom, come out, quick!"

Ms. Lanham dashed into the living room. "What's wrong?"

Gigi laughed. "We're okay. Nobody's fallen and can't get up."

"Look, Mom. This is Gigi!"

Her mom leaned toward the book, then looked at Gigi. "That's you?"

Gigi smiled and nodded. "Yes. It was during the Depression, and I had to help support my family. I couldn't afford anything in Blondell's, but I used to dress in my Sunday clothes sometimes and just walk around the store, looking at everything. They had the most beautiful hats, clothes, purses, and gloves."

"Couldn't you at least buy a pair of gloves from Blondell's?" asked Daisy.

"Gloves at Blondell's always cost twice as much as gloves from anywhere else. And there was one pair I wanted more than anything. They were blue leather, the same color as a peacock, and oh, so soft."

"Gigi, you were like a supermodel! Look at all of these pictures in here!"

"They're all me. Anyway, I was 'discovered' by a man in a suit who came up to me and asked if I was a model. At first I was frightened, but then the man showed me his pin, which said, Preston Blondell, Store Manager. I told him I wasn't one, but that I loved his store and everything in it. Pretty soon, Mr. Blondell called my mother, and before I knew it, I was getting paid to model at Blondell's fashion shows and for special customers. Good thing, too, because my father lost his full-time job and had trouble finding other work."

Daisy took Gigi's hand. "You couldn't get your gloves, Gigi?"

"No, I had to help pay the bills and buy food."

"Omigosh. It must've been so hard!"

"It was, but we always had a roof over our heads and the bare necessities, which we held onto until they wore out. My mother was always saying, 'waste not, want not,' too. I got so tired of hearing it, but it must've worked because I never waste a thing to this day."

"Mom says the same thing to me. Or, 'Daisy, you forgot to turn out the light, Daisy, you left the fridge door open'...it drives me crazy."

Gigi laughed. "Well, it's just another way you and I are alike."

Daisy put her arms around Gigi and leaned into her. "Gigi, can I spend the night?"

Before Gigi could answer, Mom, who had left the room and just returned, jumped in. "No, of course not."

"Why?"

"Because Gigi can't have you underfoot, that's why. And you have Sophia's birthday party tomorrow. You're going to that tea place, remember?"

Daisy looked at Gigi. "Are you going, Gigi? You like tea."

"I'm afraid not, dear."

"Why not? Weren't you asked?" Gigi shook her head.

Daisy looked at her mom. "Do I have to go? All Sophia and Katie talk about is horse jumping and harp lessons. And that snotty neighbor of theirs, Violet, always looks at me like I'm a germ or something. Why do they ask her and not Gigi?"

"Maybe because they don't want Gigi to be tired, which is what she will be if you spend the night tonight. And as for the party, you can't back out now. Aunt Patricia has already paid for you. You have to go."

Daisy stood up and turned away from Mom. "Oh, they won't miss the money."

"Daisy!"

"Mom, you're always talking about how easy Aunt Patricia has it. And she does! She never thinks of us, or calls to ask how she can help us. All she cares about are her manicures and golf."

Daisy sat back down and put her head on Gigi's shoulder. Gigi wrapped her arms around Daisy.

Mom sat down next to Daisy, and tried to reach out to her, but Daisy moved away in a huff.

"I want to be alone with Gigi. At least SHE looked at the paper bouquet I made for her. I don't want to spend the night at home," Daisy said with tears in her eyes.

Mom swallowed the lump in her throat. "I am so sorry, Daisy," she said and reached for her daughter's hand. "I didn't even see it. And, Gigi, I apologize to you, too. I didn't mean to argue about all this in front of you."

Gigi turned toward her granddaughter, but did not let go of Daisy. "No, I'm glad you did. You've been hurting for a long time,

Debra. I see it every time you come here, and practically every time you talk to Daisy. Yes, Don is gone; I know it's hard."

Mom blurted out tearfully, "I'm so tired, Don hardly ever pays—"

Gigi shook her head, and nodded toward Daisy. "Not now. You and Daisy have been on your own for six years now. But look at your daughter. She is a happy, well-adjusted young girl who is caring, kind, generous, and strong. She'll do anything for the ones she loves. Just like you. Don't let these tough times break your spirit and make you bitter and angry. And Daisy has such hope! Don't lose yours, or you'll never be able to move forward."

Mom sat down, and put her face in her hands. Daisy walked to her mother and put her arm around her. "It's okay, Mom. I have everything I have ever needed."

Gigi watched her granddaughter and great-granddaughter, and continued. "She will not be a bother if she spends the night tonight. She will be a comfort. What time is that tea tomorrow?"

Ms. Lanham looked at her watch. "2:30."

"Well, there's plenty of time for you to pick Daisy up and take her to the party."

Daisy moaned, "Gigi…"

"I'm sorry, Daisy, but I agree with your mother on that one. You told Sophia you're going and going you must." Gigi said firmly.

"Okay. At least I get to spend the night with you. I don't even care about tomorrow."

Gigi smiled at Daisy, then looked at Mom. "Take the time to stop and smell those roses. Paper ones, in particular, if you know what I mean. And talk with Patricia. And your mother."

*   *   *

On Sunday night, about an hour before she went to bed, Daisy had an idea. "Could I call Gigi, Mom?"

Mom was doing cross-stitch, which Daisy hadn't seen her work on in a while. Mom looked at her watch. "I don't see why not; it's not too late."

Daisy ran to the phone and called Gigi with her secret bright idea. Gigi absolutely loved it.

The next morning, Daisy walked up to her teacher, who was sitting at her desk. Mrs. Delancey looked up from those creepy glasses. "Yes?" She sounded slightly annoyed. Daisy refused to let Mrs. Delancey's tone or bulgy owl eyes unnerve her.

"My great-grandmother was a teenager during the Great Depression, and worked to help her family pay the bills. Do you think she could come in and talk about her life, since we've been studying about that time?"

For once, Mrs. Delancey smiled at Daisy. "Why Daisy, that's a wonderful idea. But is she okay with getting around? She must be close to 90."

"She IS 90, and of course she can get around. She's my best friend."

Mrs. Delancey leaned back. "Well, we'll have to make arrangements, then."

Daisy smiled at her teacher and wanted to say, "See, even people with B- brains have great ideas and something to give." As Daisy turned and walked back to her desk, she wondered, "Why can't everybody see that? I know I can."

Gigi's visit was the best school day Daisy ever had. Mrs. Delancey couldn't believe a 90-year-old woman still drove her own car, and didn't need to sit in the chair the school custodian brought in.

As Gigi spoke, Daisy passed around the worn photo album. Everyone, especially the girls, loved the photographs.

"She looks like an old-time movie star," gushed Sara Fletcher.

"It's a shame Blondell's isn't around anymore," said Fiona Nielsen, who loved shopping. Daisy looked over at Sloane, shocked. Sloane was actually quiet the entire time Gigi talked, except to ask to see the album again.

Gigi summed up her speech. "The Depression was a tough time for me; it was tough for everybody around me. But, I will always remember how it brought my family and neighbors together. It taught me the importance of strength, generosity, and kindness, and the need for hope. Without hope, no one can move forward." At that moment, Gigi looked at Daisy, smiled, and sat down. Applause and a standing ovation followed. Sloane walked to Daisy, and handed her the album. "Gigi is the coolest. I don't have any great-grandparents anymore."

Daisy smiled sadly. "That's too bad. I don't what I'd do without Gigi."

35

"What a wonderful story!" Mrs. Delancey announced, putting her hand on Gigi's shoulder. "Thank you for showing us how you helped your family survived that terrible, trying time."

"You're welcome," Gigi replied, still looking at Daisy.

Daisy repeated the last words of Gigi's speech to herself. They were almost the exact same words her great-grandmother told Mom two Saturdays ago. About her. Daisy realized that she was just like Gigi, and whatever terrible, trying time her mother faced, Daisy was going to help her survive it, and use every ounce of generosity, kindness, strength, and hope her heart and spirit had.

THAT BUBBLE OF MINE

by Joyce M. Shepherd

I blew lots of bubbles. They flew really high.
I looked in awe as they reached for the sky.

Running in circles, bursting bubbles galore,
I finally caught one before it could soar.

The morning sun made it sparkle and shine.
I thought it amazing, that bubble of mine.

As I looked inside it, a rainbow appeared.
"It's a magic bubble. Wahoo!" I cheered.

I wanted to touch it, but knew if I tried,
My magic bubble would burst with a sigh.

So I gazed and admired that bubble so fine,
And wished it would last, that bubble of mine.

37
Joyce M. Shepherd, "Hope"

THE HOMECOMING

by David A. Stelzig

I learned of momma's death from Bill McFarland, the prison chaplain. Damn fool's called near regular, for ten years or so, thinking to shame me into a visit, but this was our first face-to-face.

McFarland's deep baritone had me figuring him a big fellow. And he was. Just not the way I thought. Standing on my porch, the top of McFarland's head barely reached my chin, but from the waist up he was huge. His gigantic belly stretched against his shirt and sloped down, completely covering his belt, both front and sides. And rolls of sweaty red jowls all but buried his Roman collar. His voice was as I remembered.

"May I come in Mr. Johnson?" McFarland actually lisped, "Mither Jonthon." The stench of garlic pushed through the screen as he talked.

"What for? You already told me about momma."

"We have papers. Details to take care of," he answered, reaching for the door. He dropped his hand back to his side when he realized I wasn't moving from the doorway.

"What kinda details?"

"Funeral arrangements for one. And there's the will."

"Will?" I asked, raising my eyebrows. "What'd momma have that'd need a will?"

McFarland shrugged. "A little money. Maybe some land down near Abilene."

"Abilene? Momma still had the ranch?" My throat tightened as I pictured the source of my only long-term happiness—and my enduring nightmare.

"Think so. Left the name of an attorney."

McFarland held an envelope toward me. I pushed the door outward and accepted it, ripping it open as I walked into the trailer. The screen door squeaked loudly and slammed shut as McFarland followed me in.

There were eighty-seven dollars in small bills, which I stuffed into my shirt pocket, and a single sheet of lined, yellow paper. Momma wrote that she was of sound mind and that she wanted everything she owned to go to her only son, Carlin Johnson, me, except what it took for her funeral. Momma signed it. It was witnessed by William T. McFarland and a Juanita Hernandez. There was also a yellowed business card: Jeffrey Reynolds, Attorney at Law, Abilene, TX. His street address and phone number had been crossed out, new ones penciled onto the back.

"This says I gotta pay to bury momma," I complained, as I looked up after reading the will.

"It would seem so, Mr. Johnson," McFarland responded, nodding his head.

"What'll that cost? Don't have much money."

"Depends. Maybe a few thousand. Caskets can be quite dear."

I stepped into the kitchen area, pulled a Bud from the fridge, and popped the cap. Returning to the living room, I dropped onto the sofa, at the end near the floor fan.

"Wanna beer?" I asked, looking up at McFarland.

"No. Thank you." He took a step further into the room, closer to the fan. He stood there, legs spread, sweat running down his fat red cheeks, arms folded and resting on his prodigious gut.

"Don't got that kinda money. Guess I'm gonna pass."

McFarland sighed and shook his head, then silently looked down at the floor. I drank my beer, lit a Winston, dropped the spent match into the coffee cup on the floor near my feet.

"I can make arrangements. Keep costs low as possible," McFarland suggested. "You could contact the attorney in Abilene. Maybe Angela had some money. Or something he could liquidate for cash. You could take care of the bill when you come for the funeral."

"This don't say I gotta be at the burying," I said, holding up momma's will.

"No. No it doesn't. I just assumed you'd want to come, to say goodbye to your mother."

"Said goodbye to momma a long way back. Don't need to do it again."

We stared at each other. I finished my beer. Went for another.

"You got a phone on you?" I asked.

"I do."

"Lemme have it. I'll call the lawyer. See if momma had anything left."

Reynolds was in court, but I talked to his secretary. She hinted momma *did* have something, "assets" she called it, but wouldn't give details. I made an appointment with her boss for Friday late.

*   *   *

That had been my Wednesday. Thursday, I bummed a hundred bucks from McFarland and that, along with the eighty-seven from momma, was enough to rent a compact Chevy and buy a MasterCard from Johnny, a drinking buddy from the corner bar.

I woke slowly Friday morning, walked to the kitchen, microwaved a cup of instant coffee, carried it back, and chain smoked in bed while thinking about the family I used to have. Daddy. Momma. And, of course, Sissy. Momma's death bothered me. More'n I'd let on to McFarland. Sure I still had my anger. And couldn't forgive her. And yet, now that it was too late, I was touched with guilt for shunning her all these years.

Unlike with momma, I had a hard time recollecting a clear picture of daddy. Seems he'd been around near regular at first, but then sort of disappeared. Couldn't hardly remember him at all after Sissy was born. And Sissy? Her I saw clearly, every day, and though I fought it, probably would for the rest of my life.

About midmorning, I stubbed my cigarette, got out of bed, dressed, packed a small bag, and tossed it, along with a cooler of beer, onto the back seat of the Chevy. I pulled away from the trailer, thought better of it, went back, and wrote a note for Mae: "Momma died. Gone to Abilene."

Mae had been gone the better part of a week this time, a long time considering we hadn't had much of a fight. She'd probably be back in a day or two and I considered waiting, thinking Mae might be willing to take the trip with me. Even if she wouldn't, the truck was mine, after all, and I wouldn't have to be renting the Chevy. And it might be handy to have the cell phone. And, surprisingly, I was starting to miss her.

In the end, I decided to get the trip over with and pulled out of Amarillo heading south on Interstate 27. Usually I took pleasure driving through the pancake flat Llano Estacado of north Texas, but I was returning to Abilene, something I'd vowed would never happen. Instead of enjoying the wide horizon and the occasional windmill-fed, green fields of corn and cotton, I saw electric pumps hungrily sucking water from the Ogallala Aquifer, greasy black oil derricks, and stinging clouds of reddish-brown sand blowing across the road in advance of gathering thunderclouds.

I stopped for a bowl of chili and a couple beers just north of Lubbock and then angled southeast, picked up Interstate 20 in Sweetwater and rode that into Abilene. I had a half hour before my meeting with Reynolds, but it took that and a little more to find his address and a place to park. I walked into his office five minutes late.

"Mr. Johnson?"

"Yes'm."

"Sorry for your loss."

I simply nodded.

She was a pretty little thing; black, but lighter-skinned than Mae; a few years older than me, probably mid to late thirties; and had a body, although just a bit heavy, that gave me a great deal of pleasure to look at. She was wearing a white blouse, dark skirt, and heels, and was seated at a computer behind an oak railing that reminded me of traffic court back in Amarillo.

"Looks like you beat the rain," she commented, flashing a warm smile.

"Yes ma'am, but not by much."

"Have a seat Mr. Johnson. I'll tell Mr. Reynolds you're here."

"Thank you ma'am." I stayed standing, watched her walk to the closed door at the back of the office. Fidgeting, hat in hand, I wished I'd showered and shaved, or at least shined my boots and put on a clean pair of jeans.

"Mr. Reynolds will see you now."

She held the gate and I walked into her side of the office.

"Thank you, miss ..."

"Ryan. Noelle Ryan."

"Thank you, Noelle."

She smiled. I entered Reynolds' inner office. Noelle closed the door behind me.

Jeffrey Reynolds was well over sixty, had a ring of short gray hair around his shiny bald head, and a pointy little gray goatee that failed in its effort to hide his weak chin. The sleeves of his white silk shirt were rolled to the elbows and he wore a string tie loosely fastened with a wide, turquoise stone. A ring with a smaller, matching stone was on the middle finger of his right hand. Reynolds removed a pair of funny little half-glasses and placed them carefully on his cluttered oak desk as he stood to greet me. He was much shorter than me, no more than five foot six, and not nearly as broad.

"Mr. Johnson. I was sorry to hear about your mother." His voice was surprisingly deep for such a little guy.

"Thanks. I'm more comfortable with Carl."

"Carl then. And I'm Jeff."

We shook. More correctly, I shook. Reynolds held his little hand toward me but applied absolutely no pressure when I grabbed it.

"Have a seat, please." He gestured toward a long oak table surrounded by black metal chairs padded with green leather that looked comfortable but out of place. I sat, leaving the chair at the head of the table for Reynolds. He walked to the center of three oak file cabinets, opened the top drawer, and, after a moment, returned to the table with a thin manila file folder. He dropped it on the table as he sat.

"You bring the will, Carl?"

I took the envelope from my shirt pocket, unfolded it, and withdrew momma's yellow sheet of paper.

"Simple, to the point, and perfectly legal," he said after a quick read. "I'll keep this if I may. File it first thing Monday. Noelle can make a copy before you leave."

"Sure," I shrugged.

"Did momma have anything worth my trip from Amarillo?"

Reynolds looked at me sort of funny, then reached for the manila file.

"Well, there's a checking account with a little money ...."

"How little?"

He withdrew a small, blue checkbook from the folder. "Let's see. Just less than seven thousand at the end of the month. Haven't added interest for a while, so it'll be a little more."

I felt my pulse quicken. If I didn't pay McFarland for momma's funeral, and I had no intention of doing so, I could trade my truck for one that was practically new.

"Can I look?"

Reynolds handed me the checkbook and I leafed through the last few pages of entries.

"Looks like nothing's coming in, but you been doin' okay for yourself each and every month."

"I manage your mother's property," Reynolds responded, nodding his head. "It's about the only kind of law I do anymore."

"Property? Momma really did keep the ranch?"

"Well, yes, but there's not much left. Had to sell most of the acreage to pay house repairs and taxes through the years. And then there were her legal expenses."

"And you got that money too."

"I did."

"Shouldn't have been much, momma pleading guilty and all."

"You're right, Carl. Big costs were taxes and repairs."

"And property management."

Reynolds' expression hardened, but after a moment he relaxed, sighed, and answered. "Yes, that too. It all adds up."

"So? What's left?"

Reynolds removed a few papers from the file and slid them across the table to me. "House, couple of sheds, and about ten acres of land."

"And that's all mine?"

"Will be. Soon as the will clears probate. Shouldn't take more than a couple days."

I left what I assumed was momma's deed lying in front of me. "I'm gonna sell. Any idea what she'll bring?"

"I could check around," Reynolds offered. "Problem is, it's off the beaten path, be tough to sell as a home. And the mineral rights are gone. Best bet would be to sell it as ranch to one of your neighbors. But they won't pay much. Maybe a few thousand an acre, twenty thousand or so total. Doubt you'd get more than that."

Clearly my luck had turned the corner. I could trade my pickup for one that was actually new. I might even pay for momma's funeral. "How 'bout other stuff? Momma have anything else?"

"No. Just the furniture and other contents of the house."

"All right then," I said, standing. "I thank you for your time. Any chance getting an advance on my money?"

Reynolds made a funny little noise that was probably a laugh, but sounded more like a cough. "No. Sorry. But I can hurry the paperwork."

Reynolds stood and we walked into the outer office. Noelle was standing, umbrella in hand, staring at the deluge in the street.

"Noelle," Reynolds asked, "could you Xerox this for Carl before you leave?"

Noelle glanced at her watch, but walked over and accepted momma's will without comment. Reynolds returned to his office.

Noelle made a copy and handed it to me. "Well, cowboy, looks like you're a rancher."

"Yeah, right, with enough land for three cows."

"Goats," she laughed. "People round here raise goats nowadays. For the mohair. For sweaters."

"Goats then," I smiled.

I folded the copy of the will and placed it in my shirt pocket, tipped my hat to Noelle, and pushed the door open.

"You got a car, cowboy?"

I let the door swing back and turned to her. "Name's Carl."

"Sorry. Meant no disrespect. I like cowboys. So…Carl, you got wheels out there?"

"Yeah. Need a lift?"

"I'll trade half my umbrella for a ride to Freddie's," she suggested, shoving the handle toward me.

I offered Noelle my arm and we stepped into the downpour, paused long enough to make sure the door closed behind us, and sprinted for the Chevy.

Half the umbrella wasn't much of a bargain. I had to take off my hat and bend down to fit under it and the wind-blown rain drenched us from the waist down by the time we reached the car, parked less than a block from Reynolds' office.

I held the door for Noelle, ran to my side, slipped behind the wheel, and tossed the umbrella and my hat onto the back seat. I reached back and jerked a Bud from the hinged-lid cooler.

"Want one?"

"Nah. I'll wait till Freddie's."

"Boyfriend?"

"Yeah, right," Noelle snorted. "Freddie's as in Freddie's Bar and Grill. Over on South Pioneer."

I opened my beer and cracked the window just enough to toss the cap.

"This a rental?"

"Yeah. Why?"

"Curious. Seems small for a big guy like you. Pegged you for a Ford pickup."

"Dodge. Left it in Amarillo," I answered, not bothering to add that Mae had made off with it.

I started the engine. The windshield had fogged so I turned on the defrost and waited for it to clear. I took a slug of beer and reached for the Winstons I'd left on the floor, lighting one with my Zippo.

"Don't think you're supposed to smoke in a rental, Carl."

"What're you, the cigarette police?"

Noelle scowled at me, but then gave a little laugh and muttered "what the hell" as she helped herself to one of my cigarettes, lit it, and reached for a beer.

I opened it for her and we sat quietly.

"You a navy man?"

I glanced over. Noelle was rubbing the crossed anchor emblem on my Zippo.

"Coast Guard. Icebreaker out of Rockland, Maine."

"Nice lighter," she said, handing it to me. Our fingers touched briefly. The windows had cleared by now, so I tossed my cigarette and pulled away from the curb.

*   *   *

Rush hour traffic jammed the Abilene streets, but Noelle directed me along side streets and we arrived at Freddie's in less than twenty minutes. By then the rain had nearly ended.

"Buy you a replacement beer if you got time," Noelle offered.

"Sure. I'll park the car. Meet you inside." My luck, it seemed, continued to roll.

Parking the car though was easier said than done. It took over ten minutes to find a spot and that was three blocks away. Noelle's umbrella and my hat were still on the back seat, but I left them and walked quickly through the drizzle back to Freddie's.

The bar of Freddie's Bar and Grill was at the back of the front room. The grill could be seen through steam billowing from a rectangle cut in the wall behind the bar. The floor was crowded with a hodgepodge of tables covered in red plastic and surrounded by chairs, mostly occupied by enlisted personnel from nearby Dyess Air Force Base. The air was filled with talk and laughter and smoke. My kind of bar. As a bonus, a sideroom had an old-fashioned jukebox, two miniature pool tables, and an open space where a few couples were dancing to Willy Nelson's "Good Hearted Woman."

Noelle was in neither room. Thinking she was in the ladies' room, I squeezed up to the bar and ordered a Millers High Life. I was well into my second when Noelle slipped in beside me. She had changed into a light blue sweater and jeans tucked into shiny black cowgirl boots. There were three gold studs in her right ear, which I'm sure I would have noticed had they been there earlier. She still had rings on several fingers of each hand. I raised my eyebrows and nodded approvingly.

"My apartment's just across the alley in back," Noelle explained. "Had to get out of those wet clothes."

The guy on my left stood, giving his stool to Noelle. She smiled thanks, sat, caught the bartender's attention, and ordered a Corona for herself, another Millers for me.

I lit a Winston. Offered one to Noelle. She shook her head, took a pack of long skinny cigarettes from the back pocket of her jeans, and leaned forward as I lit one for her.

"Nice place," I suggested.

"It's a dump, but it's convenient. Good place to unwind Friday nights."

Noelle took a long drag and then reached over and touched my arm. "Carl, I'm sorry about your mother."

"Yeah. Thanks," I responded, sullenly. "Everybody's sorry."

Noelle withdrew her hand. "How'd she die?"

"Don't know. Didn't think to ask."

"Your mom died and you didn't ask what happened?"

"Nah. We weren't so close."

"No. I guess not."

Noelle sounded incredulous. After a pause, she added, "She was a good woman."

"You knew momma?"

"Well, not formally. But I talked to her. You, too."

I waited, open-mouthed, for an explanation. Noelle grinned, obviously enjoying her advantage.

"Got a divorce last year. Didn't take back my maiden name. Remember Greene's Quick Mart?"

"That was you?" Now I was incredulous.

"My parents," Noelle nodded. "I worked there sometimes."

"We were neighbors?"

"Yeah. We lived above the store," Noelle smiled. "We were neighbors."

"So you know what mamma did."

"I do."

"And why I don't feel real close."

"Yeah. I know that too. But you gotta forgive her. She had a tough life. And she was old. And tired. And probably wasn't real strong."

"She was an alcoholic. And a murderer." Tried to have it come out angry—I *was* angry for Chrissake—but my voice broke and Noelle placed her hand on my arm again, probably thinking I was feeling sad for momma. I lifted my beer and her hand slipped off. Sure I felt some sad, but I was mostly angry. And had been for more than twenty years.

Usually I kept it in. Buried. That had been easier when momma was out of mind. Before McFarland showed up. Now the wound was rubbed raw. And the beer I drank had weakened my defenses. The old anger was rising to the top, ready to boil.

I finished my beer, chugged half the one Noelle bought me, stood, and walked to the restroom. Noelle said something, but I was concentrating on fighting the blackness, the cold anger, that was attempting to take control.

I flashed back twenty-three years to that source of all nightmares: momma crying, on the bathroom floor next to the tub half-filled with water and with the dead body of my baby sister.

I pissed, punched my fist against the tile wall, and left the john, pushing through the crowd as I made my way back to the bar. One of the enlisted airmen had Noelle by the hand, trying to pull her onto the dance floor. She was shaking her head no.

"I think the lady wants to be left alone." I said it quietly, but he heard me. He should have understood.

"Not your business, mister. Better butt out."

"I'm making it my business." I grabbed the guy's wrist and pulled him away from Noelle. He took a drunken swing at me. I dodged, punched him hard in the gut, and followed with an uppercut to the chin. He folded over faster than an old roadmap. I bounced lightly, fists cocked, ready to finish him if he came up with any fight left in him.

I heard Noelle say, "Carl, don't," but paid no attention. I was listening to the blackness now. The guy *did* stagger to his feet and, as I stepped forward to put him back down, I sensed a movement beside me. I turned in time to partially deflect the pool cue swinging toward my head, but still took a glancing blow above my right ear and then turned back into a right cross from the guy who had started it all. I was out before I hit the floor.

* * *

I woke to darkness. Was in a bed of some sort, covered with a rough blanket. My head was exploding. The softest triage I could manage with my right hand found a huge swelling on my cheek and a matching knot on the opposite side of my head. I closed my eyes and lay in pain, finally drifting back to sleep. The next time I woke, it was daylight and I could smell coffee. I sat up, waited a moment for the pain to subside, and looked around.

My boots were in front of me under a small, metal TV stand. The rabbit ear antenna tethered to the fifteen-inch screen was resting on a book-laden series of shelves to the right. Behind me were two giant green easy chairs and a low table, tipped on its side and pushed against the chairs, apparently to make room for the folding cot on which I'd spent the night.

I stood. Followed the smell of coffee. The sound of running water came from the end of a hallway I passed as I entered the kitchen. The coffee pot was on a brushed-aluminum breakfast bar along with a spoon, a bowl of sugar, a bottle of extra-strength Excedrin, and a giant blue mug emblazoned with the lonestar flag of Texas. I poured a small amount of coffee, chilled it with water from the sink, and used it to down three Excedrins. I was halfway through another coffee when Noelle entered the kitchen.

She was barefoot, wearing black jeans and a yellow tee shirt.

"Morning," I smiled.

She passed me, poured coffee, kept her back to me. Not a good sign.

I tried again. "Thanks for the coffee."

Noelle turned. "So, what the hell were you trying to prove?"

"Sorry?"

"Last night. What's wrong with you?" she asked, her eyes blazing.

"Noelle," I complained, "that guy took a swing at me."

"Yeah...after you provoked him."

I shrugged. "I gotta pee. Can I use the bathroom?"

Noelle pointed to the hallway. "And then you better leave."

I went and then glanced in the mirror. Two days' growth of red beard wasn't enough to hide the giant lump on my cheek. The guy who sucker punched me must have been wearing a ring because there was a jagged half-inch cut in the center of the bump. My entire cheek and a patch on the front of my shirt were covered with dried blood. I rinsed my face and patted it dry with toilet paper. The bleeding started again, so I dabbed at it with a wad of toilet paper as I returned to the kitchen.

"Noelle, I know you're pissed. Guess you got a right…but I need a favor."

She stared at me. Said nothing.

"Gonna drive down to momma's. It's been twenty years. Place is probably changed."

"And you want me to go with you?"

"Was just a kid when I was there last."

"I don't think so Carl." Her voice was hard.

"I'll buy you a nice breakfast," I bargained.

"Thanks. No."

I walked back to the cot, sat, slipped on my boots. "Appreciate you bunking me for the night."

Noelle nodded.

"How'd I get here?"

Finally, a smile. "Friend from down the hall helped drag you. Incidentally, he's a corpsman from Dyess. Thinks you might have a concussion. You better check it out."

"Okay. Noelle, I'm real sorry. I can be an ass."

I paused at the door. "I'll drop your umbrella off on my way out of town." Then I was out and down the stairs. It took a while to orient myself, but I finally found Freddie's and then quickly walked to the car. I lit a Winston from the glove compartment, opened a now-warm beer, chugged it, opened a second, and drank it more slowly as I sat and smoked. When both were finished, I dropped them by the side of the car and drove to Noelle's to return her umbrella.

She was waiting on her front steps, walked to the passenger door, got in. "I must be out of my freaking mind."

*   *   *

After a breakfast of steak and eggs, which I paid for with the MasterCard I'd gotten from Johnny, I added ice to the cooler and we drove to momma's—soon-to-be-my—ranch.

It turned out I could have found my way without help from Noelle. Jed Peterson's windmill directly opposite our drive was an obvious landmark, although it seemed surprisingly small. The mesquites lining our driveway were now much larger, but the house, even with the recent coat of light-yellow paint, was what I remembered from childhood.

"Doesn't look in bad shape for being empty twenty-three years," I said.

"Actually, Jeffrey rented it for your mother until a couple years ago," Noelle explained.

"That would be it, then," I nodded.

I parked the Chevy near the back porch and just sat.

"Well?"

I lit a cigarette. Offered one to Noelle. She shook her head. After a couple minutes I turned to Noelle. "Feel funny bein' here. Haven't been back since the day momma killed Sissy."

"We could leave," Noelle suggested. "Until the will is processed, this might be trespassing."

I opened a Bud. It was only slightly chilled from the ice I'd added after breakfast. I lit a second Winston from the first and tossed the butt out the window.

"You smoke too much. And you drink too much."

"And you bitch too much," I responded.

She glared at me, but then took one of my cigarettes and accepted a light. We smoked in silence. After a few minutes, I opened my door, ground the cigarette with the heel of my boot, and walked onto the back porch. By the time Noelle caught up with me, I had slid my MasterCard into the doorframe to pop the lock.

"I don't think we should be doing this, Carl."

I rolled my eyes, flicked the credit card toward me, and pulled the door open.

The kitchen had a slight musty odor and the wallpaper was a new pattern, but the room still overwhelmed me with familiarity. I closed my eyes and pictured my sister, in her high chair, in front of the very table I was now leaning against.

"You're white as a sheet, Carl. You okay?"

I sighed and in a near whisper responded, "Yeah. Just memories."

"That why we're here?" Noelle asked.

"Wanted to see what momma left me."

"Maybe we should leave."
"Nah. Let's see what we got."
I pushed away from the table. Legs felt rubbery. "I'll take down here," I said. "You check upstairs."
Wasn't much to see in my survey. A table with two chairs in the kitchen, another with six chairs in the dining room, a worn sofa in front of an old TV on a small table in the living room. All of the furniture was old, but not antiques—just old. Noelle returned to the kitchen at the same time I did.
"Not much. Nice bureau and bed in the front room. Middle room is empty. Back room, by the bathroom, is padlocked."
"Oh?" I was surprised. "That's momma's. I'll take a look."
I kept my eyes diverted and crept slowly up the stairs, past the bathroom of my nightmares.
The padlock was impressive. The hardware holding it was not. One shove with my shoulder ripped the screws from the doorframe and I was in momma's bedroom.
It was as I remembered. A small dresser stood between the hallway and closet doors. Momma's bed, with its pink flowery canopy, was flanked by a Tiffany lamp on a small round table on one side, a rickety bookshelf next to the single window on the other. Being here felt good. There really had been happy times, but Sissy's death—murder, I corrected myself—had blocked them from my mind.
I walked to the window, opened the shade, and sat on momma's bed, raising a miniature storm of swirling dust. I lifted a book from the shelf and smiled. Zane Grey. *Rangers of the Lone Star.* An inscription inside the front cover read, "To my little cowboy. Happy birthday. Momma."
"Bad memories, Carl?"
Noelle was standing at the door—half in the room, half in the hallway.
"Nah," I started, and realized my cheeks were wet. I managed to blurt out, "was remembering good times."
Noelle crossed the room, sat next to me and hugged me, pressing my head onto her shoulder. For some reason, I stayed there for a second. Then I rose to my feet. I lifted the book I was holding.
"Saturday mornings, when I was a little kid, I'd lie on this bed drinking hot chocolate while momma read westerns to me. They probably bored her, but she made them real. After Sissy was born,

the three of us would lie here and momma helped me with the words as I read ABC books to her."

Noelle placed her hand on my knee. "Sounds like you were happy."

"Yeah. We were."

"But things changed?"

"After Sissy. She got sick, cried a lot. Then daddy disappeared. I think that's when momma started drinking. She'd sit in her rocker just staring, for hours on end."

"She must have been desperate."

"Guess so. Don't remember. When I was a kid, social services arranged some therapy and it took years to remember even this much."

Noelle leaned over, kissed me on my cheek, stood, took my hand.

"Let's get out of here, Carl."

I nodded and stood. As we neared the door, I noticed an old, yellowed copy of the *Abilene Reporter* on momma's dresser. I carried it to the window. The banner headline read, "Johnson Pleads to Killing Baby Daughter." There was a photo of momma in handcuffs being led out of district court by two Texas Rangers. The caption beneath the photo said that, in exchange for momma's guilty plea, the DA agreed not to seek the death penalty. The rangers were transporting momma to the Mountain View Unit of the women's prison in Gatesville.

"You read about momma's trial?"

"Sure," Noelle answered. "Everybody in Texas probably has."

"Not me."

"You're kidding."

"Shrinks wouldn't let me at first. Then I was so angry I wanted no part of it. Never even read the letters momma sent."

"Carl," Noelle scolded, "that's so wrong."

"Yeah. Maybe."

"We have the trial transcript in the office if you want to read it Monday. Unless you gotta get back to Amarillo."

"Nah. I work construction. Between jobs right now."

"Let's go to my place. You can shower and we'll get something to eat. Then you can decide what you're doing."

*   *   *

We picked up steaks on the way back to Noelle's. I showered and shaved, being careful of my cheek, and put on clean clothes. By the time I finished, Noelle had made a tossed salad and started the grill next to a small table which she had set, including two glasses of red wine, on a small balcony next to her bedroom. We sipped the wine. I grilled the steaks. We talked nervously, neither knowing where this was going.

When the steaks were done, Noelle poured herself another glass of wine. I opted for a beer and she got me a Corona from the fridge. Noelle cut a piece of meat, chewed it slowly, swallowed, and looked over at me.

"Somebody waiting for you in Amarillo, Carl?"

I shrugged. "Not sure." I told her about Mae and that she had disappeared with my truck.

"That the Dodge pickup you left in Amarillo?"

"Yeah," I smiled, "that's the one."

We exchanged small talk for the rest of the meal. Noelle poured herself the last of the wine. I walked to the kitchen, brought back a Corona, lit a cigarette, and sat in the chaise lounge on the opposite end of the balcony from the grill. Noelle came over and sat next to me. I put my arm around her and she leaned into me. We had decided where the evening was going.

*   *   *

Sunday passed quickly. We slept in, had a late morning meal of sausage and eggs, spent a pleasant afternoon talking and laughing on Noelle's balcony, and went to bed. We made love and then fell asleep watching an old John Wayne western.

*   *   *

Monday morning we woke at eight, hungry after our one-meal Sunday, rushed because Noelle was to open the office at nine. We showered and dressed, picked up coffees and egg biscuits to go, and I dropped Noelle at her office. Two minutes to nine. I found an all-day lot for the Chevy and leisurely ate my sandwich. I lit a cigarette, finished my coffee, and walked back to Noelle.

At about ten-twenty, Reynolds walked in. He stopped cold when he saw me sitting in the back corner reading the transcript.

"Carl. Didn't know you were still in town."

"Mornin'." I held up the two-inch-thick pile of paper. "Hope you don't mind."

Reynolds' eyes narrowed and they darted to the transcript, then briefly to Noelle.

"No. Of course not." He smiled, but his eyes stayed hard. "Let me know if you have questions."

"Actually, I do."

Reynolds had started to walk away. He stopped, turned back, and waited.

"We drove down to momma's. Her bedroom was padlocked."

Reynolds slumped into the chair next to me. He leaned forward, elbows on his knees, head bowed, hands clasped and nearly touching the floor.

"Angie, your mother, was an old friend. Just wanted something familiar for her. In case she got a chance to come home again."

I stared, incredulous. "You knew momma too?"

"Since high school," he nodded.

We sat quietly. After a moment, Reynolds lifted his head. "Your mother gave me something to give you." He stood and walked to his inner office.

I glanced at Noelle. "You knew they were friends?"

"Yeah," she said. "He visited her at least once a week all these years."

Reynolds came back. Handed me a small cardboard carton.

"What's this?" I asked.

"Things Angie had at Gatesville. She had cancer. Knew she was dying. Made me promise to get this to you."

I dropped the box on the floor in front of me.

"Couple more questions?"

Reynolds simply waited.

"Why'd momma plead innocent when the trial started?"

"She was in no condition to plead at all," Reynolds sighed. "I entered that plea for her. Couldn't believe she'd done that awful thing."

"But she did."

"Guess so. But for a while I thought we had a shot at an innocent verdict."

"Oh?" I asked, clearly surprised.

"The prosecution submitted photos of your sister. There were bruises and a few scratches. The ME couldn't explain the scratches. He suggested the killer was probably wearing a ring."

"Did momma have a ring?"

"She claimed not," he said, shaking his head. "Wasn't wearing one when she was arrested."

"You saying momma didn't kill Sissy?"

"No. Guess she must have done it."

"Then how do you explain the scratches?"

"Can't. Unless it was her fingernails."

"But it could have been somebody else?"

"I guess. But who?"

"How about daddy?" I asked. "He came back sometimes. And he had a lot of jewelry."

"Don't think so. The ME was going to testify about the size of the bruises. Your father's hands were too big."

"And so she changed her plea to guilty?"

"We plea bargained. It saved her life."

"She lost her life. Died in prison."

"This is Texas, son. She was going to be found guilty and she would have been executed."

*   *   *

I finished the transcript and took Noelle to an early lunch. Then I wandered the streets of Abilene, thinking. Was it possible momma *didn't* kill Sissy? I didn't actually see her do it. My only memory was me standing by the toilet, momma sitting on the floor, crying. And, of course, Sissy in the tub, dead. Could she have been killed before momma got there?

We'd never talked about it. The cops came. I guess momma called them. They took momma. Somebody else took me. The next nine years were spent in a series of foster homes. Never saw momma again. Never talked to her. Never forgave her.

But now? Was somebody else in the house? Daddy? Did I see him? Did he kill Sissy? Is that where the scratches came from?

Were his hands *really* too big to have caused the bruises or was this a medical examiner eager to help close a case?

Late afternoon, out of cigarettes, I jaywalked to a small bar, ordered a beer, and got change for the vending machine. Half an hour, three Miller draughts, and two Winstons later, still troubled, I left to pick up Noelle. She was standing on the sidewalk and hopped in when I pulled to the curb.

"Still got a couple T-bones and a six pack in the fridge," she volunteered.

"Sounds like a plan," I replied absently.

We drove to her apartment, parked, and walked up the steps. That's when I remembered the box Reynolds gave me.

"Left the box from momma in the trunk. Gonna go back for it."

"I'll leave the door open. Be in the shower."

I returned with the carton, started the grill, went to the kitchen, got a beer, lit a cigarette. The shower turned off. I slashed the box open with a butcher knife and carried it, along with my beer, into the living room.

First thing out of the box was a black, leather-covered, dog-eared bible. I dropped it on the table. I could see several sheets of lined, yellow paper with momma's handwriting still in the box.

Noelle, hair still damp, body wrapped in a flowery beach towel, walked up to me; kissed me. She sat on the edge of the coffee table in front of me and picked up momma's bible. I removed momma's writing and dropped the box to the floor. Something clunked. I laid the pages on the table, picked up the box, and looked inside. I smiled as I spied the small metal object.

Memories flooded back. Momma, holding Sissy, sitting on the back porch, watching me open my birthday present. Me, shrieking with joy as I discovered an entire Sheriff Hitchcock outfit, complete with gun belt and two six-shooters.

But the memory changed. Gradually at first, with just a hint that something bad was coming. Then in one horrifying instant the deep, ugly memory of a selfish and resentful boy sprang from its hiding place. I sank to the floor, threw my head back and roared. That God-awful day came crashing back with frightening clarity. I didn't find momma in the bathroom—just the opposite.

As I collapsed, Noelle stood, hand to her mouth, the towel falling away. She instinctively caught the box as it fell. It tipped on its side and with a small thud the damning star, my Sheriff Hitchcock ring, dropped onto the table, bounced, and fell soundlessly to the floor.

UNTAMED

by Ann Cook

No paddock, no stall, no boarded-fence limits
    To curb your spirit wild.
No saddle galls, no halter marks,
    No burrs to tangle mane and tail.
Today I saw your soulful gaze
    Go far beyond the pasture gate,
To distant plains and mountains,
    Grassy knolls and hidden glades.
Not my love, nor any science,
    Could keep you here with me, my friend.
So goodbye, my soft-eyed chestnut beauty;
    You're free to roam the stars.
Unbridled and unshod, go join that untamed herd;
    They're waiting just beyond the planet Mars.

59
THE PAST AS PRESENT

by Joanne Galantino

It was simultaneously exhilarating and calming to watch *Top Hat*. So what if Kara had seen it at least thirty times before? The music! The dancing! The gentlemen! The clothes! It was Saturday night, and there was no place for Kara to go. Well, actually, no place Kara wanted to go, no places like where Fred and Ginger danced, no places where men had to wear tuxedos and shoes that shone. Why were there no places like that today? Why did none of her friends want to go dancing, even though they complained of wanting to lose weight? Certainly no men she knew liked going except, of course, that medical resident she met ten years before. That chicken flew the coop so long ago; it was pointless to think about him. But think about him she did, on occasion, because he was the only man she ever met who liked her the way she was.

"Stop," Kara said out loud. After all, it wasn't 1935 anymore, it wasn't 1999 anymore. It was 2010. So what? IPods, IPads, technology everywhere. Kara was 33, and despite living in a world propelled by computers, she was not techno-savvy. To her, it was irrelevant, and the people who rushed out and waited in line to own every single gadget and application seemed to be the slowest to reply, if they bothered to reply at all. Kara had only a cell phone and e-mail, yet no one had to wait for her, or wonder where she was. She didn't text either, and blocked such messages from her phone (much to the annoyance of her friend, Lisa) and didn't want a plan to include them. "It takes too long to press those keys...just watch the movie, Kara," she ordered herself, humming one of the Irving Berlin tunes to get back on track. She stood up, and positioned her arms as if she had a dancing partner. She began spinning around the room, her long, blonde hair dancing along with her. She imagined her tall slim figure, clad in cotton pajamas, was instead wearing a silk, cut-on-the-bias gown, and accented with deco diamante dress clips.

*   *   *

"Come on, just get on Facebook," Lisa begged, as she paid for her lunch at Leopold's, the overpriced grocery store near Bridges and Blake, the advertising agency where Lisa and Kara worked. Kara carried her brown bag with her: Nutella, banana, and raisin sandwich and apple. She never bought anything at Leopold's.

"No way. Not after Schizo-Freddie stalked me. I don't care if he is seeing someone else. One never knows."

"You know how Facebook works. Just don't friend him."

Kara shook her head. "No. I don't even want him to *know* he could find me and reach me."

"I reconnected with a girl I knew from second grade. We did lunch a couple of weeks ago. It is sooo cool, the way you can hook up with someone from your past like that."

Cool had become the most overused word in the English language. Kara only used it to describe a temperature. As an ad copywriter, she needed to know and use a large variety of words.

"I admit, it's great that Facebook can make that happen. I just prefer not to do it."

"No biggie." The friends walked out of the store. "Can you believe it? Twelve dollars for a sandwich and chips. Good thing I brought my own drink."

Kara looked at the sandwich. "Is there a Gucci logo on the bread?"

"No, I think it's on the radicchio. Come on, let's go sit down under the tree. Toni and Leila should be there already."

Kara already knew what the topic of conversation was going to be: the reality show, *Top Brass*. Never in Kara's life had she seen and heard such unleashed ugliness: cruelty, contempt, profanity, and vulgarity, and among five blonde (hence the title) women who were supposed to be friends! It angered and saddened her to hear about their escapades. Kara watched no reality shows, although everyone she knew did. She simply kept quiet when people talked about them. Coming across as self-righteous was not the way to be.

"Hey, chickies!" Toni cried, while Leila waved.

"Hey goils!" called Lisa, as she and Kara walked toward and sat on the blanket.

"What cha got today, Kare?" Toni asked of Kara's sandwich.

"Nutella, banana, and raisins. It's fabulous."

"Don't the bananas get black?" Leila asked.

Kara held her sandwich for the girls to see. "Nope, the Nutella preserves them."

Toni made a face. I don't know, although the combination sounds good."

Lisa opened her iced tea. "Can you believe Barbara?"

Kara would've groaned, but the food going down her throat stopped her.

"I know!" cried Leila. "She totally seduced that mechanic—what's his name?"

"Giorgio!" chimed in Toni. "He can rotate my tires anytime."

"But doesn't he speak in double negatives?" Kara, who had a Master's in writing, hated it when people blatantly abused the English language. "And isn't he married?"

Lisa chuckled, and put her hand on her friend's shoulder. "You take all the fun out of everything. Why don't you just go with the flow? You got that antenna how long after the world changed to HD? Why don't you hook up with *Top Brass*? It keeps one from gossiping about coworkers."

"I watch Martha Stewart."

"I can't do any of the things she does on that show," Toni said, licking the foil from her blueberry yogurt container.

"I can do a couple of the things," said Leila, "but they don't turn out the same."

"I just buy things. It's cheaper. Anyhow, back to Giorgio, you know he was canoodling with Barbara's pool guy's sister...."

Kara didn't hear the rest of the story. She thought about her friendship with Lisa, whom she'd met when she started working at Bridges and Blake. Both women were copywriters, and it wasn't long after Kara was assigned to work with Lisa that they discovered what a great team they were. The pair won quite a few awards for their work. They even got a weekend's stay at the Plaza Hotel in New York City. Kara's niece, Mindy, was ecstatic.

"Don't forget to ask about Eloise, Weenie, and Skipperdee!" the child begged her favorite aunt. Kara inquired about those characters more for her own sake than Mindy's. She and Lisa were a perfect balance. Lisa was carefree and of the moment, always knew the latest, and never hesitated to jump on something if it struck her fancy. Kara was more practical, and needed to know every facet of a choice before she made a decision.

Kara's thoughts then drifted to her job. The agency wanted to land an account for some big company's new technology device. Mr. Bridges and Mr. Blake, each seventy-five years young, said winning the job would be "the coup of their careers." Lisa, who owned a Blackberry, three cell phones, and two Ipods, yet considered herself disorganized and behind, swore the device would put her in control of her life. Kara didn't entirely get it. Mr. Bridges and Mr. Blake put all of their faith in the two friends, knowing they could carve out magnificent copy.

"What can I say about something like this?" Putting herself in the head of a techie was impossible. It didn't help when Lisa announced in the last meeting, "Maybe I should fly solo on this one?" Kara knew she wasn't being malicious, but it still pained her to hear it.

Mr. Bridges cleared his throat. "I need you to put your heads together on this one. You know Kara brings in the practical to balance out your cool and hip, Lisa. The ads have to convey to any doubters how indispensable this thing is, not just how cool it makes one look to own it."

"Right," said Lisa sheepishly.

Kara also couldn't see spending $1,400 for something that she could accomplish with a pad, pencil, and superb memory, but her true feelings would cost her this job, which she loved. "If I worked on Madison Avenue back in the day, maybe I would've met Theodore Geisel before he became Dr. Seuss, when he was doing the Flit ads. I understand Flit," she thought.

Lisa opened her phone. "Hey chickies, we have to get back. Do you want to do happy hour at Fitzpatrick's? Kare, I know you have a dentist's appointment."

Leila chimed in immediately. "Sorry, can't. I have to meet Gary and Wilson at school. The play's tonight."

"Oh, that's right. Wilson will be the cutest little bumblebee," cooed Toni, who was unmarried, but wanted a husband and children. "I can go, Leese. How about you, Kare?"

Kara smiled politely. "I'm sorry, but I have to pass."

Lisa looked concerned. "Are they doing something serious today at the dentist? I know you said you weren't coming back. That guy, Bob, you know, the one with the broad shoulders, is going to be at Fitzpatrick's tonight."

Kara didn't know why Bob would care if she came or not. He thought plays were gay, abhorred big band music, and every time they talked and a young girl walked by, Bob completely spun his head around and had to ask Kara to repeat whatever it was she was saying.

Granted, *all* men looked, but Bob was excessive. Besides, there was no place at Fitzpatrick's for dancing.

"Maybe next week."

Lisa, who detected something was wrong with her friend, started to say something, but stopped. She could always call her tomorrow. "No problem."

*   *   *

Thank goodness Kara didn't take long at the dentist; she was in and out in forty-five minutes. "If I were a good, responsible employee, I would go back to the office," she thought. "I *am* a good, responsible employee, but I'm not going back to the office," she said aloud. Instead, Kara walked next door to the Nungasser Nursing Home where there were four elderly women sitting together and talking. From a distance, Kara could tell they were having a marvelous time. There was much laughter coming from the group. As Kara got closer, she could hear that they were remembering the days when they got dressed up to go dancing to big band music. One said she met Artie Shaw. Kara loved the music of the thirties and forties; how she wished she could've been there with them. Of course, not one of the women was texting. Not one of them talked about reality shows. Each woman was reflecting on a life well lived, full of the wonderful things Kara enjoyed—the things that made Kara an oddity among her friends and unable to find common ground with men.

"I know there were bad times way back when, what with the Great Depression and World War II, but I wish I lived during that time. I wouldn't have to do so many things alone. I don't care about being connected the way people are now; frankly, I think people are more distant today with those stupid devices. I don't want to be cool. Hip? I hate how hip looks. I...."

"Excuse me, dear, but are you all right?" It was one of the older women. Kara could tell that as a young woman, she must have been quite beautiful. She had long, dark hair, down past her shoulders, but she didn't look haggy, she looked breathtaking. She had large green eyes, framed with the longest lashes Kara had ever seen. She looked like she could've been a Varga model back in the day. Maybe she was.

"Oh yes, thank you. I'm sorry."

"There's nothing to be sorry about. You just look upset and worried," the woman continued.

"Are you looking for the main office?" asked the second woman, who was sitting in a wheelchair. Although she was unable to walk, she was sporting glittery sandals and coral polish on her toenails. "It's that way," she pointed.

"Actually, I was just walking by, and I noticed you sitting here, and it seemed like you were having such a wonderful time together. I didn't mean to intrude."

"Nonsense," said the third, whose hair was longer than the first woman's. She was wearing a beautiful jeweled headband. "We're simply reminiscing about how we used to go to all of the fabulous nightclubs in the city, dressed to the nines, and how we would swing dance to Glen Miller and Artie Shaw music—all stuff, I'm sure, quite foreign to you."

Kara's face brightened. "Oh, no, I've read, I've *dreamed* about all of those things. It sounds so wonderful to me."

"It *was* wonderful," said the fourth woman, who leaned on an exquisite walking stick topped with a brass leopard's head and decorated with spots. No utilitarian, plain cane for this lovely lady. Her nails were neatly filed and painted. "What a gorgeous shade of red," Kara thought. "It's virtually impossible to find good reds anymore. Why is that?"

The woman continued. "One of the best places was called the Scarlet Sable."

"Ooh, I loved the Scarlet Sable!" cooed the woman in the wheelchair.

"There was a fountain in the middle of the room," continued the woman with the walking stick. "Every man was handsome, and every woman was beautiful."

Kara couldn't help but think how these women were so unlike the backstabbing viragos on that skanky *Top Brass* show. They actually praised fellow members of their species. Kara felt so comfortable with the four friends, who, based on the conversation, had to be in their nineties.

"Ethel," the green-eyed woman said, "why don't you show our young friend how to waltz?"

"Me?" the woman with the headband said.

"Well, don't look at me," declared the woman in the wheelchair. The four laughed.

The woman rose. It was clear she used to be a dancer, as she was still rather slim.

"Here," she instructed Kara, "take my hand." Kara did as she was told. "Then, you do this."

Just then, the woman with the walking stick began humming *Cheek to Cheek*, one of Kara's favorite songs from the era. She started humming along.

"Wait until you get the hang of the dance," declared Ethel, "then you can sing along."

In no time at all, the two were dancing across the sidewalk. Kara and the women couldn't stop laughing and singing. They danced back toward the group, where Kara escorted Ethel back to her seat.

Kara bowed slightly. "Thank you so much for allowing me to spend time with you; it was so much fun!" She extended her hand to Ethel. "I'm Kara."

"I'm Diana," said the woman in the wheelchair.

"I'm Florence," said the green-eyed woman.

"And I'm Harriet," said the woman with the walking stick.

"It was so nice to meet you, and so lovely to visit the past. The picture you paint of it is as lovely as I imagined, and how I've seen it in books and movies," Kara continued.

"You're welcome to come to the past with us anytime," said Florence.

As Kara walked away, she heard one of the women say, "She doesn't seem upset anymore."

Kara wasn't, at least until she reached her car and drove to the mall. She should've gone home and put in *Follow the Fleet*, but she wanted to check out the shoe sale at Leighmann's Clearance Closet. The sale was so popular that it was impossible to park by the store, so she drove to the other end of the mall and entered there. The first store she passed sold computers. It was filled with people dressed in untucked T-shirts and those Godawful cargo pants. The men's faces tended to be unshaven, and the women's hair tended to be stringy and limp. Next, she passed a junior girls' boutique selling skimpy, cheaply-made clothes. Each of the mannequins wore platform shoes with see-through plastic heels. The next store was so dark, Kara couldn't see what the clothes looked like. She could, however, see a photograph featuring a close-up of a boy's undone fly.

"Great," Kara said aloud. Kara gazed at her reflection in the glass. Despite the trend favoring straight hair, Kara didn't own a flatiron. Her sleeveless pale green silk dress featured a scoop neck, slim bodice, and full skirt, suiting her perfectly. Her pumps, adorned with grosgrain bows, matched her dress and purse. If she felt like being more over the top, she would've had a hat and gloves. Seventy years ago, they would've been a necessity.

" I wish I lived back then," she found herself saying again. What was her problem? She had friends, a great job, her own townhouse, what else did she need? She could dress however she wanted, and so could the rest of the world. Why did she care so much? Why was she so sad?

I simply don't belong here, Kara realized. She was so distraught she forgot about looking for those yellow slingbacks she'd been eyeing for a year in Leighmann's upstairs shoe salon. I'm sure they didn't have tens, anyway, putting a sour-grapes spin on her rationale.

Kara got back in her car, and drove home. Tears were in her eyes. Of course, what was she going to do once she got home? She'd seen *Follow the Fleet* so many times she could recite the dialogue and dance along with Fred and Ginger. Of course, she could call Lisa and tell her she would meet her at Fitzpatrick's after all, but the thought of being in that lackluster pub with Birddog Bob made her want to cry even harder. "I have to find something else to do," she thought, wiping her eyes. "Maybe I'll go online and research that nursing home." She felt the tears dry on her face.

Even though it was four o'clock when Kara got home, she went upstairs, put on her pajamas, went to the spare room that was her office and turned on the computer. She Googled, "Nungasser Nursing Home." All of a sudden, she heard *In the Mood* blasting from her computer's speakers. The homepage featured a large ballroom where many older people were gathered and dancing. There was a large orchestra in the background. Kara looked fondly at the photograph, and smiled when she spotted Ethel, whose hair was in a bun and who was wearing a long sleeved red gown. "I hope I'm like that when I'm her age," Kara thought. "She dresses so glamorously but looks appropriate and elegant. Maybe I could learn from those women. Maybe I could meet them again." At that moment, she spied something on the home page: VOLUNTEERING. Hmmm, I wonder if I could do something on weekends?

* * *

Kara was sitting in the conference room with the fellow members of the Bridges and Blake creative team. She held the overpriced do-it-all device in her hand. "This could buy some nice tickets to some hit shows," she thought.

"Trying to figure it out, Kare?" teased Desmond Craig, a coworker so connected to everything digital and of the moment that she was sure he'd light up if he stuck his finger in an outlet. His savvy gave him an air of superiority which Kara did her best to avoid. "I'd rather have my computer crash than ask for his help," she thought.

Kara tried to smile without smirking. "I'm merely studying it."

"Well, it's not a book. You have to press buttons in order to 'study' it," he replied sarcastically, adding to his tone by making quote gestures with his index and middle fingers.

Kara did not miss a beat. "Well, if it's so self-explanatory, why does a book accompany it?" The smile never left her face.

Desmond's eyes widened, and he shifted his gaze to his notes.

Kara put the device on the table.

Lisa bolted into the room, and grabbed the gadget. "God, this thing is so cool." She began pressing buttons, seeming to know everything the thing was supposed to do without even consulting the book. "It does everything!" She put the device under Kara's nose. "Look."

Kara arched back. "Fabulous," she managed.

"Come on, it's easy. Besides, we have to come up with…"

"What's that?" Kara interrupted. She had looked down and noticed one of the screws flashed blue.

Lisa took the device back. "What's what?"

Kara pointed at the screw, which stopped flashing. "That," she said.

"That's the screw, you know, how they hold the thing together."

Desmond couldn't help but laugh.

Kara pursed her lips. "No, it looked like it glowed."

Lisa stared at it. "Glowed? That must be the sunlight hitting it."
"But the light was blue. That's not sunlight."
"Maybe it was prismatic."
"Then it would show all of the colors."
"Girl, you have an answer for everything."
"You know I'm right."
At that moment, Mr. Bridges and Mr. Blake walked in. "Having fun yet?" Mr. Blake asked.

*   *   *

At home, Kara sat down with the overpriced device in her hand. Mr. Bridges and Mr. Blake gave her permission, or rather, *insisted* she take the device home. She took them up on it, but not because she had to write about it, but because her curiosity was killing her. Not once during the meeting did anyone mention anything about the screw that flashed blue. Was it her imagination? Was it the light? No, the color of the flash was too artificial. At that moment, the screw glowed again. Kara was so startled, she almost dropped the device. What was going on? She looked in the manual. Nowhere in the book did it say anything about a glowing screw. What was this? She tried to press the screw, as if it were a button. Nothing happened. Then, she inserted her fingernail in the groove where a screwdriver would go. At that moment, the device vibrated, and then the screen showed the words, "where would you like to go?"
Kara gripped the device with both hands. "Is this a play on that Microsoft ad or something?" she wondered aloud. She started punching keys. "Well, if this thing REALLY wants to know…The Scarlet Sable, 1930s" Suddenly, Kara felt herself pitch forward.
The room began spinning (or was she spinning?). Everything around her became a brilliant crimson. Was she going there? "Omigosh," she thought. "I hope not, I'm wearing fleece pajamas covered with dancing purple hippos!" She covered her eyes with her hands. Then, she heard a band—a big band: trumpets, saxophones, clarinets—everything.
Kara uncovered her eyes. She was standing in the middle of the most magnificent nightclub she had ever seen. It *was* The Scarlet Sable! It had to be; it was just as Diana, Florence, Harriet, and Ethel described it. There was a fountain in the middle of the room. The

chairs were upholstered in red velvet, and accented with gold buttons. The tablecloths were red, too, and edged with a gorgeous gold trim. All along the wall, drawn in red, were sables dressed in tuxes and gowns for a night on the town. They looked as if they were drawn by one of *The New Yorker* artists. They probably were. Kara looked around her. Rich red drapes framed the interior. Nighttime New York City, in its art deco splendor, sparkled from The Scarlet Sable's picture windows. Everyone was dressed up: bias-cut gowns, tuxedos, bracelets sparkled, cuff links flashed. Kara turned around, catching her reflection in a mirror. She gasped. Her blonde hair was marcelled and followed the shape of her head. Her makeup was as perfectly applied as Bette Davis' at the height of her career. As her eyes went down to her gown, she nearly lost her balance. She was dressed in a black lace evening gown with veiled sleeves. In her hands was a silver minaudiere. Was this real? She began stroking the lace.

"This lace is niiiice," Kara thought. "This dress looks familiar." Could this be like the one Coco Chanel wore in her biography? "It can't be," Kara decided aloud, "because I can't afford Chanel." Who *was* she?

"Carolyn!"

"We've been wondering where you've been!"

"Have you been in the powder room all this time, dear?"

"Are you feeling all right?"

Kara turned around to see four extremely beautiful, extremely glamorous women heading toward her. Were they calling her Carolyn? They were looking right at her. Kara thought hard for a moment, and gave a definitive nod. They must be; no one was named Kara in the 1930s. And, her middle name was Lynn, hence Kara Lynn, or Carolyn! She embraced it immediately. But who were those women? She thought hard again, and then it hit her: Nungasser Nursing Home! Were they the four women she met outside the other day? Yes! Was she friends with them? Of course she would be!

"I'm so sorry, darlings. I merely lost my way," Kara explained.

"In here?" replied Diana, who was wearing a white silk charmeuse gown and matching cloak. Her hair was styled similarly to Claudette Colbert's, and was a gorgeous shade of auburn.

"You know this place like the back of your hand," uttered a confused Florence, whose green eyes and dark hair rivaled the beauty of Vivien Leigh. She wore a plum brocade gown trimmed with mink.

"Please get our friend a glass of champagne," Ethel asked a passing waiter," you know where our booth is." Her statuesque figure was perfectly suited for the slim gown of midnight blue.

"Of course, Miss Sutton," the waiter replied as he bowed, then hurried away.

"Come sit down," Harriet said, grabbing Kara's arm. Kara didn't know what was more dazzling, Harriet's beautiful face, or her pewter lame gown with the matching turban. The women immediately headed back to the table.

Kara allowed herself to be led by the women. Was she dreaming? She typically never remembered her dreams. This event was so vivid, yet felt so real, Kara couldn't help but wonder. Just then, she stopped. "This is *definitely* a dream," she decided.

In front of her stood the handsomest man she'd ever seen. In fact, he looked just like Robert Stack, one of her all-time favorite male stars. Once, when she was a teenager and out with her friends, she told them the star she most wanted to marry, if she could marry anyone, was Robert Stack. Oh, how she was chided for that one!

"He's an old man!"

"He's older than my grandfather!"

"Ewwww!"

Needless to say, Kara never told anyone else about her crush. Who was this man? He kept looking only at her, despite all of the breathtaking women everywhere in the room.

Diana took the initiative. "William, I would like you to meet my friend, Carolyn. Carolyn, this is William Warner. He is a set designer for the MacMillan Theater."

Kara gasped. "On Broadway?"

William chuckled. "Yes, on Broadway." He took her hand and kissed it gently, but his eyes remained on Kara's face. "So lovely to meet you."

It was a good thing Kara was holding on to Ethel, for her knees nearly gave out. "You, too." She couldn't think of anything else to say.

Fortunately, the waiter came with the champagne. Harriet handed it to her friend. "Drink up, Pet." Kara didn't hesitate to take it, but she didn't gulp it down. If this wasn't a dream, she wanted to remember every minute, especially with regard to this delicious William.

Diana stood up. "Well, girls, I have work to do tonight. I saw Bradford Barnsley, the perfect subject for my article on men's style . Toodle-oo."

Harriet looked at her nails. "Quite the catch, that Bradford."

"So elusive, however. Besides, Diana has her sights set on being editor-in-chief of *Maven*," said Florence.

The orchestra began playing *Cheek to Cheek*. William rose, and held out his hand. "Would you care to dance, Carolyn?"

Kara nearly fainted. No twisting this man's arm, no begging or whining on bended knee? Wow. "Yes," she replied breathlessly.

William chuckled, then took her in his arms. Carolyn glided flawlessly with him on the dance floor. Is this how it was for Ginger and Fred? Is this how it is when one is with the right person? She couldn't know already, although isn't that's what people always said, 'I knew the instant I met him'? It was a good thing Ethel showed her how to waltz the other day. She rested her head on William's shoulder. Much to her surprise, he neither flinched nor pulled away. This was almost too right, too perfect. Something is going to happen. She closed her eyes.

*   *   *

The next thing she knew, she was back in her hippo pajamas, lying in bed. The overpriced device was beside her. Was what happened real? Had she really been at the Scarlet Sable, in the past? Had she really been wearing Chanel? Had she really met a man who looked like Robert Stack, liked dancing, liked theater, liked *her*? She looked at the clock—1:17 am. "Dream or not, I've got to get some sleep."

*   *   *

"Hey, chickie, where were you last night?" Lisa cried out when she saw Kara in the parking garage. "I tried calling you, but you didn't answer. I wanted to run some ideas by you about that gadget thingy."

Kara smiled. "I love him, I—I mean *it*."

"You do? You seemed dead set against it in the meeting yesterday. Or, at least your face looked like you did."

"No, it's great. It took me places I never thought I'd go."

"What's up with you? Did you take something last night or something?"

"Sorry. No, I didn't take anything. I just think this gadget is really great."

"Well, we can't use anything in this thing's copy to say we're going somewhere. Microsoft already asked its customers that years ago. What else could we say? You're the practical one, remember?"

It helps you meet the man of your dreams. How well would it sell with *that* feature? Kara was convinced that she did not dream. And she was going to find a way to get back to see William again.

*   *   *

Kara couldn't wait until Saturday. She had a breakfast date with Ethel, Florence, Diana, and Harriet at Nungasser, and then she volunteered to help decorate for the big band event later that evening. Plus, she had a question to run by the women: Were they friends with a man named William Warner? If so, what happened to him? Did he ever marry?

"Hello, girls!" Kara greeted her friends warmly, hugging and giving each of them a kiss.

"How are you, dear?" Ethel asked, her hair in a French twist, and her long neck accentuated by dramatic gold earrings. Harriet was using a purple-colored cane, which matched her satin caftan. Diana brought some old copies of *Maven* magazine, so Kara could read her friend's articles. It was nice of Diana to let her take them home for a bit. Florence brought a photograph album.

Kara waited to look at the album after breakfast; she didn't want to damage the delicate pages. Upon seeing the first page, she gasped.

Florence put her hand on Kara's shoulder. "What's the matter?"

Diana leaned forward. "Your face looks like the one you had on the day we met you."

Kara apologized. "I'm sorry, girls. It's just this man in here. He looks so familiar to me. Who is he?"

Ethel leaned forward. "Oh, that's William Warner. Talented Broadway set designer. Won a couple of awards, too. Nicest man you'd ever want to meet."

Harriet chuckled. "Best-looking, too."

"Diehard bachelor," Diana added. "Too bad for us."

"Workaholic, you know." Florence said. "Still is."

Kara gasped again. "Still?"

Harriet nodded. "He's a resident here. In fact, he's doing some of the work for the dance tonight. He simply won't slow down."

"How old is he?" Kara wondered.

"Ninety-six," answered Diana. "Ninety-six this May."

Kara looked through the album, but she couldn't stop thinking about William. She didn't want to ask too many questions about him; it would seem suspicious and silly. What would a young woman want with a ninety-six-year-old man? Maybe in a roundabout way she could find out more.

"What's the theme of the big band event tonight?" Kara asked.

"A Night out with Duke...Duke Ellington," answered Florence.

"I think she knows which Duke you mean," replied Harriet dryly.

"I'm sorry. I keep thinking you're my granddaughter, Darby. If it's before 1985, she has no idea."

Kara laughed. "No problem. I'm an odd bird, particularly for my generation."

"You're a beautiful bird," Diana said, squeezing Kara's hand.

Kara squeezed back, and looked down. "Thank you. At least I feel like I belong here."

"I'm sure you're being too hard on yourself. I mean, you've mentioned all the friends you have who are your age," Florence offered.

"Yes, and they're great." Kara said sadly. "But I can't tell you how glad I am to have each of you. When we're together, the past is the present. Maybe that's not a very healthy attitude for me to adopt, but each of you personifies that time for me so beautifully, it's like I'm there, too."

"Well, you're going to be here, tonight, right?' Diana asked.

"I wouldn't miss it."

"Well, watch a black-and-white movie, pick out a gown and don some...what do they call them...sparklies? Oh, that's it—bling!"

Everyone laughed.

Kara chuckled. Bling was another word she chose not to use. "You use it more than I do, Diana."

"Anyhow, come as a satin doll, you know, Duke's--"

"*She knows!!*"

Just kidding, Pets," Diana teased.

Kara hugged her friends. "I can't wait." Then she rose. "I'm afraid I need to scoot. It's nearly noon, and I'm part of the decorating committee."

"Have fun, Darling."

Kara headed toward the ballroom. It looked better in person than on the website. It was a spacious, rather grand-looking place. Little decorating was required. The only person there was a tall, slim, elderly gentleman, who still sported a full head of hair. Despite his age, he was still able to move about with some ease. In his hands was a large sketchbook. Kara recognized him immediately. It was William.

"Will—I mean, Mr. Warner?" Kara began. "I'm Kara."

William extended his hand. "Call me William, please. So lovely to meet you."

Just like at the Scarlet Sable. "You, too." Kara gulped. She turned to William's sketchbook. "Are these your designs for the party tonight?"

William nodded. "Yes. Actually, everything is done. "I just need help getting everything set up. We're duplicating a nightclub whose heyday was back in the thirties and forties. Are you familiar with a place called the Scarlet Sable?"

"Yes." She felt like saying, "I've been there. And danced in your arms, rested my head on your shoulder. You looked only at me. You are the most amazing man I've ever met in my life."

"Pardon me, but are you all right?"

Kara cleared her throat. "Yes. I'm sorry. I've just heard so many wonderful things about it, that I'm sad I had to be born too late to miss it."

"You would've fit in beautifully there. Well, you can be part of it tonight. I trust you're coming?"

Kara gripped a nearby chair. "Absolutely."

William showed her his book. The sketches were vivid depictions of everything she remembered the other night. Even the scarlet sables, in all their finery, were there. Such meticulous attention to detail...no wonder William was still alive and active.

"These drawings of the sables...."

"I did those. I did the original ones for the club, too, way back when."

"You did?"

"Yes. My family owned the Macmillan Theater, and my father was good friends with Mr. Menchen, the owner of the Scarlet Sable. When I showed him some sketches of sables, he immediately hired me to do some for the club. That was my first job, and it was at that point I knew I wanted to be a set designer, which I did for fifty-eight years."

"Wow."

"I'd still be at the Macmillan, but my nephew and his family insisted I retire and live here at Nungasser. It made him nervous when I'd climb to the top of a ladder when I was eighty-six. Frankly, I think he was afraid for himself. His fear of heights is so bad, he starts hyperventilating while standing on a stepladder, second rung from the bottom . He'd make a lousy King Kong."

Kara couldn't help but laugh.

"I still draw, paint, and build things. Keeps me young, I guess. Takes me back to my theater days. Best days of my life."

Kara remembered that Florence said he was a workaholic. Maybe he just never met the right person. Maybe he's like me, and because Miss Right never showed up, he just devoted his life to designing lavish stage sets. That's because I wasn't there.

"Such a rich, fulfilling life you've led. I wish I could meet a man who loved the theater. Every time I've gone with some young man, all he does all night is tug at his necktie or look at his watch. I don't know if his shirt is choking him, or I am."

"Clearly, you've encountered some clueless men."

Kara laughed. "Don't worry, I didn't marry any of them. I was bored, frustrated, and exhausted before I got to that stage."

Before William could say anything else, some volunteers entered the room. Immediately, the topic shifted to decorating, and everyone set to work.

It was a good thing she still had the device at home.

* * *

Kara just took a relaxing bath. She spritzed herself with Chanel No. 5. She'd read a bit of history on the famous fragrance just the other day. Thank goodness it was still around, especially since every celebrity of late had come out with his or her own scent. Before she applied her makeup, she studied her book on George Hurrell photographs, selecting an image of Carole Lombard to copy. "After all, *she* snagged Clark Gable," Kara thought.

At that moment, her cell phone rang. It was Lisa. "Hey, Leese."

"Hey, chickie. What are you doing tonight? I was thinking of going to Fitzpatrick's. There's a great band playing, and you know how fabulous and frothy their brews are."

Kara couldn't just sit and *listen* to music. She had to dance to it, and frankly, the thought of Fitzpatrick's made her sleepy. In fact, she hated Fitzpatrick's, or, for that matter, any pub she'd ever been dragged to. She wasn't sitting at home alone and bored anymore. She had a choice now. She looked at the overpriced device on her nightstand. That company could make a fortune if they knew what it could really do. But Kara had no intention of sticking around and finding out how Bridges and Blake would try to sell it. She had other plans.

"I'm sorry, but I'm going to that big band event. I promised my friends I'd be there."

"Friends? Well, that'll end early. You know older people go to bed around nine or so. Why not come to Fitzie's afterward? Bob'll be there, and you know how—"

"Lisa, I *do* know. He's not the least bit interested in me. He'd date somebody still in high school if he could get away with it. Frankly, I can't stand him."

"Kara, you need to give people a chance."

"You know what? The last guy people told me to give a chance to was a habitual liar who cheated on me every chance he got. And, remember Schizo-Freddie? He was worse than the dud behind the door in the Mystery Date game. I should've slammed the door in his face long ago. Now, I'm doing it to Bob, and sparing myself some grief."

"So, you're hanging out with people who have artificial hips, instead of people who *are* hip?"

"I have never been hip, Lisa, nor do I ever want to be."

"How old *are* you, Kara…eighty-five?"

"*Ninety*-five, and then, if everything goes according to plan, twenty-five."

"What are you talking about?"

Kara looked at the nightstand. The device was flashing blue. "Lisa, I am so sorry, but I have to go—"

"Kara, what is going on? I—"

But Kara already hung up. She went immediately toward the device and stuck her thumbnail in the glowing blue screw. Once again, it vibrated, then posed the question, "Where would you like to go?" Hands shaking, she typed in the words, "To William Warner, wherever he is, nineteen thirties." Kara pitched forward. The room began spinning. The room became crimson. Kara covered her eyes. She heard a big band. When she took her hands away, she saw that she was standing in front of the fountain in the Scarlet Sable. She was wearing a pale blue silk gown with a matching jacket which was trimmed with feathers. Both of her wrists were bedecked with bracelets. Glittery clips were in her hair. Then, she spotted William. In her experience with boyfriends, they never smiled nor walked over to greet her as she arrived. Upon spotting Kara, William smiled broadly, walked swiftly to her, and took her by the hand. Kara looked down, and noticed she was still holding the device. She thought hard, but not long. "I'm *not* going back!"

She threw the device in the fountain and walked to the middle of the room to waltz with William.

BALTIMORE'S CITY HALL DOME

by Marie Edmeades

On a clear, crisp October morning not long ago my husband Paul and I investigated a part of Baltimore's architectural past that has had relatively few visitors in its over 133 years of existence. Located at 100 North Holliday Street, City Hall is only a few blocks north of the Inner Harbor. Although the chambers have been viewed by many tourists over the years, the interior of the dome has remained largely unexplored by the general public.

Dating from the late 1800s, Baltimore's City Hall is a lovely example of an architectural style known as "Second Empire French." Identifiable by its ornate windows, decorative columns and slate-covered mansard roofs, this style is reminiscent of many buildings in Paris, including the Louvre Museum. City Hall's grand portico with its double set of marble stairs was originally designed as the main entrance but is no longer used for that purpose. Now all visitors enter through a small door on ground level directly below.

Once inside we found ourselves in a tiny vestibule where our appointment was confirmed, our credentials were checked and we were asked to sign a waiver agreeing that our exploration of the dome was taken at our own risk. With the official business finished we were led up a short flight of stairs into the rotunda to await our tour guide.

Forming the core of the building, the rotunda rises almost 120 feet to the fourth floor. We craned our necks to view the elegantly decorated inner dome that caps the space. Inside the cup-shaped form, eight gently curving pilasters bend toward a stained glass oculus at the center. In a little while our perspective would be changed dramatically, for soon we would be standing above the oculus and inside the first section of the building's true dome.

Before we knew it we were shaking hands with City Hall curator Jeanne Davis who introduced us to our tour guide, head custodian Charlie Riemer. In his thirty-five years with City Hall, Charlie had made countless trips to the top of the dome. Most of these excursions were for custodial reasons. Trips made as escort to curious investigators had been fewer. Jeanne Davis has been a City Hall employee for many years; like many others who work there, she had never ventured into the dome. Not a fan of heights, Jeanne had always been reluctant to make the climb. This time she decided to accompany us on the tour.

Charlie led us to an elevator (added when the building was renovated in 1975) where our adventure would begin. When the doors opened onto the sixth floor we walked into a beehive of activity. Joining the swarm of people heading for meetings or other responsibilities, we quickly found ourselves standing before what looked like an ordinary closet door. This particular portal turned out to be a Narnia-like entryway into another world. Leaving behind the age of computers, cellphones, I-Pods and Blackberries, we opened a door to the past, a time when the greatest technologies included horse-drawn streetcars, steam engines, and sailing ships, and whose celebrities included President Ulysses S. Grant, Frederick Douglass and Louisa May Alcott.

Before us a stairway of heavy marble blocks curved gently to the right. As we ascended through the dark, narrow space our shoulders scraped along the rough brick walls on either side until we emerged, like rabbits from a hole, into a surprisingly high, sunlit room. This largely empty cylindrical-shaped area, known in architectural jargon as the "drum," serves mainly as a means of elevation for the actual dome. The drum is encircled and illuminated by twelve windows, each approximately twenty-two feet tall by six feet wide. Through them we could enjoy a panoramic view of modern-day Baltimore that the founders of City Hall could not have imagined.

In the center of the floor a twelve-sided wooden platform surrounds the oculus and supports the stained glass disk we had observed from the floor of the rotunda just moments before. From this vantage point we could see that the twelve-foot diameter disk is much larger than it had appeared from below.

After giving us some time to inspect the room and take in the serene quiet, Charlie pointed toward an elegant cast iron staircase that would take us to the next level. As we began the climb, he cautioned us not to look down or over the railing. It was good advice: the room seemed to turn with us as we slowly cork-screwed our way higher and higher to the top of the stairs. None of us wanted to risk being overcome by dizziness, but it was hard to resist looking down at the sunlight spreading like luminous fingers through the eastern windows and across the floor beneath us. Our last steps on the staircase brought us up into the "cupola." We were now inside the true dome.

The egg-shaped cupola has a very different feel compared to its companion room below. Here, instead of tall narrow windows, the room is ringed by twelve five-foot, eight-inch diameter panes whose tops can be touched by reaching an arm over one's head. The cupola's walls are exposed to show a simple yet effective system of interlocking cast iron plates that rest one atop the other. The plates curve along the arc of twelve massive iron trusses that support the structure giving the dome its distinctive shape. Here in the cupola the creativity of the building's architect and the structural engineer is revealed.

George A. Frederick, the architect, was only twenty-two in 1865 when he was awarded the contract for City Hall. He would go on to design many more structures for his native city including the Howard Peter Rawlings Conservatory and Botanical Gardens—a five-story, glass-enclosed building in Druid Hill Park—as well as several of the park's fanciful pavilions, and the Cylburn Mansion off Greenspring Avenue. City Hall, however, holds first place among his architectural achievements. Frederick was fortunate to have working beside him in this endeavor a highly talented engineer named Wendel Bollman.

Bollman owned and operated the Patapsco Iron Works in nearby Canton. At the time of City Hall's construction, he had already made a name for himself as the creative genius behind the "Bollman Truss Bridge." This self-taught engineer's design contributions revolutionized the bridge-building industry and his knowledge of cast iron construction methods was crucial to the dome's fabrication. Together with Frederick, he would earn City Hall's dome the distinction—according to a 1981 Historic American Buildings Survey (HABS)—of being "one of the finest specimens of architectural iron work in the country."

The use of iron in the construction of the building was part of a new trend in architecture. Even the United States Capitol's dome, finished in 1863, was constructed using cast iron. At the time, iron structures were considered fireproof; but as the citizens of Baltimore would discover years later during the great fire of 1904, this proved not to be the case. That conflagration, the most catastrophic fire the country had experienced since the great Chicago Fire of 1871, left seventy blocks of downtown Baltimore and more than 1,500 buildings in ruins. Many of those buildings had been constructed of iron; most notable among them was The Baltimore Sun's celebrated

"Iron Building."

Ground was broken and the cornerstone laid for City Hall on October 18, 1867 accompanied by an elaborate ceremony attended by dignitaries and ordinary citizens who had for years clamored for a municipal building worthy of what was then the country's fifth largest city. By autumn of 1875 the dome was completed. An electrically generated clock was installed in the cupola and "Big Sam," the 5,000 pound bell that sounded its hours and acted as the city's major fire alarm, was hung in the elegant "lantern" that crowned the dome. The original time mechanism which still stands in the center of the cupola is connected to the clock faces that are painted on four of the large round windows at the cardinal points of direction. This mechanism has moved the two-foot long hands of the clock for well over a century. "Big Sam" did not last as long, however. After only fourteen years of service, "Big Sam" developed a crack and was replaced by a new 7,403 pound bell dubbed "Lord Baltimore."

In order to get a glimpse of "Lord Baltimore" we would need to climb the spiral staircase that dominates the center of the cupola. Once again we wound our way up and up until, at the top of the 187th and last step of our journey, Charlie opened the cast iron door that brought us out onto a narrow, circular balcony surrounded by a marble balustrade. We shaded our eyes from the bright sun and looked down from a height of almost 200 feet to look upon a 360 degree view of the city of Baltimore.

Walking around the balcony from this height could trigger a bit of vertigo in some people, but the four of us managed to quell any queasy feelings we might have had to take in the expansive view of the city's buildings—a view that reached as far as Canton. Tucked in amongst more modern edifices, we noticed a few nearby structures that were built before City Hall was constructed: the Shot Tower on East Fayette Street built in 1828; St. Vincent de Paul's Church on North Front Street built in 1840; and, at the corner of Gaye and Ensor Streets, the six-story Italianate tower of Engine Co. #6 which has stood since 1853.

One other building caught our attention. Only half a block away at 225 North Holliday Street, a modest three-story brick structure stands in the shadow of City Hall. Although neglected by the city and not well known to the general public, it has had an eclectic history. Built around 1813 as a fine arts gallery and museum, it was later used as a school for Baltimore's African-American children. At that time it was known as "Number One Colored Primary School." Later, it became an organ factory and then even a machine shop. But perhaps this building's most important role came between 1830 and 1876 when it served as Baltimore's first City Hall.

The flash of a solitary pigeon's wings against the cloudless sky brought our gaze upward and toward the lantern. Standing against the balustrade we leaned back to peer between its fluted columns where, hidden within its dark interior, "Lord Baltimore" resides. The big bell was silent the day we visited City Hall but over the decades since its installation, famous Baltimoreans including Eubie Blake, Babe Ruth, Billy Holliday and H.L. Mencken no doubt set their time pieces to its sonorous voice.

Our tour had reached its highest point. But before we began our descent on the spiral staircases, we were invited to add our signatures on an iron beam just inside the door. We inscribed our names beside the names of those who had come before us with the hope that many would follow our footsteps to explore the grace and wonder of this beautiful jewel in Baltimore's architectural crown: the City Hall Dome.

Marie Edmeades, "City Hall Oculus"

KUME AND THE VOLCANO

by Marie E. Edmeades

A long time ago, when the world was not so old as it is now, the ancestors of the Mapuche People lived in the long, narrow country below the equator that we now call Chile.

To the north of this country was the bone dry desert. To the west was the mighty ocean. To the east were the Andes Mountains and the ancient Araucaria trees. To the frozen south was the end of the world.

In the middle of this beautiful country The People of the Land lived among the lush rain forests that covered the earth for as far as the hawk could fly. The People of the Land were strong; they worked hard to provide food, clothing and shelter for their families.

The People of the Land were brave; they never gave up their fight against the strangers from the north who tried to raid their villages, take away their land, and enslave them. Many, many times the fathers and the grandfathers, the sons and the brothers, and the husbands and the uncles were forced to leave their families alone in the villages and go off to fight the strangers.

In one of these villages where the men had gone off to war once again, there lived a little girl whom everyone called "Kume" from their word for "good and kind." Kume loved all the animals that lived in her village: the chickens, the cows, the dogs, and the llamas. She loved the colorful butterflies that flitted from flower to flower, the ibis that flew high in the sky, the noisy parakeets that nested in the trees, and the little pudus—tiny deer— that hopped among the old black lava fields. But most of all, she loved the tiny green birds who drank from the wild chilco flowers all day long.

Kume loved to watch them as they poked their long needle-beaks deep inside the blossoms to sip sweet nectar. She loved the buzzing sound their wings made as they hovered over her head, and she loved their high, sweet voices which reminded her of the tinkling sound the kaskavilla made when the machi, the village healer, shook the sacred instrument. It belonged to their machi or healer, and kept away the evil spirits.

Kume often played with the smallest of the little birds whom she named Caru Wen-uy, "green friend." One day, while Kume was playing a game of hide and seek with Wen-uy between the chilco bushes, the earth began to shake under her feet. For a moment everyone and everything in the village became silent. The earth shook again. Then Kume heard a thunderous roar. A woman shouted and pointed her finger like an arrow toward the east. "Look", she cried, "Pillan is waking!"

Everyone in the village, even the cows and the chickens and the dogs, looked toward the snow-covered volcano called Rucapillan, "the House of Pillan," where the evil spirit Pillan lived. Everyone saw the black smoke billowing from its mouth and into the blue sky above. Kume didn't know what to do. She turned toward her Caru Wen-uy in the chilco, but he had disappeared.

A cloud of dread settled over the village. Whispers of doom and destruction spread from dwelling to dwelling and all the mothers began calling to their children. Kume ran as fast as she could.

All the mothers and grandmothers, all the daughters and sisters, and all the wives and aunts waited with the children in a circle in the center of the village. The earth shook again, and more smoke rose into the sky above the house of Pillan. The dogs whined, the chickens clucked and the cows mooed mournfully, but all the women and children waited together in silence.

At last the machi came out of her dwelling carrying her sacred drum, her kaskavilla, and an earthen jar. She raised her drum over her head and beat it with a short stick—first to the east, then to the west, then to the south, and finally to the north. Then she shook it until the sacred objects inside rattled and danced. She spun around and around; first in one direction, and then in the other. Laying the drum on the ground, the machi took up her kaskavilla. As if in a trance, she walked around and around the circle waving the kaskavilla back and forth like a bird in flight.

The earth groaned eerily. Everyone in the circle reached out to touch another's hand. Everyone looked toward Rucapillan.

"Do not be afraid!" the machi said in a loud clear voice. "There is a little one in our circle who will silence the voice of Pillan and who will stand against the threat of our annihilation!"

The machi shook her kaskavilla up and down. Once again she walked around the circle, shaking the sacred instrument in front of everyone until she came to Kume.

"Kume," she said, "it is *you* who are called to go to the house of Pillan. It is *you* who will save the People of the Land."

Kume heard a strange sound, like the sound of the winter wind whistling through the ancient Araucaria trees, but it was not winter yet. She looked around the circle to see her mother and her grandmother and all the others staring at her with wide-open mouths and wide-open eyes.

The machi said, "Kume, will you go?"

The earth shook. Pillan roared once again and spat more smoke into the air. Kume could not speak. Her knees trembled like two captive rabbits and her hands felt as cold as stones. Kume thought about all those she loved—the mothers and the grandmothers, the daughters and the sisters and the wives and the aunts. She thought about the grandfathers and the fathers and the sons and the brothers and the husbands and the uncles. Kume thought about the Land and all the animals and her little green friends.

Then, in a loud, clear voice, Kume said, "*Yes!*"

The machi smiled and called Kume to the center of the circle. She picked up the earthen jar and tied it to Kume's back with a bright shawl saying, "Kume, you must carry this jar with you to the house of Pillan. You must not open the jar or let it be broken on your journey. Take nothing else with you—no food to eat or water to drink; all your needs will be provided. When you hear the sound of the kaskavilla, remember that you are not alone. We will wait for your return."

Kume turned to face the house of Pillan. Slowly, she began to walk toward the snow-covered cone in the distance. In a little while, Kume had left her village and had entered the forest. The tall, fragrant trees that surrounded her often obscured the house of Pillan but the rumbling of his voice and the ever-thickening smoke rising high above the horizon told her where he was.

Hour after hour, Kume walked through the strangely silent forest. "Where are the pudus and the foxes?" She wondered. "Where are the butterflies, the ibis and the parakeets? Why isn't the hawk hunting the rabbit? Why have they all left me alone?"

The earthen jar began to feel heavy on Kume's back. She tugged on the shawl to shift its weight. Kume thought she heard a small sound from behind her. She turned to look toward her village. Then she heard the sound again. "Is it the sound of the kaskavilla?" she wondered. Then Kume remembered the machi's words: "When you hear the sound of the kaskavilla, remember that you are not alone," and she walked on.

As the sun rose higher in the sky, Pillan's roaring became louder and louder. "I am thirsty," Kume said to herself, "but I have nothing to drink." She searched the ground looking for a stream, but she could not see one. "My mouth is so dry," she thought, "if I do not find water, surely I shall die. Perhaps there is water in the earthen jar. Perhaps I have been carrying cool, sweet water on my back all the while." The earth shook again and Pillan's harsh voice seemed to say, *"Drink or die, drink or die!"*

Kume turned her head to look at the earthen jar she carried on her back. Her mouth was as dry as the dirt beneath her feet. "A little water is all I need," she thought. But she remembered the machi's words, "You must not open the jar...all your needs will be provided."

Again, as before, she heard the small sound; like a distant kaskavilla. "What could it be?" she wondered. Pillan thundered again, his voice louder than before. Kume listened harder for the small sound. There it was again, she was certain—rippling and falling, over and over, like the sound of children's laughter. "A mountain stream!" she said aloud. Over her shoulder, Kume saw the water running freely just behind her. She knelt, scooped the icy liquid to her lips and drank until she was no longer thirsty.

It was late in the day. The earthen jar seemed to get heavier and heavier on Kume's back as she neared the house of Pillan. Her shoulders ached and her legs felt weak. Over and over again, she reminded herself that when the machi asked her if she would go to the volcano she had answered "Yes." Over and over again, she thought of her people, The People of the Land. "What if I fail," she thought. "Pillan will destroy everyone and everything I love." So Kume walked on.

As the sun began to find its bed on the horizon, Kume heard another rumble but this time it was not from Pillan. Her stomach was empty and growling for food. "All the mothers are preparing the evening meal," Kume thought. "Everyone in the village will have something warm and good to eat tonight, but I have nothing to eat."

Kume looked all around. "What can I find to eat here in the forest?" she asked herself. Her stomach cramped and pinched her as if to remind her of its need. Kume felt sad and discouraged. Pillan continued to smoke and roar. He seemed to say, "Eat or die! Eat or die!"

Kume thought about untying the shawl and opening the jar. "What if there is something good to eat in the earthen jar," Kume wondered. "I am small; just a little food would give me strength. Maybe there is flat bread and a honeycomb inside, maybe there are ears of roasted corn and sweet peppers and beans."

Her mouth began to water and her stomach grumbled again. She touched the tight knot the machi had made with the ends of the shawl, and as her fingers traced the hard tangle of cloth she remembered standing in the circle with all the women and children of the village. Kume closed her eyes and heard, as if in a dream, the high, tinkling sound of the kaskavilla and the machi saying, "It is you, Kume...you are the one." Then the tinkling changed and became instead a buzzing sound that seemed to rise and swirl above her.

Kume opened her eyes and lifted her head. Silhouetted against the sky, she saw the ancient Araucaria trees standing all around her like fearless sentinels. Under their curious, twisted branches, huge cones filled with ripened seeds lay scattered all over the ground. *"Hunger Killers!"* Kume shouted (for that is what the People of the Land called the large seeds of the Araucaria trees), and she began to gather them into her apron.

Kume was so excited about finding the seeds that she began to sing a song about them. But her joyful song soon turned to sadness when she remembered: "I must cook the hunger killers before I can eat them and I have no fire." As if listening to her thoughts, Pillan roared out once more. "No hope, no hope," he seemed to say.

The sun slipped farther and farther under a blanket of clouds; the night air cooled and Kume began to tremble. Her stomach groaned and she ached with hunger. "I am so hungry and so tired," she moaned. "Pillan is right—if I don't eat soon I will die and all will be lost."

Hot, salty tears streamed down her cheeks. She wept and wept until there were no more tears left in her. As she dabbed her swollen eyes with a corner of her apron, white ghosts, swaying silently in a rhythmic dance, suddenly appeared before her.

Kume was gripped with fear. "Are these the spirits of the dead come to take me? Am I already dead?" she wondered. More and more ghosts appeared. One after the other, they grew, rose into the air, and vanished. Kume squinted her eyes. "These are not ghosts," she thought. "They are only mists rising from a hot spring! I will cook the hunger killers in the boiling water; I will feast on their goodness, and my strength will be restored. But what shall I cook them in?"

Again Kume thought of the earthen jar tied to her back. It was just what she needed to cook the hunger killers. But in a loud, clear voice Kume said "*No!* The machi told me I must not open the earthen jar. There *must* be another way."

Kume looked around her. There, beside the hot spring, the rambling vines of the coral plant wound their way through the trees. "I can weave a basket from their stems just like my mother taught me," she thought. And so she did.

Then Kume filled the basket with the hunger killers and lowered it into the steaming water of the spring. Soon the seeds were soft enough for her to peel and eat. Her stomach grew calm and she felt strong once again.

Kume thought, "I have not died from thirst and I have not died from hunger. It is time I met Pillan at his door!"

Kume left the forest behind her and walked through the darkening night to the foot of the fearsome volcano. With each step Kume took, the evil spirit roared louder. Jets of red-hot lava leapt above the house of Pillan turning the night sky to the color of blood.

Slowly, like the tiny snail that carries his house on his back, Kume carried the earthen jar up the steep side of the volcano. Many times she slipped and fell against the hard volcanic rock as she approached Pillan but she went on. Before long, Kume came to the place where snow covered the rock. Even though her feet were bitten by the icy crystals, she continued on.

Pillan's voice became louder and more violent as Kume neared, and the earthen jar began to feel like a heavy stone on her back. Burdened by its weight, Kume sank into the deep snow, but she pushed her way onward toward Pillan. Louder and louder Pillan's voice bellowed. Now Kume crawled on her hands and knees, the weight of the earthen jar almost crushing her.

More fiery lava shot out of Pillan's mouth into the dark sky above her. Burning sparks rained down on her. They melted the snow turning it into a river that threatened to wash her away, but Kume clung to the volcano's side with all her might and continued on. The lava's heat blistered her skin and Pillan's sulfurous breath threatened to overcome her. His enraged voice became so deafening that Kume could hear no other sound.

At last Kume reached the top of the house of Pillan. She untied the knot of her shawl and carefully took the earthen jar from her back. Pillan hissed derisively, "Look at this puny creature standing at my door! Does she think her insignificant earthen jar is a worthy gift; does she wish to placate me so that I will not destroy The People of the Land? Who *dares* come to my house alone? Who are *you*?"

In a loud, clear voice Kume answered, "I am Kume! I am *not* alone! All the people and all the creatures I love are with me!"

Pillan began to laugh a loud, cruel laugh. He laughed so hard that molten lava sprayed from his mouth. He laughed so hard that the wicked force of his voice knocked Kume down; the earthen jar fell from her hands and broke upon the rocks beneath her feet.

"*No!*" Kume cried aloud.

Covering her face with her apron, Kume began to cry. Then, amidst all the noise and fury, she heard a familiar buzzing sound and a high sweet voice like the tinkling of the kaskavilla called her name, "Kume, do not be afraid!" Kume took the apron away from her face. "It is I, Caru Wen-uy. My brothers and I were sent by the machi. You have carried us with you on your back all the way to the house of Pillan."

Kume looked down at the earthen jar to see thousands of tiny green birds swarming from its center and into the air. "Do not be afraid," Wen-uy repeated as he joined them. Like a ribbon of bright green grass, the birds spiraled around the house of Pillan until, at Wen-uy's signal, they all dived directly into the mouth of the volcano.

For a long while nothing happened and Kume began to fear that Wen-uy and all his brothers were lost. But then, one after another, all the birds reappeared from the mouth of the volcano, each one carrying a small bit of Pillan's fire on top of his head. Kume heard a strange gurgle from deep inside the volcano. A small puff of white smoke rose into the air and disappeared. And then there was silence.

"Follow us home, Kume!" Wen-uy said.

Led by the tiny torches they carried on their heads and by their high, sweet songs, Kume followed her small green friends down the side of the volcano and through the forest. On and on Kume walked with Wen-uy hovering by her side; past the thermal waters where the hawks and foxes were hunting, past the Araucharia trees where the noisy parakeets were gathering seeds, and past the cool mountain spring where the pudus were playing.

"You are a brave girl Kume," Wen-uy said.

"How is it that you can speak?" Kume asked her companion.

"I could always speak," he answered. "It is only now that you understand my language."

The sun rose from its bed and Kume could see the village dwellings through the trees. As she and her green friends approached the village, she heard the machi's sacred drum beating like her own heart, calling her home.

All the fathers and the grandfathers, the sons and the brothers and all the husbands and the uncles stood in a circle with all the mothers, the grandmothers, the daughters, the sisters, the wives, the aunts and all the children. In the center of the circle stood the machi and the village chief.

When the People of The Land saw Kume coming, a great cry of joy arose among them and the circle opened for her to join them. Her green friends scattered themselves among the tree branches and the chilco flowers. The still-glowing embers that they bore on their heads made the forest seem to be on fire.

In a voice loud enough for the whole village to hear, the machi said, "*Welcome* Kume! Come to the center of the circle!"

Kume stepped forward and faced the machi.

The machi struck her drum once more and said, "Kume, you have saved The People of the Land. Your faith and courage have defeated the evil power of Pillan. You will become my apprentice and you will learn the holy ways of healing. You shall learn to listen to and understand the voices of all the creatures, and one day you will become the new machi!"

Then the machi turned toward the little green birds. "Caru Wen-uy!" she called. "Come to the center of the circle."

Wen-uy flew from his place in the chilco flowers and hovered before the machi; his swiftly beating wings buzzing like a hundred bees. Then the machi said, "The People of the Land will always be grateful to you and your brave brothers for defeating Pillan. From this time forward your kind will carry on your heads a flame that does not burn, so that all who see you will remember your great deed."

And to this day, the busy and brave little green birds who wear a crown of fire on their heads can still be seen in the long, thin country below the equator that we now call Chile.

BEAUTY OF THE STORM

by Carla J. Wiederholt

When the thunder roars and shakes the walls,
And the lightening dances through the halls,
And the whistling wind brings air so cold,
I wish you were here for me to hold.

When I hear the wind chimes fiercely clashing,
And the limbs on the trees violently thrashing,
There is not a whole lot I can do,
But fill my mind with thoughts of you.

When I feel the storm grow more intense,
There is little to do in my defense.
So I dream of you here to keep me warm.
And that is the beauty of the storm.

CAFÉ SEA BREEZE

by Karin Harrison

The man shrinks back; his hands rise in a futile attempt to dodge the punishing blows. A powerful kick targets his kidneys. The shock, as he loses consciousness, blunts awareness of the savage stabbing. He slumps into the cool sand. Shrieks from the seagulls above seem to melt into one long soulless moan.

*   *   *

Carla deeply inhales the salty air as she opens the door for business. A desultory breeze sweeps across the ocean surface while a brown pelican plunges head first into the sea. Frothy ripples expand in ever widening circles and all is quiet until he bursts from the depth and soars with ease, his throat pouch swollen with his catch.

Carla ties the apron with the Cafe Sea Breeze logo around her short, trim body. There is no denying her Italian heritage; wide dark eyes accent her oval face. Her coal black hair is pulled back and twisted into a single braid that drapes around her shoulder. A pencil-line scar trails across her left cheekbone. Her full lips stretch into a pretty smile much more frequently these days.

She steps on the terrace and inspects the tables nestled beneath the palm trees. Bird of Paradise clusters by the balustrade and extend their orange and blue flowers with lofty elegance. A few hundred yards away the deserted pier invades the Pacific Ocean with its stoic platform of concrete and steel. Seagulls screech fortissimo as they wheel above in search for morsels left behind by yesterday's crowd.

Carla sighs happily. She has found her niche at last. The painful divorce a little over a year before had nearly broken her spirit and left her drifting aimlessly.

"Carla, I'm going to retire," her father announced one morning. "These are our sunset years, and your mother and I are going to take full advantage of them." He placed his arm around her shoulder and whispers into her ear, "I want you to manage the Café."

"Dad, I don't know anything about the restaurant business. Maybe you should sell it."

Her father raised his eyebrows. "You're not serious? Café Sea Breeze has been in our family for two generations and has provided us with a comfortable living." He paused and hugged her to him. "As a matter of fact, I'm going to sign the deed over to you. It will be all yours and I'm confident that you'll continue the tradition."

During the next six weeks, Carla received a crash course in restaurant management and her parents departed immediately thereafter on a six-month cruise around the globe. Carla ran the café with the same dedication to excellence that she had observed in her father, and maintained its reputation in the tradition that brought in old loyal clients as well as new ones.

*   *   *

Scanning the beach, her attention is drawn to a man emerging from beneath the pier. He drags his hunched body forward. Each step seems to require more effort than he can manage. A worn baseball cap is pulled over dark, shoulder-length hair and extends down his forehead. Gray sweatpants hang loosely on his body as he clutches a dirty denim jacket tightly across his chest. Carla remembers seeing him before, but today he is a vision of wretchedness. On sudden impulse she waves, inviting him in for coffee. He stares blankly ahead then changes direction and shuffles through the sand toward her.

Seated at the counter, he hugs his right elbow closely to his body as his hand curls around the mug. His voice is low and strained as he thanks her with downcast eyes.

Two women joggers approach the Cafe. Carla recognizes her two friends. Maria, a pretty, petite Hispanic with a hair-trigger temperament, is deep in conversation with her listening companion. Maria uses her beautiful hands expressively as she speaks. Her short black hair curls about a bright yellow sun visor. Deep laugh lines frame her full mouth, hinting at an innate sense of humor which helps her cope with the demands of being editor of The *Zenith*, the local newspaper.

Joyce, her childhood pal and mother of two, is almost six feet tall with a well-proportioned figure. Her voice is deep and serene and washes calm over anyone in earshot. She keeps her delicate, fair complexion drenched in sunscreen.

When Maria had invited Joyce to join her in her morning jog, her friend was reluctant, but Maria was insistent.

"You need some diversion; between the kids, the house and that husband of yours, there's no time for *you*! After we jog, we'll stop at the quaint little Café at the beach. I've already gotten to know the owner. You'll like her...and she bakes the best banana bread in town."

Thus, their joint venture, rain or shine, culminates in having breakfast with Carla. During the past year, the three women became close friends.

"Good morning, ladies." Carla hands each one a steaming mug. "How was your jog this morning?"

"Invigorating!" Maria wipes her brow.

The man briefly glances at the women. Dark circles under his eyes impart deep shadows across a gaunt face and add Rip Van Winkle age.

Joyce aims her head in the man's direction and whispers, "What's with him?"

"He's homeless." Carla's tone is hushed. "I suspect he sleeps on the beach. He looked so sad this morning; I decided to offer him a cup of coffee."

"Carla, you know darned well that the beach is virtually deserted at this hour. I shudder to think what could've happened to you!" Maria chides.

"He's harmless." Carla brings out four dessert plates and begins to slice the banana bread. "I wonder if he has any family. I see so many homeless people on the beach. They beg, panhandle. Some even perform tricks; others draw on the sidewalk for the tourists. The artwork is often quite good...."

Their conversation is interrupted by a sudden thud. The women look up to find the man sprawled on the tile floor. The jacket has fallen back, revealing his bare chest. A steady trickle of blood seeps from his upper left shoulder. His right arm drapes at an odd angle across his thigh. Joyce is the first to reach his side. She checks for pulse while Maria whisks her cell phone from her shorts pocket and dials 911.

Carla snatches a stack of freshly laundered linen napkins. "My God, he's been stabbed!"

A half-inch, semi-circular puncture wound on his upper left shoulder oozes deep red blood. Joyce presses several napkins against the wound. The man remains unconscious as the women hover over him. Maria checks his jacket pocket and pulls out a creased, faded photo of a smiling young woman holding an infant in her arms. A little boy, about four, stands next to the woman. Maria tucks the picture inside her shirt pocket.

The piercing wail of the siren announces the arrival of the ambulance. The medics quickly attend to the man, and then leave for the hospital. The sirens fade into the distance. A police officer who had arrived with the ambulance questions the three women at length.

"I found this in his pocket." Maria shows him the photo. The officer clicks his tongue as he inspects it at length.

"What a shame. Looks like such a nice family. If this man dies, we may never know what happened to him." His eyebrows lift slightly and he looks up at the three women. "There are millions of homeless people all over the country and we certainly have our share here in Seaport. They're often victims of abuse." He paused. "Sometimes the same folks purposely commit crimes in order to be sent to jail for food and shelter. In police terms, we call this 'three hots and a cot.'" He grins.

"You think this is funny?" Carla retorts.

The young cop replies heatedly, "No, I don't. It's a huge problem that takes up much of our time while society decides to look the other way. On the other hand, there *are* a few programs in place designed to help the homeless get back on their feet but many are so used to the life on the street, they often choose not to take advantage of them."

"Officer, may I keep the picture for a while? I want to do a little research." Maria says.

"Sure. I know where to find you."

After the officer departs, the women sit quietly at the counter. Silence hangs like a gloomy mist.

Across the street from the Café a man lingers in the shadow of the gift shop's awning. Dressed in khakis and blue, button-down shirt, he draws deeply at his cigarette without removing it from his lips. His hands, stuffed into his pants pockets, are clenched into fists. The smoke swirls about his square jaw as he stares grimly through the window at the three figures gathered around the counter.

* * *

The sky pelts the beach with rain throughout the morning; even the gulls seek refuge beneath the pier. Carla has had few customers. She has been preoccupied with thoughts of the homeless man. The phone rings.

"Carla...."

"I told you never to call me!" She slams down the receiver. On the other end of the line the man slowly hangs up. His handsome mouth tightens into a hard straight line.

Carla stares out the window. The rain has stopped and fog curls right up to the patio, obscuring the beach in a blanket of smoky, gray haze.

The memories of her disastrous marriage still haunt her. Bill, a talented, struggling writer, had swept her off her feet. An only child, he had inherited a substantial fortune when his parents were killed in an automobile accident. Having unlimited funds allowed him to pursue his passion of writing full time.

He introduced her to a lifestyle that left her breathless. The endless parties, concerts and trips to glamorous places were exciting, and she never wanted them to end. Her parents had asked her to tread with caution, and still she married him at the courthouse in a ritual that was impersonal and rushed.

They were happy at first. Bill had several short stories published and was working on a novel. After the first year he often became bored. He spent less and less time on his writing. He would leave the house to buy cigarettes and return hours later in a drunken daze. There were times when he stayed out all night. As his drinking escalated, he became belligerent and abusive. He drew Carla into altercations that chipped away at her self-esteem. Her world had become a nightmare. She lost weight and started to smoke again, and still, she hung on to absurd hopes that he would change.

When a friend introduced her to AL-ANON she learned about the disease of alcoholism and its devastating effects on the family of the alcoholic. She sat through the entire session weeping quietly as she listened to strangers tell stories so much like her own. She learned that she had no part in the circumstances that led Bill on his path of destruction.

The harmful effect of his behavior crowded her in and she knew that she must take charge of her life and move forward with or without Bill.

One night she refused him; his drunken advances were a prelude to outright rape—not love-making. Her resistance drove him into a fury. He pinned her arms back until she cried out in pain, slammed her against the bedroom door and delivered a fierce, flat-handed blow to her face, and stormed out of the house. Her cheek was laid open by the cut from his wedding ring, yet she felt no pain. Her eyes were dry when she drove herself to the emergency room that night.

She bore the remaining scar with pride; that was the day she summoned the courage to leave him.

*   *   *

Carla sips her coffee when Maria and Joyce burst through the door.

"We've got news about the homeless man." Maria cries. "I've searched the newspaper archives. April, two years ago, there was a burglary in the suburbs of Anaheim, resulting in three deaths." She pauses with meaning.

"A mother and two children were shot point blank. The children were found in puddles of blood in their beds on the second floor, while the mother lay slumped at the bottom of the staircase with a broken neck and a bullet in her back. The coroner determined that she was shot at close range and killed instantly before being pushed down the stairs.

"It's the family of the homeless man! His name is Michael Sondheim, an accountant, thirty-eight, who was working late at his office that night—there were witnesses." Maria shows them a copy of the article. "The killer was never caught."

"His parents reported that he was depressed and withdrew from everyone. It appears that several weeks after the murders, they lost contact with Michael altogether. He had simply vanished."

"I can't even imagine a life without my husband and my kids," Joyce adds softly. "How does one survive such a tragedy?" She feels chilled despite the warm California sun.

"What's his condition?" Carla asks.

"I spoke with the doctor who told me that they expect him to make a full recovery," Maria offers. "They sewed him up and set his right arm which is broken above the elbow. Michael told the police that he was sleeping beneath the pier when he was attacked by thugs who yanked him from the sand and searched him. He had no money so they beat him just for the fun of it and stabbed him, apparently, with a screwdriver."

After the girls leave, Carla closes the cafe early and heads toward All Saints Hospital. She gets off the elevator and hesitates. Her mind runs madly through a maze of conflicting emotions. She fidgets nervously with her purse strap, and then paces ahead with determination that leads her to his room.

Michael is resting on the bed, his right arm packed in a cast. Heavy gauze binds his chest and left shoulder. Recognition quickens in his expression. "Hi," he says quietly.

"How're you feeling?" Carla asks.

"They tell me that I'm going to be fine." He replies his eyes focused intently upon her face. "It's good to see you. I used to watch you from the beach, you know. You always seemed so happy."

Carla's smile is tentative as she pulls up a chair.

"I owe my life to you and your friends…although I'm not sure it was worth saving. I should have died on the beach that day. It would have put an end to my troubles."

Carla's cheeks are flushed and her voice is low. "Your wife would have wanted you to move on with your life and find peace. Whatever happens to us, somehow we manage. Believe me, I know."

Michael stares silently out the window.

"I could use some help in the Café…" Carla's words seem to connect in rapid succession. "There's a furnished apartment on top of my parents' garage. Nothing fancy. It's small—just one room for living room and bedroom, then a tiny kitchen and bath. I used to live there. Since my father retired, they've decided to downsize and are getting ready to put their property up for sale. Nothing's definite yet, but you could stay there, at least for a while until you get on your feet again." She takes a deep breath and smiles nervously.

"You're unique. I've found that in this world most people are totally wrapped up in their own lives and don't give a damn about someone like me." Michael says with a weary grin.

"Not everyone is like that, Michael, but you've got to help yourself."

*   *   *

Maria and Joyce jog the beach. It's been three months since their encounter with the Ishmael-like Michael. When Carla announced that she hired Michael to help out at the Café, they'd been pleased.

The women are busily chatting when they spy a single runner in the distance. He waves as he approaches.

"Good morning, ladies!" Tall and tanned, his wavy hair is trimmed short. His teeth gleam white as he smiles at them affectionately.

"I'll race you back to the Café." Michael takes off sending loitering seagulls into the air, their wings flapping in noisy protest. Still, the girls have no trouble keeping up his pace.

Standing on the patio, Carla watches the three people advance when the phone rings and she runs inside to answer.

"Carla, don't hang up. I must speak with you," Bill pleads.

"I've told you not to call me anymore. Can't you get it in your head that we're through?"

"I've been watching you...."

"You have no business hanging around here."

"I know you've got a man there with you." His voice rises in anger.

"He's just an employee. Besides, it's none of your concern." Carla quickly hangs up and joins her friends.

"You look like you've seen a ghost?" Joyce, slightly winded, exclaims.

"I'm fine. It was just a crank call."

"You seem to get a lot of those lately," Michael remarks and looks at Carla thoughtfully.

*   *   *

"Michael, I'm leaving." Carla slips on her coral cotton jacket and grabs her purse and the envelope with the bank deposit. He appears from the back room where he's replacing the window molding.

"I'll finish here and lock up. See you tomorrow."

His eyes sweep over her in open admiration.

"You look great in that color." He smiles. His eyes brighten and he winks at her. Carla blushes and waves at him.

She walks across the boardwalk to the parking lot. The hush of evening settles on the small town. She opens the car door when she is violently pulled back and an arm of steel closes in on her throat keeping her breathing at a minimum. Her body stiffens.

"Don't hurt me," she manages.

"Shut up and get into the car."

"Bill!" She cringes inwardly. He reeks of liquor.

"Surprised?" He shoves her into the seat. "Move over. We're going for a ride. Give me the keys."

"What do you want?"

"I want my wife back. I know you've got lover boy working with you now. I've seen how he looks at you and you *like* it," he hisses.

She manages to sink her teeth into his arm.

"Damn you!" His face convulses with rage. He pulls his arm loose and hooks a left flush to her mouth splitting her lip. She shrinks into the seat. His eyes narrow like a big cat scenting prey; he yanks her head up. Carla moans.

"Look at me! I know you've been fooling around. *My* wife will never do that!" He spits out a grim laugh. He reaches into his pocket and pulls out a flask of whiskey. "Here, have a drink. I want you to be nice and relaxed."

He forces the burning liquid into her mouth; she gags on the liquor and her own blood. Suddenly, the door is ripped open, and two strong hands tighten around Bill's neck in a vice-grip and drag him out of the car. He is flung brusquely on the cement parking lot.

Surprised momentarily, Bill tries to focus on the tall figure standing above him. He recovers quickly. He straight-legs a foot directly to Michael's stomach. Michael doubles and backsteps. Bill regains his footing and aims a straight left to Michael's nose. Michael ducks right. Bill misses. Bill backs up and assumes a boxer's stance and bounce.

Michael merely smiles. "Never again, never again." Michael spins with whirlwind speed and lands a roundhouse kick at Bill's temple. Bill crashes against the bumper of the car and, without sound, slumps slowly into an unconscious heap. Michael kneels and sets a headlock perfect for a neck snap. He suddenly feels Carla's hands on his shoulders.

"*No*, Michael, *no!*"

"Carla, move back. I'm going to make sure he'll never bother you again!"

"Enough...please, enough! He's going to prison. It's over."

Michael reluctantly drops the unconscious man. He rises and faces Carla. His breath comes in heaves. Carla moves toward him and he gathers her into his arms. She buries her bloodied lips, her tear-streaked face in his chest.

He holds her close to him, and wind blows gently from the east—whispering, misty, and full of promise.

Joel Furches, "Vineyard"

SYMPHONY OF A WOMAN

by Joyce M. Shepherd

She is a gift you wished for,
With skin as soft as a goose's down.
Her breath is as soft as a feather
That tickles your smiling fancy.
She is a miracle, a daughter.

She is a fierce protector,
As well as an honest critic.
Unconditional love is her forte,
With shared moments her treasures.
She is fortunate to be a sister.

She is a woman with purpose,
Spreading her wings and soaring.
Nourishing her inner spirit,
The beauty of life surrounds her.
She is a loving child of God.

She is a life partner and friend,
Sharing the joys and sorrows.
As she stumbles along life's path,
A strong shoulder gives her support.
She is a cherished wife.

She is a vessel for life,
Feeling a hiccup and thumping foot.
Quickly marching forward,
She embraces the circle of life.
She is in awe. She is a mother.

She is a most fortunate woman
With a heart filled to overflowing.
Her biggest role is just beginning.
It is the trophy at the finish line.
She is inspired. She is a grandmother.

DIGGING WITH A PURPOSE

by Leslie B. Picker

The howling winds rattled the windows that frigid night in January while my husband struggled with each breath. Holding his hand, and murmuring comforting words, I hoped he knew I was there. He died as the sun rose on that cold, cold day.

I was vaguely aware when the crocuses crested in March, their tiny blossoms reaching above the snow-covered ground. I even smiled at the burst of lemon yellow when the daffodils greeted the longer days. At the beginning of April, I noted the cherry blossoms, saw the forsythia, and glimpsed the dogwood, but the iris at the end of the month made me melancholy remembering that I planted those lilac rhyzomes when my son was still in diapers.

Going to work, returning home, and going about daily living was like slogging through knee-high mud. Everything was an effort. Making meals to nourish us (we ate out...a lot), paying bills, and even keeping the house decently clean were chores that I barely had the energy to perform. Though both of us were adjusting to the absence of his father, Aaron at fifteen seemed to get back into his life much faster than I. I put on a brave face and forged ahead into my new circumstances.

The hyacinths and then lilacs bloomed, and I brought the cut flowers into the house, hoping the fragrance would lighten our mood. It was so difficult a period, those first few months. The phone calls from friends and relatives became less frequent. It seemed like I was in a tunnel, with no light at the end.

Towards the end of May, I became aware of the patterns of sunlight on the windows as they filtered through the fully-leafed trees. In wonder I walked outside one Saturday morning and realized it was full spring! The climbing roses had buds, and by the chimney, the tiger lily was roaring. I chuckled; the dandelions were in full bloom all over the lawn. For the first time in months I felt energized—I wanted petunias, zinnias, impatiens, marigolds, and salvia...*and* tomatoes, peppers, and squash! There was so much to do!

Although the core of sadness remained, I realized that there would be good days now. I found that having a purpose was a way to get through those difficult times, and planting May flowers was the first step.

MY SEVEN DECADES WITH POLIO

by Peter Raimondi

My life changed tremendously in 1936 when I was just two months shy of my ninth birthday. The day was Sunday, a crisp morning in September. As I came down the stairs of our two-story house on Cordelia Avenue and went into the living room, my mother called to my attention that I was limping. The look on her face was full of fright. She called for my father and, when he saw that I was limping, he tried to reassure my mother. Perhaps the only thing wrong with my leg was that I had slept on it wrong and had cut off the circulation. Dad massaged my leg to see if that would help. My limp persisted. Even at the age of eight, I could see how upset my mother and father were.

Our close-knit Italian family practically owned our street and the red brick and stone houses that we lived in. My grandparents Pietro and Nickolina, Aunt Helen, Aunt Lydia and my Uncle Paul—all lived just across the street. Next door were my Aunt Melina and Uncle Victor and their three children, Mary, Lenia, and Tommy Serano. Upstairs in their rented apartment lived my Uncle Joe and Aunt Jenny Comma. They were all soon in our house trying to reassure my mother and father—and me—that everything was going to be okay.

My mother and father, like all mothers and fathers, wanted the best for their children. Perhaps my sisters were short-changed though. Most of my parents' attention was on my health problem. I am really very sorry if my sisters did not get the attention they should have gotten as they were growing up. My mother and father were consumed with getting their son back to being able to walk again.

My mother, I am sure, was already convinced that I had polio. No one had a phone in our family but one of our neighbors called Doctor Julius Glick, our family practitioner who made house calls. I think that his charge for house calls was $2.00. Dr. Glick soon arrived and decided that I should be admitted to the hospital. I am sure he felt as my mother and father did—that I did indeed have polio.

Soon a big red ambulance arrived and my Aunt Helen, who called me Petey Boy, carried me down to the ambulance. Almost everyone in my family called me Petey Boy. Boy, I thought I was really important to ride in such a big red ambulance.

I was taken to Sindenham Hospital. Today, Montebello Hospital is on the same site. A spinal tap was performed and it was confirmed that I had contracted polio. Back in those days 30,000 to 40,000 men, women and mostly children came down with this dreaded disease each year in the United States alone. There were many polio patients who needed the help of an iron lung to breathe.

In this hospital my left leg was placed in a plaster cast. I realized that something was wrong with my leg when my leg fell out of bed when I turned over and I could not get my leg back into bed.

The dark years began when I was transferred to Kernan Hospital under the care of a Dr. Galven. At this hospital I was placed in a full body cast from my hips down to my toes. My legs were spread apart in a V shape and there was a piece of wood or something that kept my legs apart. The heels of my feet lying on the bottom of the cast really hurt. I cried a lot. Cutting holes in the bottom of the cast did not stop the pain. The edges of the cut just made the pain more intense.

After a time this cast was removed but my left leg had lost all of its power to move. I was furnished with a half cast that I was required to wear only at night. One day I showed the doctor that I could flex my left thumb out of its joint. Bingo, another cast was put on my left hand to keep it from moving. The doctors determined that I had polio in both legs but, thank God, my right leg recovered except for my little toe.

As a result of the polio, my left leg developed about two and half inches shorter than the right. This leg also withered and was not as big, as muscular as the right leg. Due to circulation difficulties, my left leg was (and still is) very cold in the winter.

My stay at Kernan hospital was probably less than six months. From there I was transferred to Children's Hospital. There I was placed under the care of Dr. George Bennett, a world-renowned orthopedic doctor. The team of Mr. & Mrs. Henry O. Kendall headed the physical therapy department at Children's Hospital. They probably didn't make more than $1200.00 a year but they were a great team. Mr. Kendall called me "Pedro."

There are those people who I remember who were very kind and compassionate to me while I was in the hospital. There was Miss Dorsey, my nurse, who told me I was her very first patient who went into shock after being operated on. And there was Beulah, another nurse, who always kept me laughing. Miss Feldman, my physical therapist, worked with me almost every day to get me back to walking again. On occasion, my mother would bring homemade strawberry shortcake for the nurses to enjoy. This was also a treat for me.

I can remember the excitement that my parents had when they first read about a wonderful Austrian nurse who was doing such a marvelous job with polio patients in her own country. Her name was Sister Kenney. The method used by Sister Kenney was not to let the affected muscles wither away by placing those legs and limbs into a plaster cast as was done with me, but to keep the affected muscles moving with physical therapy.

When my parents approached the doctors who were treating me, they tuned her out and seemed to regard Sister Kenney as a quack. This was a shame for the many people who had polio because Sister Kenney's treatment was effective and helped many polio patients be free of leg braces. Sometimes the medical profession can be arrogant and too slow to accept progressive ideas. New ideas and methods should be accepted as soon as they're proven safe and effective.

Dr. Bennett decided I needed an operation that would keep me from slouching over because I had lost the use of some of my stomach muscles. I didn't want any part of this and I cried and cried. I know this broke my mother's and father's hearts for they had to convince me to have this operation. The way they did this was in promising me they would come behind the hospital each night and toot the horn and flash the headlights on their car so that I knew they were with me and visiting outside of the hospital. This was a great comfort to me. The nurses would push my bed to the window so I could wave to my sisters Marie and Lenita standing on the hill outside my ward on Sundays.

I was extremely sick after the operation on my back and left leg. Ether was used to put me to sleep. All I can remember is that I shook violently, was cold, and vomited repeatedly.

One day a Mr. Bruno came to measure me for a leg brace at the hospital. I believe that my first leg brace cost around $75.00. My last leg brace, not very long ago, cost about $8,000.

My first experience in standing up was extremely difficult. My legs felt like they were on fire and had pins and needles in them. I had a hard time walking with this new brace. The brace had a band that wrapped around my back and was buckled in the front of my stomach twisting my body when I walked. Learning to walk with this brace took me years. I had to be careful of my limitations in movement.

Disabled people are always looking for something that will give them stability as they walk—a handrail or a wall. This becomes second nature as they learn to walk again. There were many times that I fell and I walked on crutches for many years before I started walking with a cane.

One of the big events while I was in the hospital is one that I have never forgotten. One day all of the children from the local hospitals were taken to the Hippodrome Theater to see *Snow White and the Seven Dwarfs*. Martha Ray, the comedian, was on stage and walked among us children cheering us up with her style of comedy. Many children, like me, were on gurneys.

Next came the long convalescing at home. It was not easy for either my parents or me. The League for Crippled Children furnished me with a wheelchair. This happened because of the March of Dimes that I believe President Roosevelt started. He was also a polio victim.

My mother never complained as she carried me up and down the fifteen steps to my second floor bedroom. I probably weighed close to one hundred pounds, maybe more. Her unselfish efforts to make my life easier even though I was disabled continued throughout her lifetime. My mother was my best friend. There are millions of stories—mine is certainly one of them—that prove the unselfish devotion of mothers.

I know that I must have had my mother read me the story *Robinson Crusoe* at least a hundred times as I was recovering at home. A boy's imagination is wonderful. Mine always put me into the characters in the book.

My father kept me busy with his war stories about World War I. We talked for hours with me asking all the questions. Dad had a great deal to do with my progress by going about his relentless efforts to find a better way to improve my leg brace. For years I wore a built-up lift on the bottom of my shoe. This lift was about two and a half inches high. My father convinced the brace manufacture that the lift *could* be put inside my shoe. It was his determination and his reiteration that if I persisted, I would succeed.

Later in my life my wife Joan came up with another idea which saved us lots of money. Instead of buying a second pair of shoes and altering them, she suggested that I buy a size larger shoe.

This has worked out fine.

My mother and father never tried to keep me from doing anything that I wanted to do because of my disability. My childhood friends never treated me any differently than they did before I came down with polio.

That wheelchair that was furnished by the League for Crippled Children really got a workout! My friends Will Mead Snyder and Roy Whiteley took me everywhere that I could possibly think of going. And when I say everywhere, that means wherever they could push, pull, wrangle or wrestle that wheelchair with me in it!

Mom would have died early if she knew what we did. There was a large cherry tree in Gallagher's orchard from which dangled a large hemp rope. All of the boys would jump off of one of the large branches with this rope and swing back and forth like Tarzan of the movie fame of those days.

Everybody went to see Tarzan. The cost of a movie trip (usually a couple of features and some shorts) was about thirty-five cents. If you went on Saturday you could see a double feature. They were usually cowboy pictures. Every kid had his own gun and holster.

Of course, I could not climb on the large branch, but Will and Roy would get me out of the wheelchair and I would grab the rope with both hands and my friends would pull me back as far as they could up the incline to the tree trunk and then, with a push, let me go flying through the wind. Lots of fun! But if Mom had known, I would probably not be here to write this story!

The only time in my life that I received a spanking resulted from an adventure begun when the three of us, Will, Roy and me, arrived at the bottom of the Western Maryland Railroad tracks on Rogers Avenue. As we were curious and adventuresome boys, the next logical step was to get up on the bed where the trains actually ran. From the bottom of this incline to the top of the bed where the trains ran was probably thirty feet of granite, fist-sized, loose rock.

There was no way that Will and Roy could push or pull that wheelchair with me in it to the top of the train tracks. So, naturally, we decided that Will would grab one hand and Roy would grab the other hand and they would pull me up the stone and coal-dust incline on my stomach. You can imagine the result. When I got to the top I was as black as the ace of spades from my face all the way down the front of my clothes to the tops of my shoes—there may have been rips in my clothes; frankly, I was too dirty to tell. When I got home and Mom found out that I had been on top of the railroad tracks, I received my first spanking with my britches pulled down. Mom was not angry so much because of the dirt all over me, but because I could have been killed by a speeding train. For my part, I was not so greatly hurt by the spanking as by the total embarrassment of having my britches pulled down by my Mom.

As the last episode shows, I wasn't a perfect kid. Far from it. I got into lots of trouble when I went to school, and I fought with my sisters like most boys do. I can remember teasing both of my sisters whenever our mother made cream puffs. I would squeeze the cream out of the puffs and tell my sisters that it was pus out of a dead man's ear. This little ploy didn't work. My sisters would say, "Be quiet, Petey!"

I might as well mention my experience with cigarettes. All of us boys were smokers. My problem was that my mother always caught me. Not with the cigarettes, mind you, but because I came home with singed-off eyelashes and eyebrows because I held the matches too close to my face when trying to light my cigarette. Mom would say, "Have you been smoking?" And, of course, the answer was plain to see. Got caught again.

During the war we had to turn in our toothpaste tubes to get another tube of toothpaste. Anything made of rubber was also hard to get. Will and Roy got me my first job. They both delivered the *Baltimore Sun* for Mr. Carter who lived not far from our houses. Mr. Carter could not get rubber bands to put around the newspapers before they were delivered. My friends suggested to Mr. Carter that if he would give me old bicycle tubes, I could cut rubber bands for him. The deal was made and I was paid the sum of one dollar per thousand rubber bands that I cut. My mother and sisters all helped me with the cutting.

Another thing that I remember was the enlistment of my friends Will and Roy into the service. Will joined the Merchant Marines and Roy joined the U.S. Marine Corp. I was devastated because I could not join their efforts in fighting for our country. But I soon did my small part to contribute to the war effort. I decided that I would start a scrap metal drive for the war in an empty lot across the street. Mr. Bentz, a veteran of WWI and one of our neighbors, told me that it wouldn't work.

Well, despite his pessimism, our neighborhood *did* begin to pitch in. This small pile of scrap grew to a large mountain of metal. Scrap metal was coming not only from our immediate neighborhood but also from other neighborhoods in all directions. I was so proud when the U.S. Army came with three dump trucks to pick up this scrap for the war effort, I felt really good when Mr. Bentz gave me the "thumbs-up" signal.

Over my lifetime I imagine that I must have had more than twenty braces made to order. Getting used to the new braces was always a challenge. They would often break. The leather would tear my skin because of the constant rubbing. About three or four years ago my mother-in-law saw a new type of brace that was being made by a company in Abington, Maryland. I went there at her insistence and was fitted for a new brace. This brace was made of space-age metal—titanium!

This discovery and improvement all came about because some fourteen years ago I shattered my polio leg at the hip. This occurred when our dogs Sam and Maggie tried to pass me as I was going up the stairs; I twisted my body and fell like a rag doll. People say that animals are dumb, but this is not true. Both Sam and Maggie became very quiet and still. They knew that something terrible had happened. If they could have spoken they would have told me how sorry they were for causing my problem. This was the worst pain that I have ever experienced in my life. A metal bar was installed in my leg and hip. As a result, I cannot sleep on my sides or stomach—I have to sleep on my back. For the next fourteen years I walked on crutches. I was afraid to go back to the cane I was using before I broke my hip because I was afraid I would fall again. Moreover, my left leg had been broken below the knee about twenty-five years ago. Walking on crutches presented additional problems. Both shoulder rotator cuffs were being worn out.

My new brace gives me the confidence to start walking with a cane again after so many years on crutches. Thank God my mother-in-law saw this new brace at the Harford Mall!

Titanium may be light and strong but it isn't perfect; during the first week of May 2006, the new leg brace broke in half. I fell to the kitchen floor injuring my right shoulder. It is now more than a year after that fall and I believe my shoulder will never be the same.

Despite my disability, I always did almost anything that I wanted to do. The only thing that I really missed was dancing and running. I can remember before I was eight how I loved to run up and down the sidewalk in front of our house with the wind hitting me in the face. My legs kicked high as an antelope behind me as ran. Sometimes, I thought I would fly!

My father continued finding new ways to make it easier for me to adjust to my disability. Like most boys, I wanted to learn to drive and when Dad bought a new 1939 Plymouth, my chance to drive became real because of what my father did for me. First, he taped a block of wood on the clutch. I would pick my leg up beneath the kneecap and place my left foot on the clutch. Then I would push down on my knee with my left hand until the pedal would move. I took my driving test in that Plymouth and the instructor never even noticed what I was doing to shift gears. I passed on the first try and I know my Dad was very proud of my accomplishment. (So was I!)

My wife Joan gave me my first dancing lessons. Now, *that* took a lot of patient coaching! My wife encouraged me to dance with her and, thanks to her, I was able dance with my mother at my mother and father's fiftieth wedding anniversary. The same priest that married my mother and father was there as was Dr. Glick who treated me for polio many years ago.

Two of the most pleasant times in my life were the two summer seasons I spent at Camp Greentop for crippled children in Thurmont, Maryland. Close by was the camp that the president of the United States would visit. Back in those days I believe it was called "Shangri-La." Today it is Camp David. On occasion, the President would visit us. This was always a major event for us all.

Our headmaster for the camp was Vest Marx, a very distinguished gentleman with white hair and a heavy white mustache. Our cabins slept eight boys with two counselors. Ray Swartzback and Mr. Frantz, our pair of counselors, both came from Baltimore. Mr. Swartzback had a great deal of influence with boys. I believe that Mr. Swartzback became a minister and Mr. Frantz was the head of the X-ray department at Maryland General Hospital. Each evening, Mr. Swartzback would pay each boy a visit at bedtime and would talk about the day's events and what each of us could do to improve. He would always end or start his conversations with, "Look me in my good eye!"

There were many fun times for the boys and girls at this camp. When the moon was full, we would all gather in a semi-circle around an area that was set up with benches carved out of logs. In the middle of the semi-circle was a large pile of stacked firewood. Mr. Marx, in full Indian headdress, would stand on top of a large outcropping of rock that was above and beyond the near-circle where the children were all seated. Then, raising his hands to the full moon, he would say that if the Great Spirit looked down kindly on this gathering, we would have instant fire in the firewood that was stacked. Our eyes must have almost popped out of our heads because, presto, the firewood burst into flames! Sometimes one of the lady counselors, dressed in full Indian costume, would sing for us. We all sang songs and had hot dogs and soda.

Many years later, I took a drive up to Camp Greentop. The semi-circle was still there and so were the benches. As I stood there I could see those wonderful evenings unfold exactly as I did when I was a little boy. I *did* discover how this instant fire was started by the Great Spirit but, of course, I cannot reveal His ways. To this day, I do believe the Great Spirit was at that gathering of boys and girls those many years ago. The camp, and its magic, is still there every summer for other disabled children.

There was a large swimming pool. We had a large open field where we would play ball and other games; the butterflies were a constant and wonderful distraction. They were absolutely beautiful in their many colors. We caught black snakes and kept them in glass aquariums. Mice would fall into the bathtub in the infirmary after falling off of the overhead logs. We would feed these to the black snakes who became our pets.

One time as I was going to the latrine, I came across a black snake or, rather, the snake crossed *my* path—suddenly! I can tell you that my feet never touched the ground as my crutches carried me as fast as I could run back to the cabin yelling, "Snake! Snake!" Boy, did I receive a reprimand from Mr. Swartzback. I think that I had our whole section in an uproar because of my yelling. In my defense, that snake must have been five or six feet long.

Friendships developed fast for all of us. Fun was everywhere and at every moment. Sometimes half of the cabin's kids with one of the counselors would get up around four in the morning and leave a trail for the other half of the kids to follow after the early-risers two-hour lead. Our hikes ended up in Foxville, a one-house town where we could buy all the candy we wanted for about five cents.

Going to church in Thurmont on Sundays was also great fun. Coming down the mountain in that old 1940 Ford station wagon was full of thrills. We would take turns yelling to the counselor who was driving to go faster. A ranger lived in a log cabin at the bottom of the mountain. He looked as if he were from the Old West with a six-gun strapped to his side and a beat-up Stetson on his head.

There were all types of activities. There was a small zoo. It had some wild local mammals but mostly native snakes. Not far from our camp was a CCC camp. This camp of hard-working men was set up to pursue public projects and kickstart employment during the Great Depression. Our visit was always on Wednesday so we, too, could watch their movies with them in the outdoors.

When I was ten, I had my first overnight camp-out near the Cunningham Falls. They had built canvas bunks so that none of us had to sleep on the ground. I remember lying there looking up into a night as clear as sequins on a panther, counting all the stars as far as I could see, taking in the wonderful smells from the moist ground and the pines and hemlocks, and listening to all the night-hunters of the forest. The background rhythm was the sound of the rushing waters from the falls. I thought how lucky I was to be enjoying all of God's wonders. This was a small piece of heaven. I felt very secure under the sparkling stars. Wonderful sights, smells and sounds—music for a quick and sound sleep.

All good things must come to an end. As we approached the end of the camping season many of us reflected on the wonderful times and friends we met during our eight weeks at Camp Greentop. The day soon arrived to say goodbye. Every child—and counselor—shed some tears. Almost every moment I spent at Camp Greentop is still engraved in my memory and heart.

With those memories of the camp in my heart are those people—my mother; father; sisters, Marie and Lenita; my wife, Joan; my mother-in-law, Ruth; my children, Christopher and Jennifer; and my many friends during my illnesses and rehabilitations—who encouraged me to go on.

None of them asked anything in return and I have been wealthy in their love and friendship. I have been blessed to have so many people unconditionally *for* me. God bless them all.

Dianna J. Zurinsky, "Moss on the River"

STAR DATE

by JoAnn M. Macdonald

Have you looked up at the stars on a clear moonless night? Have you wondered about those twinkling stars—their nature, size, age and future? The young girl who later becomes the adult protagonist in the film *Contact* certainly does. This young girl, portrayed by Jodi Foster, could have been modeled directly on one of the most remarkable women of the nineteenth century, Maria Mitchell.

Maria, "Mah-RYE-ah" as her family pronounced it, Mitchell looked up at the stars night after night with her father from the time she was tall enough to climb the ladder to the roof. She was the third of ten children and the only one to take an interest in her father's hobby. He built a rooftop "walk" on their house in order to set up his telescope and observe the night skies. Maria and her father spent many nights in the cold of the winter and very warm, balmy nights in the summer "sweeping the sky," as Henry Albers recounts in his book *Maria Mitchell, A life in Journals and Letters* (14).

Nowadays, it is not unusual for girls to study astronomy. Consider this, though—Maria Mitchell was born on August 1, 1818 on Nantucket Island off the coast of Massachusetts! In those early years of the United States of America, most girls were not encouraged to learn anything except household chores like cleaning, cooking, sewing and weaving. Maria was very fortunate to be born of parents like William and Lydia Mitchell. They were avid readers, especially her mother. She had been a librarian before she married William and instilled the love of books in her children. Both parents wanted their children to be learned adults so they encouraged them to read and study everything.

Maria's favorite subject was mathematics, especially calculations. "Sweeping the sky with a telescope, she and her father would observe eclipses and make calculations of the movements of the planets" (Albers 14). She counted the seconds for her father while they observed a lunar eclipse. Maria stated in her journal: "This time was noted by me; I was 12 ½ years old. M.M" (Albers 9). A later journal entry dated March 2, 1845 reads: "I 'swept' last night for two hours, by three periods. It was a grand night— not a breath of air, not a fringe of cloud. All clear, all beautiful. I really enjoy that kind of work, but my back soon becomes tired, long after the cold chills me" (Albers 43, Gormley 51, and Wright 67).

Even with the stresses of the weather, Maria was a mentally strong and physically healthy girl, traits which later would prove to be assets in helping to raise her younger siblings because she was older and unmarried when her mother became ill. She did not consider herself to be a beauty—far from it. Her dislike of her own facial features carried into her adulthood. To Maria, her negative assessment of her attractiveness discouraged her sociability with boys and later, men. It would direct her path to astronomy—her passion. She never married (Gormley 48).

Albers' *Maria Mitchell: A Life in Journals and Letters* reprints a poem she wrote in 1853:

> Did you never go home, Sarah,
> It's nothing so very sad,
> I've done it a hundred times, Sarah,
> When there wasn't a man to be had
>
> And I've done it a hundred times more
> When I've seen them stand hat in hand
> I've walked alone at the door,
> And they continued to stand. (20)

*   *   *

Nantucket can be a cruel place when the rime settles in or the winter winds blow off the Atlantic Ocean. As with most New Englanders, the Mitchells were determined to make their homes comfortable and safe and their lives meaningful. They were a sensible and close-knit family who exhibited admirable values. All of the children shared in the household chores. Albers tells us: "Maria's task was what she called an endless washing of dishes" (17). According to Albers, in her journal many years later when considering her childhood as part of a large Quaker family, Maria would reflect on those formative years on Nantucket Island. "Our want of opportunity was our opportunity—our privations were our privileges, our needs were our stimulants—we are what we are partly because we had little and wanted so much, and it is hard to tell which was the more powerful factor" (22). Albers continues: Mr. Mitchell was "a highly skilled astronomical observer" (10). He had no formal training, yet he was able to earn money by rating the instruments—the chronometers—which were essential to determining longitude on the whaling ships. He was respected for his accuracy in calibrations. Under her father's watchful eye, Maria learned to do the calculations of the instruments (Gormley 9).

The United States whaling business flourished after the War of 1812 with Nantucket Island the main northeastern port for as many as eighty ships. A formative incident occurred when her father was away at business and old Cap'n Bill Chadwick of the good ship *Baltic* came to the Mitchell home for calibration of his ship's chronometer (Wright 21). The captain frowned when he learned that Mr. Mitchell was unavailable, "for a chronometer only one second off would cause a ship to be a quarter mile off course" (Gormley 9). Mrs. Mitchell, known as a good Quaker and a most honest woman, looked doubtful, and the captain was even more dubious when Maria spoke timidly but then added with determination, "Thee knows I have often watched father [do the calibrations]" (Wright 21). Then, according to Wright, "from under his [the captain's] dark brows, he looked Maria up and down" (21). One can imagine his apprehension with the mere girl of fourteen in a gray dress, starched white apron and white cap who was eager to set his ship's chronometer. With no one else on the island to do the calibration, he had no choice but to trust in her self-assuredness. She proceeded to successfully recalibrate the instrument (Gormley 10, Macdonald 2, and Wright 21).

Her father was her main teacher in her younger years although she did attend the local school for a few years. With no higher, formal education available to her she was self-taught. Eager to earn her own way, at seventeen she placed an advertisement in the Nantucket newspaper announcing the opening of her own "school for Girls for the purpose of Instruction in Reading, Writing, Spelling, Geography, Grammar, History, Natural Philosophy, Arithmetic, Geometry and Algebra" (Albers 15). She maintained the school for a year until the newly-built Nantucket *Atheneum* with its well-stocked library beckoned. Maria obtained a librarian's position there and closed the school (Macdonald 1).

She took advantage of the opportunity to read many books, and so taught herself German, Greek, Latin and calculus. The last was really to advance her knowledge of astronomy. The *Atheneum* offered Lyceum lectures by noted Unitarians and Transcendentalists—individuals of progressive and often similar thought—Bronson Alcott, Elizabeth Peabody, Henry David Thoreau, Ralph Waldo Emerson, Lucy Stone, Elizabeth Oakes Smith, William Ellery Channing, Horace Greeley and Theodore Parker. Maria was influenced by these open-minded and logical thinkers who supported her beliefs in a more positive theology than that of the many Christian denominations which frightened the faithful with tales of hellfire and damnation. She resigned her Quaker membership in 1843; she later aligned herself with Universalism concepts which include salvation for all without the need for a personal savior (Macdonald 2).

"She unambiguously described astronomy as 'the study of the works of God,' and her diaries are filled with references to church services she attended and sermons she heard" (Albers 22). She may have been the first American woman scientist but she retained her strong religious beliefs.

The year 1847 would be an exceptionally important one for Maria. She had been watching a particular patch of the heavens for many nights. One particular point of light, a "fuzzy star," had caught her attention (Gormley 42). Suddenly, one night she became excited. She had calculated its position and it had moved! Yes! It moved night after night! She had discovered a comet. She had been watching and hoping for such a phenomenon. And there it was. William Mitchell recorded, "This evening at half past ten Maria discovered a telescopic comet five degrees above Polaris. William Mitchell, 10 mo 1, 1847" (Albers 26 and Gormley 42).

Again, from Albers: "William Mitchell wasted no time in notifying his friend William C. Bond, director of the Harvard College Observatory, about his daughter's fortuitous find" (26). Would another astronomer somewhere in the world publish the discovery of the same comet and submit his discovery with a date preceding hers? World communications were exceedingly slow. The long wait of several weeks to perhaps months for a reply would be nearly unbearable. Finally the fateful letter arrived—one year later. It stated Maria Mitchell was recognized for discovering "Comet Mitchell 1847VI" (Albers 30).

This "star date" determined the path for the rest of Maria's life. She was awarded a gold medal from King Frederick VI of Denmark. He had established this prize in 1831 for anyone who discovered a comet (Albers 28 and Gormley 40). Letters of introductions from American astronomers helped to open the European scientific doors to her. It was not an easy task, however.

Not all male scientists were eager to meet a female scientist. Undaunted by these men, Maria held fast to her desire to view the universe from the Vatican's observatory.

Albers records a brief account from her journal regarding her attempt "to visit the Astronomical Observatory situated in the Roman College of the Jesuit Fathers":
> I was ignorant enough of the ways of all Papal Institutions and indeed of all Italy to ask if I might visit the Roman Observatory. I remembered that the days of Galileo were days of 2 centuries since. I did not know that my heretic feet must not enter the sanctuary, that my woman's robe must not brush the seats of learning. (121)

With covert assistance by a well-connected priest, Maria was finally granted permission to visit the observatory, but only in the daytime!

Other honors came to her over her lifetime celebrating her status as a woman of science and, especially, as an *American* woman of science. From *The Book of Women's Firsts*, by Phyllis J. Read and Bernard L. Witlieb and *What Every American Should Know About Women's History*, by Christine Lunardini, Ph.D., these are Maria Mitchell's achievements: She was the first woman appointed to the American Academy of Arts and Sciences (1848), the first woman elected to the American Association for the Advancement of Science (1850), the first woman to be elected to the American Philosophical Society (1869), and a founder and first president of the American Association for Advancement of Women (1873). Posthumously, Maria Mitchell was elected to the Hall of Fame of Great Americans (1905) (Read and Witlieb 294 and Lunardini 63).

Moreover, her teaching career began in 1865 at Vassar College as the first woman professor of Astronomy. She led the way for women to find careers in science and, equally important, to reach their potential. According to Albers, she told her women students:
> For women, there are undoubtedly great difficulties in the path, but so much the more to overcome. First, no woman should say, 'I am but a woman.' But a woman! What more can you ask to be? Born a woman, with an average brain of humanity, born with more than the average heart, if you are mortal what higher destiny could you have? No matter where you

> are nor what you are, you are a power. Your influence is incalculable. (258)

And as one would expect, Maria was an advocate in the Woman's Rights Movement. All of the notable women of that time—leaders such as Elizabeth Cady Stanton and Susan B. Anthony—were her friends and compatriots in the struggle for the right to vote, for equality in professions, and for reforms in education and health issues for women (Gormley 89). Growing up in a warm, loving and encouraging family enabled Maria Mitchell to become the astronomer she dreamed of becoming and—perhaps more than she imagined—a role model for women.

At her funeral in June, 1889 on Nantucket Island, Vassar's President James Monroe Taylor eulogized Maria Mitchell. These words are an excerpt from his eulogy as recounted by Albers:

> If I were to select for comment the one most striking trait of her character, I should name her *genuineness*. There was no false note in Maria Mitchell's thinking or utterance. Doubt she might and she might linger longer in doubt, but false she could not be. …This genuineness explains also a marked feature of her religious experience. She would not use the language of faith often because it did not seem to her that she had clearly grasped the truths which came through faith. It would be a grave error to infer from this that she was not a *religious* woman in a true sense. She was always a seeker of *truth*. …She fulfilled the exhortation of her friend Dr. Channing, 'Worship God with what He most delights in, with aspiration for spiritual light and life.' (323)

The little girl who looked at the stars and wondered what they were and how far away they were eventually had a wonder-filled date with the stars—Maria Mitchell discovered her comet and, in so doing, discovered her destiny.

Works Cited

Albers, Henry (ed.). *Maria Mitchell: A Life in Journals and Letters.* Clinton Corners, New York: College Avenue Press, 2001.

Gormley, Beatrice. *Maria Mitchell, The Soul of an Astronomer.* Grand Rapids, Michigan: William B. Eerdmans Publishing Company, 1995.

Lunardini, Ph.D., Christine. *What Every American Should Know About Women's History.* Holbrook, Massachusetts: Adams Media Corporation, 1997.

Macdonald, JoAnn M. *Maria Mitchell.* Boston, Massachusetts: The Unitarian Universalist Association, Unitarian Universalist Historical Society, Dictionary of Unitarian Universalist Biography, 2005.

Read, Phyllis J. and Bernard L. Witlieb. *The Book of Women's Firsts.* New York, New York: Random House, Inc., 1992.

Wright, Helen. *Sweeper in the Sky: The Life of Maria Mitchell.* Commemorative Edition. Clinton Corners, New York: College Avenue Press, 1997.

CLOUD DANCER

by Susan C. Buttimer

Here we are!

Up, up, into space, into the sky
   With the fresh wind on our faces,
     And the drumming, humming in our ears.

      Out, over the sea
        We soar like a bird on double wings,
         For this moment,
           We have gained the perception of the gulls.

        Below, the ocean breaks,
       Away, over and down,
       Visually pulling us toward the shore.

    Above,
    A tough gust of wind
   Tosses us skyward.

   Through flight,
  Though seemingly suspended alone,
We participate in a Universal song.

Today, over the sea,
We danced in the clouds.

RETURNING

by Lee Bruce

Arriving in our hometown for our forty-fifth high school class reunion, my friend and I noticed many changes. As we drove down Broad Avenue, we spied people who looked like those we had known in our youth, but no one we actually knew.

Years ago our business district was small. One could walk the entire length in less than ten minutes. Often it took considerably longer because of visiting with friends and neighbors. My instructions, firmly given by my Mother, were to keep moving along with no stops at Handelsman's Drug Store. She had little appreciation of my needing a cherry coke. The local drug store held our only soda fountain and a druggist who loved children.

Many of the shops were wooden, most painted white with green or black trim. The A&P was the only barn-red structure. It was strange but I could hear Mother's voice directing me. "Be sure to have Mr. Dolfi choose the strawberries. He will know just which ones to send." Across the street the butcher shop was white but had black framing the large windows. In those windows were displayed large baskets of seasonal vegetables and dressed chickens hanging upside down. "Be sure to explain to Mr. Wasicek that there will be twelve here for dinner Sunday. Ask him to choose a nice roast for me."

*   *   *

Now, as we moved along Broad Avenue near Frank's gas station, we passed the movie house. The large marquee said "CLOSED" but in my mind's eye I saw, "Children 12 cents, Adults 35 cents." We saw that Yencsik's Market had relocated, the music store had closed, but the gray porch-paint-colored hardware store was still in business. What a perfect choice of color since they sold lumber and paint! Two funeral homes separated by four nicely kept homes brought us to the end at Roley's Garage. During WWII, when there were no cars manufactured, the garage was converted to a bowling alley. The really good news was that they also had a soda fountain—cherry cokes, here we come! I lived in that neighborhood and can remember going to sleep to "rrrrrrrrrrrBam, rrrrrrrrrrrBam!"

As we remembered the various businesses we were reminded of the smells of baking bread, melons piled high in front of the grocery stores, the waxy scent of the bank, perfume of flowers at Irwin's Florist Shop, and the coffee mills grinding Eight O'Clock coffee in the mills at the A&P.

Next to the drug store a plain wood sign said, "SHOE REPAIR." Not *shoes* repaired" because you would take only one shoe if the need was singular. Bruno was the shoemaker's name. He didn't make shoes; he repaired them. With stained hands he also fixed purses, leather aprons, and holders for various tools. Wide boards, freshly oiled to preserve them, added to the aromas of shoe dyes and leather. The shop was dark. As one's eyes—and imagination—adjusted, one could almost see Bruno in the back of his establishment smile and wave.

More vivid than my memory of Bruno or his shoes is my recall of the sparkling clean window beneath the sign. Mrs. Puppelle, Bruno's wife and the woman who perpetually cleaned that window, had coal black hair, soft brown eyes, bright red lipstick and fascinatingly lacquered nails in the same shade of red. When business at the shop was slow, she did handwork. If one arrived early in the day one could smell the vinegar used in the water to clean that window.

Each child who attended Graham Street Elementary School found this woman to be beautiful. We were not big spenders. We made our purchases one penny at a time. If one has never had to decide between three green leaves or three orange slices one may have missed an experience of a lifetime. These were major decisions. We wore our "candy buying" faces as we entered the store. If one were to look really troubled about the choice, one might miraculously find two green leaves and two orange slices in the tiny bag. I wish I could remember her name,...Genna, Sarafina, Carmella...one of those musical sounding names. It seems so important to remember.

As each school year began a new group of children for her to help and love and learn about came to her shop. They, too, would experience her golden cash register and the wonder of the glass candy case. What a delight. Each child would meet Bruno's wife with the bright lipstick and polished nails. They would become, with the tiny paper bag of treasures, one of the children of Our Goddess.

For me this town and its people are still so vivid. Mr. Lambert had been the caretaker of the cemetery. I see his lined face and blue eyes. Sounds of accordian music float from the windows of Joey's bungalow. I can taste the cream puffs from Valdesarri's Bakery where I went with my Uncle Bob to celebrate his return to town.

Others will bring their memories to the reunion of friends tonight. We come from all over the country, enriched by a lifetime of experiences—successes, failures, degrees attained, dreams—whether followed or foiled. We come to affirm friendships and to renew ourselves.

As we stood in the local cemetery where we had come to lovingly honor our parents, I began to laugh. How inappropriate. We had seen no one in town that we recognized but here were the names of so many we knew and remembered. What a peculiar place to feel youthful. Friends, neighbors, relatives—all were represented in this hallowed place.

As children born in the Depression, we grew up with very little money. We were, however, extremely fortunate to be a part of this time and this town. We learned to be frugal—a skill to serve us well in later life. Most valuable of all, we were loved, safe, and happy. If urban sophistication were what you sought, you would never have been happy in our town. We were. It had consistency. Work hard. Love God. Worship regularly. Respect family values. A handshake was as binding as any paper contract. Early in our lives we learned the rules for living.

When a Polish mother-of-the-bride and the Italian mother-of-the-groom met to decide the menu for the wedding reception, they could not agree. Potato salad and pierogies versus meatballs and ravioli. Each mother was committed to honoring the expectations. The Compromise: two receptions, one in the church social hall and one in the local Italian lodge. Thankfully, we had only one Catholic Church, the neighbors joked.

Food was our rate of exchange. I did English homework for Sondra's ham cappicolla sandwich. If you needed a paper typed, you called Elma or Dolores. Math and science were the domain of Tom or Bill. Each had a favorite, a skill and we bartered freely. We knew our academic strengths and what was in most family pantries.

Many of my classmates were fortunate recipients of Mrs. Crawford's coffee cake, my Mom's apple pie or Mrs. Fee's orange-frosted cookies. One could easily get an invitation to dinner in most homes. You had to call home first so that your family knew where you were. At a friend's home you ate whatever you were served. With family, one could choose according to tastes, menu, and inclinations—sometimes even splitting the meal with the main course at one house and dessert at another. It helped if one had lots of aunts, honorary or legitimate.

So many names remembered and forgotten. I *do* wish I could remember the name of the "candy lady." I need to know her name. I will ask Elma. She married a local boy. If she doesn't remember, someone in her card club will. We had to call her Mrs. Puppelli because we were just kids. It was a very personal relationship she had with all of us. It is important to know *all* of her name.

AUDREY GETS DRAWN IN

by Joanne Galantino

"Have you tried that new video game, *Crusaders*? It's really awesome!" raved Trent Osborne as he was leaving school with his friends, Jake Clemson and Justin Walker.

"No! Can we play it when we get to your house?" Jake replied.

Ms. Hutchins intervened. " 'May,' Jake. "You say, may."

Jake looked at Ms. Hutchins. "For crying out loud, it's Friday," he wanted to say. Ca—I mean—*may* I forget about Language class until Monday?" Instead, Jake turned to Trent and said, "*May* we play it when we get to your house?"

"Of course, you ca-*may*," said Trent, laughing.

"Cool!" cheered Justin.

"But now you guys sound like my grandmother's soap." Trent put his two friends in headlocks, and the three stutter-stepped toward their school bus.

*   *   *

Audrey Emerson watched the three boys. Trent, Jake, and Justin had been friends since Pre-K. They all liked the same things, they played the same sports, they even sounded the same. Audrey sighed as she hoisted her backpack higher on her shoulder. How she wished she had a friend like that. She knew it wasn't possible. Every single one of the girls played some sort of sport and Audrey was as coordinated as a bull on roller skates. She tired easily when she ran. She couldn't turn cartwheels, and the thought of using her head to stop a soccer ball gave her a headache. She didn't care as much about the first two things, but her dislike of soccer was a problem. Her father played soccer in high school and went to college on a soccer scholarship. He was always tossing a ball around, begging her play with him.

"Wouldn't it be great to get a sports scholarship, like I did?" he would ask her. Audrey wanted to tell him that the school she hoped to attend didn't even offer athletics, but she didn't want to hurt her father's feelings. He simply didn't understand her different dreams. All Audrey wanted to do was draw. After homework was done and books were put away, out came the paper, pencils, and crayons. She'd been at it since she was two years old. Her mother even taped drawings in Audrey's baby book to prove it.

Audrey walked slowly to her bus and sat down near the front, by herself. Just like in school, she had no one to talk to or anything to talk about. "I don't care," she thought. "At least I'm one of the first stops." She overheard two of her classmates, Madison Adams and Alyssa Rainier, talking. Naturally, the conversation was soccer.

"I hope it doesn't rain tomorrow," Madison said worriedly, "or else our game will be canceled."

"I know," agreed Alyssa. "I have been practicing every day after school. My poor mother has two big bruises on her legs from where the ball hit her. I've never seen such colorful marks. Some parts of the bruises are *yellow*."

Madison groaned. "Ughh. The only yellow I want to see is on our soccer uniforms. That is, if we ever get any."

Alyssa rolled her eyes. "Yeah, our logo was lame last year. Some of our opponents laughed at it."

"I remember," Madison complained. "Anyway, maybe your mom can borrow your brother's old guards and stuff."

"Yeah," nodded Alyssa. "At least she didn't get hit in the face. No makeup in the world can cover soccer bruises."

Audrey shuddered. No way was she going to subject herself to a ball like that. Her father once broke his nose playing soccer. To hear him tell the story, Audrey thought, it sounded as if he *liked* it. "I'll stick to drawing," she decided. No injuries there, unless she stabbed herself with a pencil and got lead poisoning. Audrey looked up in time to see the bus driver pulling in front of her street. Audrey grabbed her backpack, said goodbye to the bus driver, and walked home.

Mrs. Emerson opened the door before Audrey rang the bell. "Hi, Dear," she said, giving her daughter a hug.

"Hey, Mom," Audrey hugged her back.

Mrs. Emerson had been sewing a mod-style jumper for Audrey. One half was black, and the other half was white. It had a cool white plastic belt with a red buckle, too. It would be perfect with the shiny black flat boots Gram sent her for her birthday. Mrs. Emerson held it up.

Audrey gasped and grabbed the garment. "Omigosh, it's awesome, Mom!" she cried. "It'll be perfect with my black boots, black tights, and red turtleneck."

Mrs. Emerson smiled. "I was thinking exactly the same thing. You may even borrow a couple of my bangle bracelets."

"*Yes!!*" Audrey shrieked, hugging her mother again. "Thank you so much!" Audrey herself was just learning to sew. So far, she knew how to sew on buttons and once made a small pillow, but that was it. Mrs. Emerson could sew anything, and her things always turned out better than the pictures on the patterns. Audrey longed to design dresses and sew them. It was so much fun to wear things that were like no one else's.

"I'm so glad you love it, Honey. It'll be a perfect way to face Monday. Whenever I had a new dress to wear to school, going there was easier and much more fun."

Suddenly, Audrey looked down. Her face became so downcast Mrs. Emerson thought her daughter might be ill.

"What's wrong, Baby? Did something happen today?" Mrs. Emerson knew Audrey had no close friends, and she never asked to have anyone over, or to host sleepovers. Of course she worried, but because her daughter was always drawing or doing things by herself, she figured she was simply a loner and therefore content. But now, something was terribly wrong. Were there bullies? Mrs. Emerson clutched Audrey's shoulders. "Please tell me what happened."

Audrey put her new dress down carefully, and wiped her eyes. "I'm sorry, but for me, no matter what I wear, going to school is never easy and it's never fun. I have nothing in common with anyone there. No one is ever mean to me, but no one ever comes up to talk to me, either." She put her arms around her mother, and cried.

Mrs. Emerson held her and said, "Well, it sounds like you need to start talking to your classmates. The girls may think you don't like them." She let go of her daughter and walked to a table scattered with Audrey's drawings and art supplies. She picked one up and held in front of Audrey. "Did anyone ever see your drawings? I could see you making a lot of friends that way."

Audrey shook her head. "No, they only care about soccer stuff. Just like Daddy. He never asks to see my drawings. All he ever talks about is playing soccer and earning a scholarship. No art school has athletic fields on the campus—they have studios."

Mrs. Emerson put her arm around her daughter. "Daddy will see, and so will the kids at school. Come on, let me show you how to put a zipper in your fabulous new jumper. It's a challenge, but I know you'll get the hang of it." The two walked into Mrs. Emerson's sewing room.

*   *   *

Mr. Emerson was a little late getting home. Mrs. Emerson and Audrey were already eating when he walked in. "Sorry I'm late, ladies," he said, kissing each of them as he sat down to dinner. "Everything looks great, Lisa," Mr. Emerson said as he helped himself to salad. "Guess who I ran into today while I was finishing up with my last sales call? Charlie Bartman. He said he has a nine-year-old daughter in Audrey's class. Do you know her?" Mr. Emerson asked, spooning spaghetti on his plate.

Audrey nodded. "Yes. Olivia Bartman." The most aggressive girl athlete in the 4th grade. Audrey didn't dislike her; she just didn't hang around her. Olivia was very popular. Everyone always wanted her on their teams because she practically guaranteed victories.

Mr. Emerson continued. "Anyhow, Charles was telling how Olivia got her soccer team to the finals, and scored the winning goal in the championship."

Mrs. Emerson started, "Greg..."

Mr. Emerson spooned sauce on his spaghetti, then sprinkled on some Parmesan cheese. "That Olivia sounds like quite a gal." He looked at Audrey. "You've heard me mention Charlie Bartman. Why didn't you tell me his daughter was in your class? There's a scholarship with that girl's name on it."

"Greg..." Mrs. Emerson began again.

Audrey put down her fork. She was beginning to feel a bit sick. "I don't really know her," she responded weakly.

Mr. Emerson didn't notice his wife or his daughter. "Well, you can invite her here, and get to know her that way. Maybe she could help you work on your soccer moves. Who knows, maybe you could both get sports scholarships? Maybe you could appear in *Sports Illustrated's* Teen Stars section...."

It was too much for Audrey. She stood up.

"Why don't you adopt Olivia?" she shouted. "I don't *ever* want to play soccer! I don't want to work on my soccer skills, because I don't have any. I don't want gross yellow bruises. I don't want a broken nose. I just want to be a fashion designer and have friends. I am an artist. Don't you like artists? Don't you like *me*? Do you wish I was another type of daughter? If so, why don't you go to my school and trade me in!" Audrey stormed out of the room, sobbing.

Mr. Emerson stared at the doorway. He was stunned. He had never seen Audrey so upset. "Lisa," Mr. Emerson started. "What have I done?"

Mrs. Emerson looked at her husband. "Audrey just revealed to me how sad and lonely she is. Frankly, she needs to go up to the kids at school and talk with them. I'm sure they know about other things besides soccer."

Mr. Emerson looked hopeful. "Well, maybe if I told her some facts about the game, they'd...."

"No. And it's time you accept our daughter for what she is. Audrey is an artist. The awards and scholarships she wants will come from her drawings, not goals, or laps, or points." Mrs. Emerson wrapped up Audrey's dinner and put it in the refrigerator.

Mr. Emerson felt terrible. He was about to get up from his seat and go to Audrey's room when he sat down again. "Great," he said.

Mrs. Emerson picked up the bowls of leftover spaghetti and sauce. "What?"

"I almost forgot. Since we weren't going anywhere tonight, I invited Charlie, Beth, and Olivia over for coffee and dessert around 7:00."

"I wish you would've called. I don't have time to bake anything now."

"No worries. I'll run to Simon's Bakery and pick up some cookies. I'll get some of those mint chocolate ones."

Mrs. Emerson sighed. "Poor Audrey. She was so upset today. Oh well, she can practice talking with just Olivia. She has to open up."

Mr. Emerson ran out the door, "It's all good! They'll be here at 7:00!"

Mrs. Emerson looked around the house. At least everything was straightened up. She thought, "I'll get some cups, saucers, plates, and napkins, and be done with it. But first I have to talk to Audrey." She walked up to Audrey's bedroom door and tapped on it gently.

"Audrey? Baby?" The door opened slowly. Audrey was standing in her pajamas.

"What is it, Mom?"

Mrs. Emerson entered her room "Honey, you have to change. We're having company. Go put your school clothes back on."

Audrey didn't want to change. "Who's coming? Can't I stay in my pjs?"

Mrs. Emerson went to Audrey's hamper. "No. It's Mr. Charlie, Miss Beth, and Olivia," she replied. "You have to get dressed."

"What?!" Audrey shrieked. "Why?!"

I'm sorry, dear, but Daddy thought he was doing a good thing. You know how he feels about soccer."

Audrey removed her pajamas angrily.

"And you know how *I* feel about it. Can't I pretend to be sick so I can put my pjs back on? Then I can stay away from everybody. We just studied about rhinoviruses in science."

"No, you can't be rude. Olivia is your guest, no matter how much you dislike her."

Audrey slipped on her school pants.

"I don't dislike her, I'm just not *like* her. We're like night and day."

Mrs. Emerson handed Audrey her socks.

"Well, in life, you'll meet people who you won't feel comfortable with, and you'll need to be as kind to them as to someone whose company you do like."

Audrey pulled on her socks, not caring if the heel of one was on the top of her foot.

"I hope she doesn't bring a soccer ball with her."

"You mean you don't want to turn on the outside lights and run around with Daddy, Mr. Charlie, Olivia, and the bats?"

Audrey made a gagging motion.

"Come on," Mrs. Emerson said as she put her arm around her.

Audrey was at her table, coloring her latest fashion drawing. It was a lady wearing a pink gown with long white gloves. She copied it from a 1950s picture of Gram. It was hard to believe Gram's waist was ever that tiny. It was Audrey's favorite photo of her, and she kept it framed in her room.

The doorbell rang. Mr. Emerson leapt up from his chair.

"It's the Bartmans," he said as he walked swiftly to the door. Mrs. Emerson followed him. Audrey stayed seated until her mother motioned sharply. Audrey put down her crayon, and silently walked toward her parents. Audrey felt awkward as she faced the Bartmans.

"Hey, Greg!" bellowed Mr. Bartman, shaking Mr. Emerson's hand. He motioned toward his family. "You remember Beth. And this is Olivia." Mr. Emerson's eyes lit up. "So this is Olivia! Put 'er there, Soccer Star!" He said, extending his hand. Olivia shook it.

"Nice to meet you, Mr. Emerson,"

Audrey noticed she didn't have a soccer ball with her, but she was wearing one of those expensive Glenville Elementary Yellow Jackets T-shirts. "That bee design is terrible," Audrey thought. "I can't believe they sold that for $25." Obviously, Audrey didn't own one; besides, she was allergic to bees.

"Olivia, you didn't say hello to Mrs. Emerson or to Audrey," said Mrs. Bartman. "How are you both?" she asked pleasantly. Audrey looked at the ground. "Fine," she slowly replied.

"How about some coffee?" Mrs. Emerson offered. "I have milk for the girls." She walked toward the kitchen. "Greg picked up some cookies from Simon's. Have you ever had their chocolate mint sandwiches?"

"Oh my gosh," said Mrs. Bartman. "I looove those cookies. I could eat a whole dozen. They're addicting!" She began helping Mrs. Emerson put out the plates.

Mrs. Emerson chuckled. "Me, too. That's why Greg bought a whole bunch of them." Everyone sat down. Mrs. Emerson looked for Audrey, but she wasn't in the room. Just as she started to get up, Audrey entered with paper and pencil in hand.

"Audrey...," Mrs. Emerson began.

"I can talk and draw at the same time," Audrey replied without looking up. Mr. Emerson looked at his daughter.

"Undivided attention, Audrey," he said firmly.

Mrs. Bartman looked at Audrey's drawing. "Oh, Audrey, may I see?" Audrey, bewildered, looked up.

"Sure," she answered. On the paper was a picture of a yellow jacket. Audrey drew her bee with an angry face and a really big stinger. Mrs. Bartman was smiling.

"This is terrific, Audrey. Much better than our last bee, the one on Olivia's shirt. The person I hired to create that used clip art."

Audrey spoke up. "I think clip art is cheating."

Mrs. Bartman laughed. "Charlie, look at this drawing. Don't you think this is a better bee than what that other artist did?"

Mr. Bartman took the drawing.

Olivia joined in with, "Yeah, that other man wouldn't draw soccer cleats on the bee, either. Remember?"

Mrs. Bartman nodded sadly. "I know, I'm sorry. We were in such a rush that time. And we had to sell those shirts for $25.00! Thank goodness we didn't have a lot made. We would've been stuck with them."

Mr. Bartman and Mr. Emerson looked at the drawing together.

"Honey, this is terrific!" Mr. Emerson noted. "It really shows the team's fighting spirit."

Mr. Bartman nodded. "It would be great to get uniforms with this bee on it."

Olivia suddenly stood up. "That's it!"

Mr. and Mrs. Bartman looked at Olivia. "What's it?" they asked together.

"Why can't we get a yellow shirt with *Audrey's* bee on it...and black shorts with a smaller version of her bee on one leg? That would be *so* cool!"

Audrey stared with her mouth open. Was this really happening? Olivia put her hand on Audrey's shoulder, and handed her the drawing.

"Do you think you could add cleats to your bee?"

Audrey immediately set to work, putting a soccer shoe on each of the bee's six feet. Olivia watched her draw.

"Gee," she remarked, "you draw so fast!"

Audrey smiled, not putting the pencil down until the picture was done. "Thanks," she said, holding up her design.

Everyone at the table applauded.

"Mom...Dad," Olivia asked, "could we please take this to the printing place?"

"Of course," said Mrs. Bartman. "We can go after practice tomorrow afternoon." She looked at Audrey. "Thank you so much, dear. The girls will absolutely love this."

All Audrey could do was smile and nod. Olivia beamed. I can't wait to tell the other players."

*   *   *

Mr. and Mrs. Emerson took their seats at Henley's Ice Cream parlor. Audrey was sitting with Olivia and the rest of the girls' soccer team. A bee with a very large stinger and cleats, just like the one on the players' uniforms, was painted on each player's face. Thanks to Mrs. Bartman, Audrey was now in charge of team spirit and publicity. She drew posters and banners and painted the players' faces before each game. Olivia brought one of the banners into Henley's.

"Audrey, could you start off signing the banner? We need to have all the signatures before we hang it up at school on Monday."

"Yea!" chorused the girls.

MOVING DAY

by David A. Stelzig

The winds of yesterday, still strong and steady, choked the sky with dust, diminished the morning sun to a dull, blood-red disk hanging above the distant Wassach Hills. Fine, hot sand, howling in from the plains, stung my ankles and must also have tormented the oxen though these patient beasts simply turned from the gale. They waited, eyes nearly closed, for my next command.

The sand swept beneath the wagon, now heaped high with all we owned on earth. It beat against the house, the shed, the barn, then circled to the leeward sides and deposited in huge tapering dunes. Smaller drifts sheltered behind fence posts and the fallen, broken remnants of a scarecrow that once stood guard over green and fertile fields...and behind the simple, pine cross I'd planted on that dreadful day, we laid Rebecca to rest.

Dear, sweet Rebecca, just three when she passed. For a vanishingly brief period, the light of our lives. Then the onset of the great drought, afflicting us now for nearly a decade and a half, as if heaven itself mourned the loss of our daughter.

Martha was there, kneeling by the grave. Head bowed. Shoulders sagging. Unmoving. Camouflaged in the dirty air by her long-sleeve, ankle-length, brown cotton housedress.

I trudged to her and silently stood for a moment, my hand resting on her shoulder, before quietly saying, "It is time old woman. It is time."

A sigh rippled through Martha's body. Then, with an arm around her waist, I helped her to her feet, thinking again how frail, how like a tiny bird she had become.

As we approached the wagon, Martha stopped by the small oak chest I'd left on the ground. She stared at it, then looked to me with dead, sunken eyes, her thin face creased in pain, her arthritic hands pressed tightly against her cheeks.

"Martha, there is no room," I explained.

She simply nodded and I lifted her up onto the seat. I walked to the back, looked down at Martha's treasured melodeon case, then bent to one knee and caressed the intricate rose pattern carved into the chest by Martha's father so long ago, so far away. I untied the saddle for the horse we no longer had and let it fall to the dirt. I lifted the melodeon box, tied it securely in the place vacated by the saddle, and joined my wife on the wagon.

Martha squeezed my knee. She rewarded me with a small smile. Her parched lower lip cracked, exposing a thin, red line of blood. I rested my hand on Martha's. I flicked the reins. The oxen strained forward. We began our trek to life, to hope, beyond the blowing sands.

140
Leslie Picker, "Prie Dieu"

141
GRAVE POTENTIAL

by Sarah Shilko-Mohr

I lay on my side blinking. Slowly my vision returns and the etchings on the gravestone come into focus. The tombstone reads, "Arbiter Banyon, born 1997, died...." There is no death date. There never will be. The gravestone is a prop, a temporal portal marker, placed there by the likes of me.

Traveling in time is brutal. I collapse spread-eagled atop the moist leaves—certainly a softer bed than the hot sand of ancient Egypt of my last trip. Recuperating, I listen to the sounds of the fall evening. Autumn-colored leaves rustle gently in the wind. Peepers sing a sweet song—a sound rare in the cluttered future. The waning sunlight cues tiny, timid creatures to begin their nightly forage for whatever sustenance lies sheltered under the bed of fallen leaves. An owl watches and waits. I too wait as my body slows its outcry at being torn apart, spread across the elastic sheet that is time itself, then reassembled at a specific configuration of elemental particles and physical forces.

I am as naked and hairless as a newborn baby. Human flesh can barely survive the assault that time travel wreaks; inert clothing doesn't stand a chance. But it's my job and I love it. Why do it? My unique past and present life...*and* that certain determination drives a halfback in football to be abused and broken in pursuit of getting a pigskin from one end of the field to the other. Or the insanity which pushed those brazen and brave souls who paid outrageous fortunes to be the first to venture into outer space strapped into something as fragile and unpredictable as a giant firecracker. Death means nothing. It's the *living* that matters; pain is just a tolerable side effect of whole body exhilaration and mind-bending awe. I have that certain type of in-your-face recklessness that is part of the personality profile the Foundation requires of its Portal Marker Maintenance employees.

The damp air is creeping into my bones. Time to get started. Even though I'd made sure there was no Arbiter Banyon for twenty-five years in either direction (therefore no grave visitors), a naked, bald man covered in tattoos lying prone on a grave could raise a ruckus on the off chance some exploring dog was pursued by a frantic owner or more likely, some graveyard game of "I dare you" was set forth by the local trick-or-treaters. All time trips are now scheduled on Halloween. The Foundation learned the hard way through a dozen snafus. The Directors settled on Halloweens as arrival dates because unusual looks and weird occurrences could be explained away as either elaborate costumes or misguided pranks.

Since only my body can make the trip, my instructions are tattooed on my skin. I am a veteran traveler and running out of space. I will need new flesh soon. Not exactly a pleasant operation but a necessary one since I am nowhere near wanting to retire. Pulling myself to a sitting position, every muscle screaming in protest, I turn my calf out as far as I can to review my checklist. In my time configuration, privileges are granted on how much you give back to society. Not above self-serving negotiations, I've assured myself of receiving some real perks by taking on extra requests. These requests are hieroglyphically encoded inside a triangle, indelibly inked into my flesh, their meaning known only to me—at least in this timeframe; I am an open book to my compatriots of the future. Venturing out of the graveyard will break with Foundation protocol; I'm only a Maintenance Inspector. But this trip, I have an ulterior motive; a private mission that's not marked anywhere on my body but carved indelibly in my soul—something I need to prove once and for all and worth jeopardizing my career, if it comes to that.

I roll to my knees grimacing and then, with only the slightest hesitation, put my index finger down my throat. Gagging, vomiting violently, I expel my cargo onto the flattened leaves where I've rested. Puncturing the seal of the regurgitated capsule with a purposely ragged, talon-like fingernail, I wait as the contents draw moisture from the night air and reconstitute into my costume. The clothing pack sucks every ounce of humidity within a five-foot radius making me feel warmer in the process. The night chill has become more profound since I'd arrived and I am grateful for the clothing with no sense of the ridiculous as I am soon garbed in what used to be called a pirate costume. The placement of a gold earring and hook hand eludes me for a second and I briefly consult my calf tattoo for instructions. I work quickly since one of the pitfalls of time travel is that the memories of where I came from begin to fade as soon as I arrive. This side effect will not leave me stranded; time has a way of correcting itself, like a huge rubber band springing back into shape, but it could make for some awkward moments explaining to superiors and favor requestors why I didn't complete my mission.

The "Aargh!" I practice is followed by gravelly coughing. My voice is raspy, the vocal chords not quite reconfigured to wholeness. I will need another good hour before my organs function at optimal levels and my blood runs fast and warm through my veins. I stand, cringing and curling inward at the ripping stabs in my muscles. Thrusting my hands into the pockets of my pants, I pull out an eye patch. Then I bring out an archeologically-retrieved handful of current-era paper money purposely saturated in benign bacteria to survive the journey. With a practiced deftness, I pluck my eye from its socket, covering the empty hole with the patch, and place the biologically altered ocular in a natural-looking crack in the back of the grave marker. The biomechanical orb immediately begins sending nerve-thin tendrils deep into the crack where the mechanics of the time portal are hidden. As the orb takes its readings, I use my good eye to inspect the state of the cemetery's continued viability as a portal station. Rarely disturbed or visited in the dead of night, cemeteries have proven to be efficient areas for constructing the special doorways. With indigenous materials available for the majority of construction of the linking stations, the only hazards lie for those risk-taking engineers who are sent with no grounding beacon, relying only on critical math, to add the final elements expelled from the confines of their stomachs. We'd lost some good travelers during these construction projects. History recorded each as homeless, a migrant John Doe or Jane Doe, but we knew better.

Temporarily putting aside the hook hand, I fall to my duties. Turning my mind to identifying hazardous scenarios that could potentially damage the marker, I look up for overhanging branches, electrical wires, or even squirrel nests threatened by high winds. None of the other nearby headstones is crumbling or cracked or threatening to topple over. This part of the graveyard is old and abandoned, the family names worn away by decades of eroding weather. But people of this era are loath to disturb their dead, even the long forgotten ones, and that keeps this spot safe from intrusion. Nonetheless, I will check for any real estate or construction signs when I go into town. Eventually, all the dead get turned over and built upon. The Foundation simply can't predict just when that will be for this particular Time Travel Station.

The iris of the eye device closes; its wet tendrils retract from the crack in the granite. I reinsert it into my socket, scanning the data it has retrieved. All is well. It's turning out to be a pretty mundane maintenance check. And yet, to actually witness the unrecorded, mundane moments of the past has become the passion of the future. What seemed so unimportant before has now proven to be the foundation of what lays ahead.

I bend my knees, arch my back, utter another "Aargh." Nothing in my throat cracks, screams or breaks. Weaving in and out of the gravestones, I spy the lights at the edge of town and head toward them.

There is a certain Zen-ness about the act of walking. The rhythmic rock of the hips, the counter-swaying required to balance on one leg while bringing the other forward. Where I come from, walking is outdated; peripheral-ready Segways transport the masses everywhere. Plugged-in, hooked-up, wheels where legs used to tread. Better to accommodate the constant influx of data transmitted through eye and earpieces and output through electronic gloves that have become common attire. We are all knowing, but without really seeing and with limited hearing. Busy, busy, busy, alone in a crowd.

Subconsciously, I repeatedly rub my thumb against the side of my index knuckle. It's a deep-in-thought quirk I've practiced since childhood for no apparent reason, a tic of unknown origin.

"Hey Buddy! What do you think you're doing?!"

Apparently, I am not immune to the isolationist influence of my time, as I have just stumbled over a pair of legs attached to a filthy, bleary-eyed bum sitting propped against a wall. I had been oblivious to his presence. Protocol for the situation escapes me and I respond with the reaction that will be appropriate in this man's very distant future.

Studying his condition, the bottle wrapped in brown paper, the filth of his clothes, the grease flattening his hair to his withered and spotted skull, I blurt out with genuine curiosity,

"Have you no greater potential?"

We're big on living up to your potential where I come from. Studies of potentialities begin at conception and continue in every facet of life from that point forward. Then, with the greater understanding of physics and time travel frontiers, the influences of the past melded into the grand question of, "What can I become?" Even past life regression is given a second look, but from the different angle of the past, present, and future coexisting and intricately connected. I'd participated in the esoteric experiments myself on several occasions. Not living up to your potential was as close to criminal as my time got.

The gist of the bum's mumbled expletive was clear. Withdrawing some of the crumpled bills in my pocket, I tossed them in the direction of his stained crotch. Pulling myself back into character with a muted "Aargh," I continued down the sidewalk.

Human traffic was becoming denser. There were even some goblins and ghosts running the streets with jack-o-lanterns swinging from their small hands. They, however, took one look at me and steered clear, pausing only momentarily before taking a skirting course. Out of the corner of my one eye, I saw the pink neon sign of my destination.

The "Hanorin's Bar" sign stood out brilliantly in the darkness of night. Heading for the heavy wooden door directly beneath its glowing light, I paused momentarily just before entering to pull down the stocking covering my calf to check my list. In that instant, I realized I had left the hook hand in the graveyard.

"Balzer!" I spat before I could stop. Was it the time travel effect that had me leaving part of my costume behind or simple human error? Human error could hurry my transfer to another "department of potential pursuit"; better to chalk up the forgetfulness to fading memories associated with time jumping.

I pulled open the door to the bar and, with a resounding "Ahoy there, me hearties," made my grand entrance. Shaking what should have been my hook hand, I swaggered into the room, crying out my practiced "Arrgh!" The resulting laughter and applause, to which I gave an exaggerated bow, allowed me the time to scan the perimeter.

And there she was. She sat at the very end of the bar, on the last stool, deliberately pulled into the shadows of the corner. She had been watching me until I looked in her direction. Catching my glance, she quickly looked down and wrapped her hands tightly around her drink. I continued my pirate show of Halloween spirit and slowly made my way to her end of the C-shaped bar counter. I stopped just this side of the curve—far enough to not be in her space but close enough to strike up a conversation. Turning around to the bar crowd, hoping the eye tattooed on the back of my head would amuse her, I took a pirate pose and bellowed to the patrons,

"Safe port has been made. Me cargo's been unloaded. Me ship's in good repair." The truth…though no one but me knew it.

"Let us drink hearty and be merry, me buccos. Drinks are on me!"

The bartender stood behind the counter with a cocked eyebrow and sardonic twist to his mouth, which turned to a wide-mouthed smile as I unloaded my pocket of the wad of bills and slapped them onto the counter. I laughed, in character, reading on his face that the bills would more than cover the tab. A small wave of relief ran through me since I wasn't quite sure how well the scientists had outfitted me for the journey. I stole a swift glance to the sheltered woman. The atmosphere changed almost imperceptibly.

"And bring me some grub! I've had naught but fish and millet these long weeks at sea."

The bartender pushed a menu across the slick surface. I tried to match up the symbols on the menu with the hieroglyphics on my calf. The translation wasn't coming as clearly as I would have liked as my mind was more concentrated on the girl than on the requests for indigenous food substances the Benefactors had asked for. I looked at the short menu and gambled.

"Everything looks good and it's been a long journey." Another veiled truth. "I'll take one of everything!"

The bartender threw his head back and laughed. For him, it was going to be a profitable night.

"Does that go for your drink order, too?"

I secured my welcome for the night by responding with another slap on the bar and a robust, "Set me up! One of everything, Swabbie!"

I tipped my non-existent hat to the mouthed thanks from the imbibing patrons. As a woman dressed in what I could only imagine was a skinned cat costume began to slink her way in my direction, I discouraged her intention by turning my back on her and directing a question toward the girl shrunk into the shadows at the end of the bar.

"What about you? What'll you be drinking?"

A fleeting glimpse, a tight-lipped smile, shoulders drawn tighter inward, a slight shake of her head and a dismissing wave of her hand. She wanted nothing to do with me. Everything about her said, "Leave me alone!" But I suspected there was more, much more under that veneer.

I gave her a moment, calculating my next move. My thumb rubbed my knuckle in rhythmic strokes.

In the background, I heard cell phones ringing. In the mirror behind the bar I saw the reflection of people sitting at tables with their laptops open and running. Turning, I scanned the gathering, pity and abhorrence battling within me.

"You're in a bar filled with living, breathing people!" I wanted to scream. "Disembodied voices, electronic information are not a substitute! You don't know how bad your disconnection is going to get. Wired up to your data devices, you're just going to be more alone than you ever believed possible!" Instead, I merely sighed.

I turned back to the living, breathing human being I so earnestly sought.

"What's your name?" I tossed out, leveling a gaze into the shadows.

Her return stare was filled with panic. But she looked me straight in the eye. And then it happened. The arc across time struck her. I saw it, but she only *felt* it and it dazed her for a moment. The open-mouthed gape, her eyes turned more inward even though they stayed fixed on me. And then, her shoulders relaxed, the grip on the glass loosened, her mouth closed and the soft lips turned up into a smile. Whatever her reservations about me, she seemed to have come to the conclusion I was trustworthy. I'd seen the arc, felt the connection, but more than that, I sensed the eddy that formed in the fluid rush of time. It set up a tension, the rubber band consistency being stretched out to encompass the new ripple.

She cocked her head, "Do I know you from so…" she began, but cut short her question; it sounding too much like a come-on. Ruffled, confused, she lowered her eyes and muttered, "Lucy." Then, with more resolve, she raised her head and voice and said, "My name is Lucy."

Lucy. I had a name now. I was shocked how the wispy sound of it warmed me. Lucy. Suddenly, I wanted to know everything about her; needed to know how she had become a part of my life. The rubber band stretched further.

She had said more, but I hadn't heard it. I took a chance and moved one stool closer. "What was that?" I ventured, seeing none of the former trepidation in her eyes, although a certain rigidity remained in her shoulders as I moved nearer.

"What's your name?" Lucy asked softly.

Balzer! Not again. I could not remember my name. I was pulling a total blank. Ad-libbing, I threw out the most recent name I had been called—"Buddy" as in "Hey Buddy, What do you think you're doing?" I saw it received as acceptable. I also felt the eddy expand in the liquid pool of time. The tight center pulled at me in contradiction to the stretching this meeting was causing.

The bartender had lined up shots in front of me along with a tall glass of foaming amber fluid. Plates of indigenous food substances created a slowly forming circle out from the glasses. I started on the left and planned to work my way to the right until I had consumed an acceptable portion of all of them. I threw down one of the shots and let out a hardy "Aargh!" in response to the fire that started in my throat and exploded in my stomach. Lucy giggled and the band grew tauter.

I didn't see her drink in my line up. "What's that you're drinking? I don't have one."

Returning to shy nervousness, she waved her hand and turned away, muttering, "Oh, you don't want one of these." She wasn't looking at me; she had withdrawn into herself yet again.

I concentrated on the plates of food while I ran through possible questions that would get me closer to her without eliciting the bolt of panic she always seemed to be on the verge of. I continued to eat and drink as I ran through scenarios. Some of the patrons made quick stops on their way out to thank me again for my generosity, but they seemed a little disappointed as I'd dropped the pirate routine in my preoccupation with my more urgent quest. I swiveled back to my grub and saw Lucy staring at me with a quizzical expression.

"What is it?" I asked as gently as possible.

"You just dragged your sleeve through the ketchup on the French fries…but there's nothing there. And your costume doesn't have any seams." She looked at me suspiciously, her eyes demanding an explanation.

I recalled the hook hand lying on top of a grave marker. Having been detached from my body, it would have disintegrated by now. Nothing non-biological, or more specifically, nothing could make the trip that was unable to blend to the harmonics emitted by the energy bands of time. It was always a gamble that such things like the money would withstand the violent forces that time travel wrought. The costume was not made of fabric but of a material that was grown and was still living. Not only did it provide a current-era disguise, it also served to gather atmospheric data, collect any skin flakes shed from my body and provided a shield against any pollen, dust or microbes I might pick up. Collecting hair wasn't a problem. The rest of my body was as bald as my head and would remain so as a side effect of time travel—a trip as searing as a meteor burning through Earth's atmosphere.

"Aye, lass. I've sailed to many lands. Made port in many an exotic and mysterious isle, I have. It was in one of them I procured this magically woven cloth." I closed my banter with a wink and a nod.

She looked at me strangely for a heartbeat, "Is that where you got those tattoos?" Her tone implied she didn't necessarily approve of my body graffiti, but didn't want to offend me either. It was the opening I was looking for.

I leaned conspiratorially in her direction and took comfort when she didn't balk.

"Let you in on a secret." Her eyebrows raised and I continued, "It's all fake. Washes off in a single shower."

She laughed. A relieved laugh, a reassured laugh. The tattoos had scared her. Somehow her thinking they were not real gave me the stamp of normalcy. The last vestige of stranger assessment had been made and I had passed. Until I picked up the next shot glass and saw the caution return. I set it back down, calculating what benefits I would have to give up in the future by coming back with less than requested on the list, and decided this was more important. I stood and had the bartender remove the detritus of my "to do" list, moving one stool closer to Lucy.

I asked her, "What brings you out tonight?" I tacked on "landlubber" just for good measure.

Again, she gave me the wan smile and the dismissive hand wave. And then she did the damnedest thing. Withdrawing, turning inward, she began rubbing her thumb across her index knuckle. I gasped at the affectation. I couldn't back off this time. I needed to know the truth.

"No, really. Tell me, what brought you here tonight?" I pushed, struggling to remain nonchalant.

She answered, good-naturedly rolling her eyes to the ceiling, "Oh, just a little personal celebration." Pausing, without looking up, she added, "I completed the restoration of an antique atlas today." And the nervous tic returned to her hand.

Bypassing typical social drivel, I leapt to the heart of the matter. "And as you restored the maps, did you wonder about all those countries and dream of sailing down the rivers, climbing the mountains, and trekking the deserts?"

I'd hit a nerve. Lucy gaped at me in astonishment. Her "Yes" was breathy.

"I'll bet you love history, too," I posited, looking for further commonality between us.

"I *love* history," was her quiet reply.

Searching for another bond, I said, "And I imagine you are a woman of deep passions," and watched as she blushed from her neck to her hairline, her hands fluttering over her empty glass. I turned and snapped for the bartender, my welcome still fully established. The pile of bills had rapidly diminished, without a word from me, and made their way to the cash register and the bartender's pocket.

"Another drink for Lucy." The barkeep looked at Lucy, having forgotten what she was drinking and almost surprised at seeing her sitting there.

"Ah, it's ah, just tonic and lime."

"No gin?"

"Right. Just tonic and lime." She never looked at him. And then as an afterthought, called out, "I'll pay for it." She would not risk ingratiating herself to me. I let it go. I was sure I knew her heart even though she barricaded it against disappointments and pain.

"So *are* you going to take that trip to Tahiti?" The words weren't out of my mouth for a split second when I realized my error. I'd moved too fast. Her pale look of shock just confirmed it.

"The brochure sticking out of your purse," I said quickly, pointing to the travel pamphlet that had slipped up out of its pocket when she'd retrieved her wallet. Observation of details is my life and livelihood.

"Oh, oh, well, oh...," she stammered and smiled and then shook her head. "Probably not."

"How come?"

"Oh, I was just looking at it. Not really my style... you know, vacation, ah... traveling."

And there was the telling difference between us.

"You're *afraid* to go, aren't you?" And I saw how deep the truth was in that. She'd barely had the courage to venture here tonight from her stark apartment. She lived on the meager income of a solitary book restorer rather than risk going out in the world. Even in her appearance, she went out of her way to remain unseen. Plain, mousy hair. Drab, cloudy-day clothing. The hands that gripped her glass were unadorned—not a single ring, no polish on the clean, rounded nails. Except for one thing. She wore an Egyptian symbol on a chain around her neck. One lonely piece of color in a sea of bland.

"You ought to go. Tahiti, I mean. It could change your life." I wanted to sound upbeat without thinking about the consequences to my own life.

Her flitting smile tried to cover so much. "You're a confident man, aren't you? I'll bet *you've* traveled," she said looking up at me with a hunger that hurt.

"Sure, Lucy...on both counts. But I didn't start out like that. Building confidence, taking a trip—for either, you start with baby steps. Take a risk, savor the risk, *embrace* the risk."

The eddy became a whirlpool. An undertow dragged at me, shortening my time here with every word I spoke.

"Baby steps you say" and her hunger became ravenous. She moved out of the dark corner and into the light. And finally, we talked and all the while with the undertow of liquid time taking on a force that threatened to disintegrate me before her eyes.

I listened as Lucy slowly stripped away the layers covering her suppressed dreams, revealing her depth for wonder even as the elastic bands of time tightened around me to a suffocating tautness. My mind raced as I recognized myself in her. Her burning intensity held me.

The lights blinked last call.

I couldn't move. I didn't watch as Lucy got up and left. I didn't see the buoyant lift to her step that hope generated. I didn't see the smile that was lit from her soul or the sparkle in her eyes. I didn't see the straightness of her spine as she reveled in the idea that a chance encounter with a stranger had changed her forever. I didn't see the dreamy expression on her face as she walked out the door and into the path of an oncoming car. I only flinched slightly when I heard the thud and the screams from the horrified bystanders.

The band snapped. The undertow ceased, the eddy smoothed out, the ripples receded. Time corrected itself with only the lingering sense of *déjà vu* left to puzzle those who sensed it.

I had known she would be here tonight. Known how and when she would die. And although the people of this time not only did not disturb their dead, and were meticulous in recording the minutiae of their deaths, those facts only confirmed *when* but so little else. I had come to know her, Lucy, through this past-life regression. Felt her buried passion, her inability to break free of fear. Experienced her death as my own. Again and again. I'd known as well as I knew myself that in her last moments, Lucy had vowed to put aside her fears and fulfill a life of passion. There was no paradox; I'd had nothing to do with it. It was the completed restoration project that began the spark that blazed. And it was snuffed out too soon to be realized for more than a moment.

I had not found the proof I had sought. In that regard, I had found no certainty that the woman I saw when regressed to moments before my own conception was the repressed woman in the bar. Or that Lucy had been reincarnated in me and her caged passions were being played out through my life. I was no surer now than before, that when Fate asked, the soul of Lucy had begged to be allowed to live again and fulfill the life she'd denied herself in this one. But if…just if…she was reincarnated in me, I would continue, for as long as possible, to pursue what had become *my* passion for the dangerous, the new, the mind-bending and awesome. And in that pursuit, I would honor and live up to the potential for both myself *and* my illusory Lucy.

IMAGINATION

by Joyce M. Shepherd

There are castles in the sky.
    There are angels in the snow.
        There are fairies in the forest—I've seen them.
        I know.

There are tea parties with rabbits.
    There are yellow brick roads.
        There are monsters in the closet—I've seen them.
        I know.

There's an island full of pirates.
    There's a glass-encased rose.
        There's a knight in shining armor—I've seen him.
        I know.

There's an awfully friendly dragon.
    There's an Aladdin lamp that glows.
        There's an elephant that flies—I've seen him.
        I know.

They say it's my imagination;
    Stuff will change as up I grow.
        Grownups can be so silly—I've seen them.
        I know.

    If I *have* to grow up, there's one thing I *surely* know.
    I'll *keep* my imagination and take it everywhere I go.

NIGHTS OF TERROR

By Karin Harrison

Spring 1945

Sirens wailed into the night. Helen bolted up, groped for the matches and lit the candle stump. She heard the grandfather clock in the hallway strike the midnight hour. She yawned and jumped out of bed. Another sleepless night to be spent in the dungeon, she thought as she reached for her glasses. The sirens had alerted them every single night this week. She couldn't remember when she had the luxury of a whole night's sleep. A quick peek in the mirror revealed an attractive forty-year-old woman of medium height, dressed in a loose fitting navy blue sweat suit. Salt and pepper curls fell down her forehead. Green eyes stared back at her through wire-rimmed spectacles.

Who was this woman? A mere shadow of who she used to be. Her face was pale and gaunt, with dark shadows under the eyes and prominent lines around the mouth that had dug deeply into the skin. She shrugged and reached for her shoes. There wasn't much time.

Helen rushed into the children's bedroom.

"Paul, Bessie, wake up."

She gently lifted four-year-old Anne from her bed. The toddler screamed in protest. Helen sighed heavily.

"Hush sweetheart."

She brushed a kiss across the fuzzy red hair of her youngest child who clutched her beloved, well-worn Teddy firmly by its ear.

Paul, her oldest child, disentangled his body from the sheets and sat on the edge of the bed. At fourteen, he was tall and thin. His hair was tousled, his eyes half closed as he stretched his long legs. Across the room, his sister did not stir.

"Paul, make sure Bessie gets up. I'm going to wake Omi and Opa." Helen hurried out of the room. Anne rested her head against her mother's shoulder and, with her thumb in her mouth, drifted off.

Paul rose and padded across the room.

"Rise and shine, Bessie."

He tugged on the bulky down comforter which kept Elisabeth safely ensconced in a world of happy dreams. When she didn't move, he yanked it off the bed.

"Leave me alone, you ogre!" She buried her dark head beneath her pillow. She was nine years old and resented being bullied by her brother. Since her father was at war, Paul seemed to have taken on an unprecedented authority. She noticed that her mother often consulted with him. He was allowed to stay up later than his sisters did, a rule she often challenged. Five years difference in age between them was such a trifling thing and she was certain that her maturity more than equaled his.

Helen and her family occupied the first floor of the three-story apartment complex together with her parents who had lost their home during the very first air attack. Their house had been located on Bahnhofstrasse opposite the railroad station, an area that initially suffered the greatest losses. The bombs hit their targets with precision and annihilated the entire district. The ensuing inferno lasted for days. Only rubble and ruins remained where once stood magnificent, proud buildings dating back over a hundred years.

The beautiful Wildenheim castle resembled a ghostly shell of scorched sandstone; the staggered remains of the four towers rose from the ruins lamenting their demise to the heavens. The gardens bordering the perimeter, once a colorful patchwork of diversified flora, had been overrun by a variety of proliferating weeds and brush. Two gaping craters had swallowed several of the huge, gnarled oaks, planted two hundred years before by order of the king.

The bombings continued, night after night inflicting deadly destruction that wiped out nearly eighty percent of the city. The loss of their home with all their possessions had a profound effect on Helen's father. Hermann had become defiant and stubborn, whereas Rosa, his wife, dealt with the situation in a more practical manner; survival was utmost in her mind. They had been through this before. Hermann had fought in France during World War I where, during a scouting mission, he stepped on a land mine. He spent many weeks in the field hospital, and despite primitive conditions, the surgeon managed to save his leg; the recovery left him walking with a painful limp. Rosa guided her husband with unwavering firmness and support through the difficult recovery period.

She failed, however, to get him to join the Nazi Party and, as a result, he became the subject of repeated harassment by the Gestapo who frequently hauled him to their headquarters for questioning. When they failed to intimidate him, they resorted to torture. On one occasion, they forced Hermann to stand up naked for hours in a cold room. His crippled leg sent pain spasms through his entire body. When he collapsed, they revived him and the torture continued until he was no longer able to stand up. They could not break him. He despised their party and everything it stood for and suffered their wrath with stoic resignation. Eventually, they decided that he was a harmless old man and left him alone.

*   *   *

Helen walked toward the livingroom, which served as a bedroom for her parents. She knocked on the door.

"He refuses to get out of bed." Dressed in a sweater and wrinkled wool skirt, Rosa stuck her head through the door. They had been sleeping in their clothes for months, ever since the night attacks had begun. It saved time and frustration and got them to the shelter more quickly.

"Do you want me to talk to him?" Helen asked.

"He says let the whole house fall on him; he doesn't care anymore." Rosa sighed. "You go ahead and take care of the children. I will deal with him."

Helen gave her arm a reassuring squeeze and headed for the large hallway closet. She snatched the canvas bag containing candles, matches, and blankets, and followed Paul who was walking toward the apartment entrance door, dragging the sleepy Elisabeth behind him. Rosa and Hermann tagged along. Helen glanced at her father and he stared at her defiantly. His expression softened when his eyes fell on Anne and he reached for her. He gathered her up into his arms. Anne whimpered softly and pressed her sleepy face against his, oblivious to the emerging stubble on his cheeks.

The family hurried down the steps toward the rear of the cellar where the air shelter was located. Helen and her gang were always the last to arrive. The other tenants were sitting on wooden benches, their faces taut and grim. Helen nodded at the Stringers, who lived on the third floor together with their daughter-in-law Mary. The owners of the property, Mr. and Mrs. Brenner, occupied the second floor and had arrived a few minutes before Helen. Mrs. Brenner sat with her head bowed in devout prayer and her arthritic hands clutching her rosary. She was a big woman with small eyes that glinted malevolently from beneath lowered lids as her large bosom heaved in rhythmic succession. A huge mole on her chin sprouted dark fuzz. Her husband, a ruddy, stout man, sat next to her, his face stony and eyes fixed upon the tattered bible resting on his lap.

The nights in the shelter were long and exhausting. The room, no larger than a four meter square, was small and stifling. Constructed of concrete reinforced by steel, the shelter provided minimal safety if the building were hit. Plain wooden benches lined the damp walls and four metal chairs crowded around a small table in the center of the room. The tenants had brought their own candles and placed them on the table. There had been no electricity for months.

Mrs. Brenner scowled when the first floor tenants made their entrance. She mumbled under her breath. The Brenners were childless and had zero tolerance for children. Helen's brood was the cause of continued annoyance and Mrs. Brenner missed no opportunity to express her disapproval of Helen's parenting skills. The landlords had imposed stringent rules upon their tenants. Each family was allotted a small section of the garden to grow vegetables and flowers; however, the children were banned from that area or anywhere else on the surrounding property. Mrs. Brenner's kitchen window allowed a clear view of the backyard, and she watched routinely in hopes of catching the unsuspecting villains in any wrongdoing. The kids were always in trouble and Helen had to summon all her diplomatic skills to placate the complaining landlords.

Mary Stringer jumped from the bench and hurried toward Helen to lend a hand. Tall and thin, Mary was an optimist which showed in her laughing eyes and dimpled cheeks. She had only been married six months when her husband was called to war. Helen and Mary had a common bond; their husbands were missing in action, and they'd had no news in over a year. The two women had become good friends as they commiserated. Helen was certain that she would have gone mad without Mary's support during the long hours in the shelter.

"She's been hyper since we got here," Mary whispered casting a furtive glance at Mrs. Brenner.

"I'd give anything not to have to come down here," Helen muttered. "There are times when I am tempted to punch her ugly face."

Mary suppressed a giggle and resumed her seat next to her parents.

Anne's quiet sobs had escalated into ear piercing screams; they'd discovered that her beloved Teddy was missing. Paul offered to search for him in the stairway, but Mr. Brenner had already locked the heavy steel door. Hermann rocked Anne gently in his arms, to no avail. She began to howl and then decided to hold her breath. Hermann quickly handed the child over to her mother. Mrs. Brenner watched the scene with dour contempt. She pointed a crooked finger at Helen and whined, "You'd better shut her up. I'm getting a sick headache."

"A headache should be the least of your worries," Hermann declared.

Mrs. Brenner rolled her eyes and shifted her bulk on the bench. The rosary beads jangled ominously as she shot disapproving glances at her frightened tenants.

Helen paced the small room rocking Anne in her arms. Eleven steps one way; she had counted them a hundred times. She glanced at the people lining the walls. They sat slumped in resignation and silently awaited their fate.

There was a time when their lives were filled with laughter. It was so long ago. Helen closed her eyes to the poignant memories and mocking ghosts. She could almost smell the fragrant breeze that swept across the river that Sunday afternoon as she sat close to Fritz in the small boat. High up on the cliff, Wildenheim Castle rose proudly, a sentinel, an ageless landmark whose pinnacles of towers, spires and turrets could be seen for miles. For centuries, it was home to the royal family of the King, who ruled the state quite often with more vigor than wisdom.

On that afternoon a lifetime ago they had finished their sandwiches and the children enjoyed the last of the small desert cakes. The boat drifted aimlessly. Paul and Bessie had cast their fishing lines and waited patiently. It was a carefree, happy day. Helen turned to her husband and drew his face close to hers. His eyes, an incredible, indefinable shade of hazel, searched hers.

"What is it? You're acting mysteriously today."

"I'm very happy," she sighed, eyes downcast. "I wonder if it'll be a boy or a girl."

His sat up abruptly causing the little boat to sway precariously.

"Dad, stop it! You're chasing the fish away!" Paul shouted over his shoulder.

"Darling, is it true?" Fritz pulled her close to him.

"Yes. I'm afraid you'll have another mouth to feed. I just found out yesterday. We'll have our baby in May." Helen whispered, "Shall we tell the kids?"

Later on that afternoon, they strolled in the beautiful gardens of Wildenheim Castle, and watched the glorious sunset from the terrace.

* * *

Anne sighed in her sleep. Helen softly kissed her on the cheek. What was to become of them? The children deserved a chance at a life free of fear and starvation. Every day she fought to provide them with the mere necessities and she worried that the trauma of the nights in the shelter would inflict lasting emotional damage though Rosa assured her that the children would be fine and told her to quit worrying.

Helen passed a fleeting look around the room. Everyone was quiet, even Mrs. Brenner. Bessie, sleeping soundly, had cuddled up next to her grandfather. Helen smiled at her oldest daughter. Bessie had inherited Fritz's dark hair and strong, square chin and, like Fritz, Bessie was able to fall asleep in any position at any given time; sometimes she nodded off at the dinner table and they had to carry her to bed.

Helen caught Hermann's eye. He'd been watching her and nodded reassuringly. Like Bessie, she felt an intense urge to crawl on his lap, as she used to when she was a child and the world was crowding in on her. He always managed to make her feel better. Helen blinked and her eyes welled. He winked at her, and she gave him a bittersweet smile. She knew what he was thinking, one day at a time, one day at a time. She sat down next to Mary.

The faint drone of airplane engines penetrated the thick walls with increasing din. They held their breaths. Heavy thuds echoed briefly in the distance and then the noise came closer. High pitched whistles melted into a succession of fierce blasts that rattled the building. The earsplitting sound of an explosion filled the shelter, and chunks of plaster fell on the terrified group.

Mrs. Brenner screamed, "We're hit! We're going to die!" She covered her face.

The Stringers held on to each other, expecting the worst. Hermann put one arm around Rosa and tightened the other arm around the sleeping Elisabeth. Anne woke up and clung to her mother, sobbing quietly. Helen glanced at Paul. His eyes were filled with fear as he looked at his mother. He was shaking and she pulled him to her.

"I'm *afraid*," Paul said through gritted teeth.

"So am I. It's nothing to be ashamed of," Helen whispered. She closed her eyes as her lips moved in silent prayer: "Please don't make my children suffer. If we are to die tonight, let it be quick."

Helen focused her gaze straight ahead. "Where are you Fritz? Are you still alive?" she wondered. Just last week she spoke with her best friend Inge, who showed her a letter from her husband dated over a year ago but which had just arrived. There was no return address. The two women decided that maybe their husbands were fighting on the Russian front. Only two days later, a bomb leveled Inge's house and buried everyone beneath a mountain of concrete, plaster, and wood. The explosion was heard all across the Godelsberg community. Fragments of rock spewed into all directions and eliminated any remaining window within a half a kilometer. When the sirens had signaled that it was safe to leave the air shelters, the neighbors had discovered the horrible sight. They worked feverishly to dig out the people buried beneath the rubble. Everyone pitched in, even the children. It took hours to clear away the chunks of concrete. Then they heard a faint noise; someone was banging on a pipe. It was a sign of life, but they lacked the tools to speed up the rescue and by the time they dug through that evening, the only survivor was Ben, Inge's German shepherd. There had been no way to get word to Werner, Inge's husband, if indeed he was still alive.

*   *   *

A familiar sound came from the distance. Helen opened her eyes. There it was again. The chime sequence of the Grandfather clock in their apartment announced the fifth hour. Five melodious chimes suddenly were the most beautiful sound in the world. She heaved a sigh of relief.

Paul craned his head. He jumped up. "The planes are gone!" he cried.

Everyone strained to hear. Mr. Stringer let out a sharp breath. "Yes, it's over. We made it through another night." The cold room became alive with effervescent chatter as all burdens of tension had been lifted and their spirits rose. They knew there would be other nights like this but that thought was pushed aside as they reveled in being alive.

Within the next hour, the sirens signaled that it was safe to leave the shelter. Mr. Brenner unlocked the door and pushed it open against its grinding protest. They filed out of their nightly prison, one by one, with Mr. Stringer leading the way. With silent apprehension, they crept up the stairs. No obstacles blocked their way. The house seemed to be intact. Helen followed her parents, carrying Anne in her arms. Paul and Elisabeth were right behind her. She heard Rosa suddenly gasp, "*No!!*"

"What is it?" Helen quickly stepped around her mother and spotted the huge crater in the backyard where the gardens used to be. Chunks of earth and bits of greenery had been scattered across the property. A black pall of smoke hovered over the chaos of mangled wire fencing and uprooted fruit trees. The ramshackle garden shed had been reduced to smoldering embers.

The group stared at the sight in silence. The bomb had miraculously cleared the house and detonated in the garden.

"Wow, were *we* lucky!" Paul exclaimed and then everyone began to speak at once. They laughed and hugged each other in a happy convergence that included even the Brenners, who seemed to have shed their hostility for the time being.

Helen bowed her head and whispered a quick prayer, "Thank you, for keeping us safe."

Rosa stepped forward and studied the area. "Our precious crop is gone. What are we going to do now? We'd be better off dead."

"Mother, don't say that. We are alive; that's what matters. We'll manage…somehow." Helen's voice was strong, void of the forebodings clouding her mind.

"How much more are we supposed to take? What have we done that must be punished like this?" Rosa's voice was husky with tears.

Mr. Stringer took several steps forward. "We'll clean up the mess and plant again—that's what we'll do. We're going to create a community garden where the shed used to be. There is enough room left for planting. It looks like Helen's peach tree survived and the apple and pear trees in the Brenner's section by the rear fence look tall and strong. We'll work together and share equally," he said firmly. He stared boldly at the Brenners who nodded reluctantly.

"Mutti, look," and Bessie pointed to the horizon. The eastern sky was ablaze in beautiful variations of red, purple, orange and peach—a spectacular atmospheric display that accompanied the rise of the sun and dispelled the gloom of the night. Helen looked up. Ever-widening bands of golden rays embraced the town and lit up the hollow towers of Wildenheim castle in a celebration of life that filled their hearts with hope. They had survived one more night. A new day had begun.

ODE TO SUMMER

by Ann Cook

When summer comes, I greet the golden sun
    As it bids good-morn the fertile earth.
And with lightened heart join gilded shafts of sunlight
    Along the winding garden path.
Beneath dawn's blushing sky, I glimpse the diamond
    Dewdrops that cling to bud and bough.
I cherish field and woodland cloaked now in morning mist,
    And we haunt this honeyed byway,
        The wary stag and I.

When summer comes, from lattice-shaded bower,
    I behold the cloistered lawn.
To wonder at the noble oak,
    Hushed now in the midday calm.
The lily pond sleeps dark and deep
    Beneath its creamy blooms while in this time of sultry sun,
    Like me, the garden rests.
Neither bird nor beast any longer stir; they await
    A cooling breeze.

When summer comes, the sun slides down a Midas path
    To usher in the torrid night.
Again I stroll the garden lane and spy a ray of sun;
    It lingers on a Grecian maid, so ageless and demure.
When robins nest, and fireflies lift to join the twinkling stars,
    In the silent dusk, a shadow among shadows,
        An owl takes flight.
Again, the garden air is heavy with perfume but the cooling
    Storm will stay well north.

164
Ryan Twentey, "Architecture II"

TURNABOUT

by Mary Beth Creighton

I knock on the wide door and ask if I can come in for a visit; caterpillars are always polite. I hear a quiet "okay." I stick my head around the door cautiously—this patient may not be ready for a visit from a five-and-a-half-foot insect.

"Oh, thank you," I say.

The old man's eyebrows rise at the sight of my make-up and green hair. He's so thin and small. In my eyes, the hospital bed instantly takes on the form of the Sta-Puf man from Ghostbusters about to swallow this wee morsel. His face is wrinkled and pale, but his dark eyes are alert and watchful as I step into his room.

"Hello!" I say cheerfully. "May my friend come in too?"

He hesitates for a moment but then nods his approval. I wave Daffydil in and make introductions. "I'm Katy the Caterpillar and this is my clown friend Daffydil." I circle a finger around my right ear. "She's a little daffy."

"I…ah…I'm Hank Shaffer." Perplexed, he looks at our costumes; our rainbow of colors now defeat his sullen beige and white room.

My facial features are over the edge. Skin covered in alabaster white, huge painted crimson nose and cheeks to match. I have a mile-wide red smile and high black eyebrows with ebony laugh lines at the corners of my eyes. My florescent hair is crowned by black antennas and matches my medium-green caterpillar body. I have purple and light green spots and wear pink and black knee-high socks and pink shoes—camouflage is no use when you're a human-sized insect.

Daffydil is wearing a frilly white dress with red polka dots, a big yellow apron, and matching pantaloons. Her kaleidoscope shoes have flower designs on them and a big daffodil is sticking out of her funny little hat. She has rosy cheeks, a heart-shaped nose and puckered red lips.

Mr. Shaffer looks down at his bony hands then up again tentatively. "Why are you here?"

"We're here to see you," I reply. "*And* clown around. I must warn you though, we *are* a little silly."

"Yup," agrees Daffydil. "I even had to go to the doctor because of sillyitis. Want to see my x-ray?"

Mr. Shaffer nods. Daffydil whips out an "x-ray" out of a large apron pocket and holds it in front of him. "My doctor said I've got butterflies in my stomach." He looks at the butterflies in Daffydil's x-ray and glances my way.

"I told you she's daffy," I say. "Hey. I'm learning magic. I'll show you my new tricks, but I need your help. Do you know any magic words Mr. Shaffer?"

"Ah...abracadabra?"

"Perfect!"

Quietly, Mr. Shaffer watches as I perform my new rope trick. I take three pieces of rope and tie them end to end. I wrap the rope around my hand and ask Mr. Shaffer to say the magic words. When I unwrap the rope, the knots are gone.

"Ta da!"

"That's pretty good," Mr. Shaffer says.

"Thank you."

Next, I show him my empty change purse and drop in a white square of paper. I wave my hand over top and ask again for the magic words. Mr. Shaffer looks truly surprised when I show him the paper has disappeared and a one dollar bill has materialized in its place. "Just don't ask me to turn it into a one hundred dollar bill. That never works."

"Never," Daffydil agrees. She starts looking for floating dust bunnies in his room. She flits around with her duster, swiping high and low in the air.

Mr. Shaffer starts to look amused. I think I see the corners of his mouth twitch when I show him my runny nose. It's plastic with little feet. When I wind it up, it bobbles across my palm making a whirring noise.

"That's more like a walking nose," Daffydil quips.

I ignore her and gently wipe my "runny nose" with a tissue.

"I was in WWII," Mr. Shaffer says suddenly.

I straighten up and give him a respectful salute. "It's a special honor to meet a veteran. What branch of the service?"

"Army. I drove a jeep." He sits up a little higher in his bed. "I have a heart problem. I've had five operations and I've been in and out of different hospitals for months."

"My goodness," says Daffydil.

"Have you met any clowns at the other hospitals?" I ask.

"No...." He pauses and his dark eyes take on a sparkle. "Well, come to think of it, I *have* met quite a few clowns, but they were only *accidental* clowns."

Daffydil and I crack up at his joke and double over. His laughter joins ours. It's sweeter than syrup on pancakes. We've made a connection. We haven't cured his heart but we've definitely helped it.

"We're going to leave you with some happy healing bubbles," Daffydil says. She gets out her bubble container and pulls out a tiny wand. She gently blows into the wand and tiny bubbles float across Mr. Shaffer's bed. He smiles and tries to catch one with his hand.

Then he looks at each us. "Thank you for visiting me."

"It's been our absolute pleasure," I say. Daffydil nods in agreement. "Here's a picture to remember us by." We each hand him our silly photo.

"If no one believes you met some clowns," says Daffydil, "just show them our pictures."

He smiles again, but his eyes glisten like shallow pools. "You're the first visitors I've had."

"Well, we hope you enjoyed the visit as much as we have!" I say.

"I *have*!"

A dietary hostess appears in the doorway. She knocks on the open door. "Dinner is here, Mr. Shaffer. Maybe I bring in your tray now?"

"Yes, please." His cheeks flush and his eyes crinkle endearingly. He doesn't look so small now, the Sta-Puf man is held at bay. "I am a little hungry."

Daffydil and I wave goodbye and leave Mr. Shaffer to his dinner. Outside his room, it's my turn to have eyes that glisten.

AT THE END OF HIS ROPE

by Ann M. Cook

Eight in the morning and Jacob was halfway through his third cup of coffee. From his office on the tenth floor he looked at the heavy smog hanging over Los Angeles. He decided it would be late afternoon before it lifted.

"Damn. No wonder I want to get the hell away from here. This kind of weather is enough to drive anyone nuts. What I want is warmth and sunshine, mostly sunshine, something to cheer me up," he mused to himself. He drank the last of the coffee, slammed the cup near the pot and settled into the big leather chair.

Without focusing on its content he took a file from the in-basket and flipped through the five pages of information. On the surface nothing appeared unusual, only that he would be headed for the East coast. "Not if I can help it," he said aloud.

He was aware his boss Doug was watching from the glass-enclosed office and, when he was motioned in, he took the file with him. Doug frowned and pointed to a chair. Jacob sat down stretching his long legs along the mocha brown carpet.

"I don't know what's going on with this case, but it seems odd. I need you to handle this one. Hope you're not taking time off in the next week or so."

Jacob suddenly felt a twinge of disappointment. For the past week he had considered putting in for retirement and now he was being asked to take another case. A case that would take him away from home for no telling how long. He was sixty-two years old, tired of working, tired of traveling, and tired of hearing tales of why life insurance policies should be paid to the bereaved even though they were not the beneficiaries. He cast a glance at Doug who was looking at a copy of the file.

"Would it matter? I don't particularly want to go east but I don't suppose I have a choice."

"You're right...at least not now. Have you looked at the file?" Doug asked.

"Not really, I only glanced at it...what's it about?"

"A woman's dead and her husband—Bradley Harper—has applied for the insurance, two mill. He's only had the policy six months and that ol' gut feeling says something's not right here."

"How old was the woman? She had to take a physical exam. What killed her?" Jacob asked.

"She was young...mid-twenties. The husband contacted the agent...said his wife was lost at sea. I don't know what in hell that means, but it sure sounds suspicious to me. If she *were* a CEO of a large company okay, but I checked on her and nowhere did I come up with her name other than she was married to a ship's captain. Do the investigation...see what's going on." He handed Jacob an envelope containing an airline ticket and expense money.

"Yeah. Wouldn't be the first husband to slowly and carefully plan a wife's death. He doesn't kill her right away...he takes his time. This *does* need looking into," Jacob said.

"I told the agent to tell Harper we need to process the claim but we'll use the delay to investigate the death. We'll hold him off as long as we can. Hope this is enough petty cash; if you need more use your expense account. Your flight leaves tonight so you'd better get ready. Let me know in the next day or two what you find out."

*   *   *

In the heat of a July afternoon, the temperature already at ninety-one, Jacob Ivanson arrived at his destination, Willow Creek, a small waterfront development just south of Baltimore. He parked the rental car at the end of the street and stepped out onto the tree-lined roadway. After the air-conditioned car the heat was oppressive. He removed his sportcoat and tossed it in the back seat.

He was impressed with the big Colonial homes, neatly trimmed lawns, and boats of all sizes—Bayliners, Grady Whites, Whalers—tied up at private docks. He found the address of the claimant and the first thing he noticed was the big catamaran tied at the pier. About forty-five or fifty feet of what looked like custom work. "Wow!" He realized he had spoken aloud. The sleek blue and silver craft bobbed lazily on the incoming tide. The house appeared to be vacant.

Before knocking at the door he decided to talk to some of the neighbors. He wanted to get the feel from the neighbors: did they know the dead woman, did they know the husband, what did they know about the couple together—any good dirt they could tell him.

As Jacob stood on the sidewalk, a woman came from the side entrance of the house next door. She appeared to be in her late fifties or early sixties. Her lightly tanned skin was nicely accentuated by a white dress. Red and white jewelry, red shoes, and matching purse completed her outfit. Jacob found her poised and attractive. She smiled as she went to a red Mustang parked in her driveway. Before opening the door, she looked at Jacob.

"May I help you? You seem to be lost," she said.

"I don't know if I'm lost or not; I'm looking for the Harpers. Do they still live here?"

"Bradley does." The woman hesitated then added. "Maria died a while back."

"I'm sorry to hear that. Was she sick?"

Jacob immediately regretted asking such a direct question, but he wanted to learn more before she left. She turned from the car.

"No. On the contrary, she seemed very healthy, always working in the yard. Always cleaning windows, things like that. She made me feel bad about my own windows. That activity's a pretty good sign she felt healthy."

"What did she die from? Auto accident?" Jacob asked.

"Not an auto accident, a boating accident. Maybe I shouldn't be talking so much, but it was a freak boating accident and she didn't even like boats."

Jacob was about to ask why Maria didn't like boats but was interrupted.

"Are you a detective or something?"

"What makes you think that?"

"Strangers don't usually show up on our street. They don't park their cars and walk around looking at houses and boats."

"Oh!" He must have been spotted right away, he thought.

"Especially tall, good-looking men: gray at the temples, well-dressed. You're too...ah...*sophisticated* for the role of the traveling salesman." She smiled.

Jacob decided he had better be truthful about his reason for being here. This woman was perceptive and he decided he needed a neighborhood ally.

The woman went on, "You seem interested in Maria's death and you didn't seem shocked to hear she's dead. I watch a lot of TV, especially detective and murder mysteries. I think you might be a detective...you act like one."

"You're very observant and clever. I'm here to investigate an insurance claim. I'd appreciate any information you could give me."

He handed her his ID and waited patiently while she studied the details. She gave back the ID.

"Hello, Jacob. Welcome to our part of the world. I'm Cecile. You no doubt noticed I live next door."

"Yes, some of that sharp detecting of mine."

Cecile seemed relieved to know someone else was suspicious about Maria's death. She smiled again, somewhat tentatively, and appeared to make a decision.

"I can tell you what I know. It might not mean a lot, but I'm suspicious of Maria's death, especially the way she died. Sarah, that's my friend, she and I felt it strange she died at sea."

"Is Bradley at home? I understand he's a ship's captain and spends a lot of time at sea."

"He's at sea right now…everyone calls him Brad, he likes that better than Bradley."

"Why do you think Maria's death is questionable? You must have a good reason," Jacob said.

"Maria told me over and over how she hated boats and the water and she didn't know why she ever married a captain of a ship. He's captain of one of those big container ships; they go all over the world."

"Did she ever say why she *did* marry him, especially since she knew he was a ship's captain?"

"How much do you know about Brad and Maria?" Cecile said. She looked directly into Jacob's eyes as she spoke. He liked that about the woman.

"I don't know them at all. The first I heard of either was when my boss told me I was to investigate the claim."

"I don't know where Brad came from, but Maria was from a small town near the Panama Canal. She met Brad and he swept her off her feet—he's that type of man, a real charmer. In one week they married and he brought her here to live. He bought this house just for her. She told me he had been married before and he wanted her to have a brand new house, a place they could share with no bad memories. She liked everything except that boat."

"That's a beautiful cat, why didn't she like it?"

"I don't know exactly, she just hated it. She liked the house on the water and she liked to garden, but she didn't want to go any farther than the beach. That was her limit. She spent a lot of time alone, but she loved her deck and the view."

Jacob looked across the water. The pristine beach, the graceful untrimmed trees, the flurry of life among the cattails. This tributary of the Chesapeake Bay would be an ideal place to retire. For an instant he imagined himself lounging on a deck overlooking this quiet inlet, a Miller Lite and ham sandwich on a table next to his favorite lounge chair,

"It's strange then that she died in a boating accident, isn't it?" he said.

"Yes...it's really weird. Everyone here was stunned. We all liked Maria, even though she stayed mostly to herself."

"Do you know when Bradley will be home? I'd like to talk to him."

"Brad hasn't been here for several weeks. Sometimes he's gone for months; it depends on where his ship is sent. The gardener comes once a week to mow the lawn. Other than that, no one comes around," Cecile said.

"Nobody has come to visit? What about the funeral? How about her relatives?"

"There was no funeral, only a short memorial...terribly brief, really. Her body was never recovered. Brad acted like Maria never existed."

"When you talked to Bradley, how did he seem?" Jacob asked.

"That's part of the mystery; no one has information as to how or when she died. Brad acted very weird. He came home, said she was dead, and left almost immediately. He was very unemotional. No tears, no breakdown—he could have been talking about an old dog he had put down."

"Did Maria ever talk about her relatives? Surely she mentioned them, maybe where they lived or when they might come to visit," Jacob said.

"Last week some people did knock at the door, but they didn't stay long enough for me to ask who they were looking for. They may have been relatives or friends of Maria. They looked a bit like her and I *did* hear them talk among themselves—it sounded like Spanish."

Cecile looked at her watch. "I've got to go...some of the other neighbors may be able to tell you more. Sarah knew Maria better than I did. My friend Herb will be here later today; maybe he can tell you something. He was the first one to talk to Brad and he'll be able to tell you more of Brad's behavior. To me, Brad isn't a very likeable person. Of course that's *my* opinion."

Jacob wanted to hear more. He noticed her hand tighten on the door handle. He knew she was uncomfortable talking about Maria's death. He gave her the opportunity to say more. She didn't find this easy so he waited.

"What else can you tell me?"

For a long moment she looked at Jacob and then turned to the boat. When she turned back her eyes filled with tears.

"I can't talk now. Maybe later. I'm too upset right now." With that she got behind the wheel of the Mustang and sped down the street.

Jacob wanted to hear more about the death of the young woman. He hoped the other neighbors were as quick to open up as Cecile. He also wanted to talk to Herb. He could learn a lot from talking to the neighbors. After all, he thought, sometimes the neighbors know more about people than those people know about themselves.

Jacob looked after the red car until it turned the corner. He checked the time in California and dialed his boss's private number.

*   *   *

"It's early but you might be right on the money with this one," Jacob said in reply to the husky voice on the other end of the line.

"I knew it! Something told me that son-of-a-bitch killed her. That gut feeling seldom fails. When men marry young women, especially young naive women, and take out a fat insurance policy, sirens and lights should go off. You usually can tell by the amount of the policy. She wasn't a CEO either, was she?"

"Not hardly. Just a young woman who appeared to simply want a good life. Wait, did it *say* she was a CEO on the application?" Jacob asked.

"Not specifically but it did refer to potential earnings that could exceed two million," Doug replied.

"That's a lot of money for a young girl who worked in the office of a shipping company. She was a receptionist, not an executive like her husband would have you believe. And that was before they were married; she hasn't worked since. It appears he lied on the application. That puts him in trouble right there."

"Well, take your time. Find everything necessary to make a case against this guy."

"I will. By the way, this is a really nice area. I wouldn't mind living here...you know, retire to a life of fishing and boating." Jacob might as well brace Doug for the inevitable.

Jacob could hear someone in the background. He hoped Doug wasn't pulling in additional personnel. He wanted to solve this case without any help. It would mean a big bonus, and that bonus would really help in getting that retirement place, maybe in a neighborhood like this.

He never realized the east coast was this attractive. The people were equally attractive. Emily had died six years ago and he now found himself wanting company. Cecile, this woman he had met only this morning, made him acutely aware of how lonely his life had become.

"This fellow Brad isn't home and he might not show up for a while. Do you want me to stay until I talk to him?"

"It depends on what you learn from the neighbors. I hope you won't be more than a week."

"I will want to talk to more locals. It'll be several days. I'll call again after I talk to them. And Doug, in the meantime, get somebody ready to replace me. I'll be retiring when this case is over. I've had enough." He punched the off button. He didn't hear Doug's reply.

"You *can't* retire—you're my best investigator!"

*   *   *

The temperature still hovered at eighty-five when Jacob knocked on the neighbor's door on the other side of the Harper residence. A slim, dark-haired woman answered the door and invited Jacob into the cool interior.

"I saw you talking to Cecile. I figured you would be coming here sooner or later. In fact, the whole neighborhood was expecting you. What took you so long?"

Jacob handed his ID to the woman. "Just to be sure you can trust me," he said. While she checked the ID, he was deciding this woman was as attractive as her neighbor Cecile.

She studied his face and compared it to the photo before

returning it.

"Nice," she said.

Jacob fumbled his ID into his wallet.

"I'm Sarah." She extended her hand. Jacob thought it warm and friendly. "Come sit down, it's really hot out there. How about a beer?"

"Not now...maybe some other time, okay?"

"Sure."

"My company's questioning Maria's death. It seems strange, her dying at sea...her husband has a sizeable insurance policy on her life." Jacob chose his words carefully.

"I feel so bad about Maria's death. The poor girl lived a horrible life with Brad. She tried to say she was just being a good wife, but I knew better. She was *scared*. Not only did he make ridiculous demands, he never wanted her family to visit. She was so homesick when she first moved here, but he forbade her to contact her family. There were times I overheard them arguing about her relatives, and I often caught her crying because she was so lonely."

"Well people *do* argue. It's not too strange for wives to be upset when their husbands aren't home with them." Maybe Sarah was making too much out of a small disagreement. "Did she ever tell you she wanted to go home?" Jacob asked.

"*Lord,* yes! She wanted to end the marriage. She was a good Catholic girl and she was too scared to say she wanted out."

"How about the other neighbors, was she friends with anyone else? Were they aware of how she felt?"

"I really don't know. Cecile and I were the closest. Maria stayed to herself. Only spoke when she was spoken to. Cecile and I made her talk. We more or less forced ourselves on her."

"She was lucky to have you two as neighbors."

"I guess so, but we should have done more. Why is it we always think of things we should have done after it's too late."

"I don't know. Things always seem clearer after the disaster's over," Jacob said.

"You're so right. I wish I'd have seen the warning signs though."

"Can you tell me anything about that catamaran? I understood Maria was afraid of the water," Jacob said.

"That's the oddest thing. That monstrosity showed up about four months before Maria died. It was a surprise to the whole neighborhood. A boat that size is a rarity around here. We all wondered how Brad could afford a boat like that."

"How often does he take it out? It appears to be ocean-worthy. He could probably go around the world in a boat that size," Jacob said.

"That's what Maria was afraid of. Brad kept telling her they were going on a long vacation, possibly three or four months. She didn't want to go, but she was too afraid to say so. She always did what Brad wanted."

"I'd like to talk to the dealer that sold it to him. I'd like to know what something like that costs."

"You'll have to go to France. Maria told me some outfit in France made it special order for Brad. He told them what he wanted and they made it to suit him. It's certainly ostentatious. Too much boat for this neighborhood."

"Have you been on board? Can you tell me what it looks like?"

"I was aboard it just once, just to see what it was like. It's pretty enough: a big kitchen area on the top deck, very elaborate. It has all the latest appliances and gadgets, microwave, dishwasher, even a wine cooler. There's also a big main room with beautiful furniture and a bar—you should *see* the bar, all wood and mirrors. In fact, the entire boat is teakwood and burnished brass. There's plenty of room for several people and it's big enough to sail the Caribbean or Mediterranean, if that's what you like."

"On the boat…would everybody be…close…within sight of the others?"

"I suppose…except when they were sleeping. That boat has sleeping quarters in either pontoon. On each side of the boat there's a flight of steps going down to a separate stateroom. Each suite has its own private bath and is entirely separated from the other one. I wondered what would happen if there were a fire and one had to get out of the stateroom. Those pontoons are dark, no windows or escape hatches. At least I didn't notice any, but surely there would be a way to get out. It was scary."

"It sounds scary. Did Maria take to it at all?"

"Heavens, no! I often saw her sitting on the deck of the house staring at the boat, nearly in tears. She dreaded going out in any boat, let alone that one."

"Did she ever say why she didn't like boats and the water?"

"Her father was lost at sea. I think he was a sailor and his ship sank during a storm. His body was never recovered. I think Maria was afraid the same might happen to her. She was rather superstitious and believed in things recurring in one's life. Mostly the bad things, like her father's death."

"Very disturbing. I can imagine that must have been especially traumatizing for a little kid."

"Yes, and it was all compounded by her own mother! Her mother claimed her father had sinned and received the ultimate punishment for his offenses. It had to do with her mother's belief in a JuJu cult. She was evidently a firm believer. Maria was scared she might do something bad and be punished, and for her, punishment would be death, or so she thought. I thought she was into the cult way too much. She seemed obsessed with death. I imagine that's why Brad didn't want Maria's mother visiting. I heard them arguing about that a *lot*." Sarah paused. She seemed to be trying to recall something. She looked at the boat.

"Is there anything else you can tell me?" Jacob asked.

Sarah paused for a moment, sipped her iced tea then leaned forward. "Yes…about two weeks ago a cleaning company came and gave the entire boat a good cleaning: *everything*, inside and out. I figured Brad was probably going to sell it, but Cecile said that Brad told her he was coming for the boat later. So maybe he *isn't* going to get rid of it," Sarah said.

*   *   *

Herb had his head under the hood of the red Mustang. He wiped his hands and introduced himself.

"I really don't know anything about cars but I find the complexity fascinating. Just look at that V-8!" Herb said.

Jacob estimated Herb to be in his late sixties. He seemed sturdy, good-natured, and built for power—not speed.

"I don't know much either, only that they need gas and occasionally, some oil. These days it takes a computer to understand them," Jacob said. Then he added, "You know why I'm here so I'll get right to the point."

"Yes, Cecile told me. She said you'd be back."

"What can you tell me about Brad and Maria's marriage? A man's point of view is sometimes different than a woman's. I know

Cecile and Sara mean well, but I need more than just suspicion and feeling. It's important we know the facts. I can't move on anything I can't prove." Jacob needed evidence of at least fraud. If he could *prove* Brad was responsible for Maria's death, even better. No two million dollars for Brad, a bonus for Jacob's nest egg, and, perhaps, some justice for Maria.

Herb paused for a moment. He looked toward the house. He could see Cecile in the kitchen preparing lunch.

"Cecile is still upset about Maria's death. She keeps telling me that Brad killed Maria and nothing is going to change her mind. I've tried to ask her why she is so sure, but she just looks at me and tells me I wouldn't understand."

"Wouldn't understand what?" Jacob asked. He leaned against the bright red fender.

"I don't know. Maybe it's a woman's intuition to *feel* things like that."

"How did *you* feel about Brad? How did he seem to you?"

"Like a bad actor playing sad."

Before Herb could say more Cecile called them inside.

The coolness of the house felt good and, while Cecile brought ice tea, Jacob glanced around the comfortable room. Traditional furniture—navy and cream sofa, wood-and-glass tables and gold-framed family photos. Mirrored-back walls reflected the manicured short stretch of lawn, the sparkling water, and the hardwood on the far shore. To access this tranquil scene, sliding glass doors led to a wide deck. Pale green chairs and umbrella made the deck very inviting with impatiens and fern adding color. The deck looked almost tropical. Jacob approved.

"I understand you were the first to speak with Brad," he said looking at Herb.

"Yes. I happened to be outside when he came home. He went directly into the house, not saying anything, not even hello. After a few minutes, he came back out and over to where I was. And, would you believe it? Very matter-of-factly he told me Maria was dead. Just that—Maria is dead—and would I mind telling Cecile?"

"No red eyes, no hunched-over shoulders?"

"Not in the least. I couldn't believe he was that calm. Of course, he may have been in shock. I can't really say one way or the other."

"What else did he say?"

"Only that he didn't have very much time, and would I tell Cecile."

"You mean he didn't want to tell Cecile himself. That was cruel. He knew they were good friends, didn't he?"

"Yes. I told Brad I wasn't going to do it. That he would have to. He said again that he didn't have time, and I asked him how much time would it take to tell Cecile? He claimed he had appointments with his lawyer and insurance company. He also had to make arrangements for a memorial service. That was his excuse. I told him bluntly to make time."

"So he finally *did* come in and tell you." Jacob addressed this to Cecile.

"Yes, after I insisted it was his responsibility," Herb said.

"Did he say what happened? How Maria died?" Jacob looked at Cecile for an answer.

"He said they were in the Gulf of Mexico when Maria fell off the boat and drowned. He and her mother looked and looked but couldn't find her. At first they thought she was somewhere on the boat, but after a thorough search they realized she wasn't aboard. He said he thought she was in her mother's bedroom and her mother thought she was in Brad's room, so neither missed Maria for a time."

"I didn't think Maria's mother would be with them. Evidently they were closer than you thought."

"I guess so. They must have picked her up in Panama. Maria never mentioned her mother going. Maybe Brad wanted to surprise Maria by taking her along, although I doubt that," Cecile said.

"Did Brad say where they were when Maria disappeared?"

"He said they were close to the Yucatan Peninsula, in Mexican territorial waters. He also said he hadn't thought to notify the American Embassy, only the Mexican authorities. They did an investigation into Maria's disappearance and determined it to be a boating accident. Are you going to Mexico and check into the case?" Cecile asked.

"No, I'll contact them and have them fax a copy of the report. These days we don't have to travel everywhere and I can't think what a trip down there would tell me anyway. A phone call is all we need."

"Why didn't he notify the American Counsel? They might have been able to do something. He should have notified them," Cecile added.

"Brad probably didn't want too extensive an investigation. If he had something to hide, by waiting, much of the evidence would have been contaminated. He's a pretty smart cookie. If he did kill her, he had everything figured out—even to having a witness aboard...a darn good witness at that."

"It's hard for me to imagine someone so cruel. He's a psychopath...a demented killer. I can't believe I lived next door to a murderer and never suspected." Cecile took Herb's hand. Her eyes filled with tears and she wiped them away with a Kleenex.

"Even the cleverest make at least one mistake. It may take a while...sometimes *quite* a while, but he'll make a mistake and we'll get him. Sooner or later it'll be payback time."

"I sure hope so. If there's anything we can do, let us know," Herb said.

"I'm going to look at the boat. I don't need to look inside; just a quick check on the deck from which we assume she fell or was pushed. I've got a court order."

"Sure, help yourself...and good luck."

*   *   *

Jacob went aboard. The tide was high and the boat and pier were on the same level. He walked the boat's full length noting there were no signs of it *ever* having been at sea. "Good cleaning job," he thought. At the stern Jacob noticed a piece of rope trailing into the water. It originated from a hatch covering; a storage area. Brad had told Cecile and Herb he thought Maria had been emptying garbage when she lost her balance. Brad said he had noticed the bags of garbage were gone, presumably from this very storage compartment, and figured Maria and the garbage had fallen overboard, maybe from a sudden ocean swell causing the boat to rock.

Jacob pulled the free end of the rope from the water. He held it for a moment studying its waterlogged end. It was severed on an angle, a clean cut as with a sharp knife. It was odd; most yachting ropes are not simply cut on an angle. They are finished neatly with the end securely fastened either with crimped metal, twisted smaller rope, or a finely braided loop. He dropped the rope back into the water.

Finding nothing more of interest on the boat, he stood for a moment gazing at the shoreline of Willow Creek. Where the shoreline curled to the right, the sinking sun caught the rolling wake of a small boat. That bright sun turned the waves into undulating bands of gold.

"Beautiful!" he said aloud. All along the shore fireflies rose to meet the twinkling sparkles of dock lights and emerging stars. Until well after dark, he strolled the neighborhood admiring the homes and the quietness. He was certain this was an ideal place to live. He wanted escape from the flashy and youth-oriented California hubbub. This was much more his style. It might take a while to find the right house, but when he retired he would have time. A good realtor would find him the right place. Peace, quiet, and release from the attempts to make things right for the stockholders of West Coast Life Insurance.

Returning to his car, he sat for a minute imagining a rockfish bending his rod tip. As he put the key in the ignition he noticed a car backing out of the Harper's driveway. Before starting his own engine he waited until the car passed. The driver was a man, about thirty-five, blonde hair and full beard. Jacob wondered if it was Brad Harper. The only reason he could be here was to get that Catamaran ready for a voyage to God knows where. Jacob decided he would check on it tomorrow.

*   *   *

At the motel a message was waiting—a call from Doug. Maria's mother had requested to see the investigator. She wanted to talk about her daughter's death. She was in Baltimore and left a number.

So the group at the house *had* been family and Maria's mother was in town. He wondered what she could tell him. He copied the hotel address and, after a hurried call to make sure she was available, headed north on the ever-crowded Interstate 95.

She was waiting in the lobby. A petite, composed, dark woman with cropped ebony hair. She appeared to be about forty-five. Maria's mother wore a turquoise dress with a geometric print of Incan motifs. She introduced herself as Rosita Garcia.

He identified himself and asked if she would be more comfortable going somewhere else.

"Yes please...somewhere else," she said.

He called a cab; it would be easier than trying to find

somewhere to talk while driving the rental. Jacob told the taxi driver to take them to an out-of-the-way café. The ride was in silence, the heat oppressive. They found a booth at the rear of Coffee Beanery and More.

After they ordered coffee Rosita clasped her hands as in prayer.

"Senor Jacob. I am very angry and very…how you say…upturned…no, no, upset. I know what Brad did and I cannot let this man, this dog, escape justicia, ah…justice. I am a little afraid, pero," she said over her clasped hands.

Jacob wanted to reassure the woman she would be safe, but he wasn't sure exactly how much danger she might be in. He waited until she lowered her hands to the table.

"You don't have to be afraid…just tell me what happened on that boat? What happened to your daughter? You must tell me…*por justicia*," Jacob demanded.

"He let her die. I know he did. I know he killed her."

"What did you see," Jacob insisted.

"You must not let him know you talked with me…si?"

"I won't let him know, but you have to help. You were there, you know what happened." Jacob took a small recorder from his briefcase, laid it on the table and flicked the on button.

"What happened the night Maria died? We have to know *exactly* what happened. Tell me what you saw."

Rosita clenched her hands, swallowed once and looked at the recorder.

"I saw him. He was holding a rope and Maria was also holding the rope. She was trying to put it around her waist. He kept tugging on it."

"What time was this? What were you doing on deck?"

"It was around one-thirty. I could not sleep. The ocean is beautiful at night, the moon on the water, the waves. I also wanted to be with Maria. I knew she was scared, so I thought I would keep her company. So she would not be all by herself. He did not see me. They…fight, ah, argue."

"Why didn't you say something, get between them? It might have helped."

"I was scared, scared for my own life." Rosita let a sob escape. "I always knew Brad was a bad person, from the first time I met him I was afraid of him. I never thought he would harm Maria, so I started down to my room when I heard her cry out. I went back up and saw Brad standing with a knife in his hand. Maria wasn't there anymore and he just kept looking over the back of the boat."

"Did he know you were there?"

"I do not think so. I hid in the stairway for a minute then went to where Brad was. He seemed surprised to see me. He asked how long I was on the deck. I did not answer. Then he said he and Maria had a talk and she went to the cabin."

"Rosita, I want you to be available as a witness. You need not be afraid of Brad. He won't be out of jail for a long time."

"How can you be sure? Justicia en America? I see the TV. Your justice, always too late."

Jacob took her hand. He looked into her tear-filled eyes.

"In the state of Maryland there is a so-called Slayers Rule. That means anyone who intentionally causes the death of an insured person cannot collect the benefits. He'll get no money. And if he's found guilty of her death in a murder trial, he'll spend the rest of his life in prison."

"But he'll say he didn't kill her. He's very...clever, he has a way that makes you believe him," Rosita said.

"A jury will find him guilty. We'll have to trust the jury."

Rosita looked at Jacob. She looked weary, there were dark circles under her eyes. The anguish of Maria's death showed. After a moment she smiled. The tears were still there.

"Maria was going to leave him. She had plans to come home. Now I will never see her again. I know she is in heaven, but it is hard to know I will never see her again in this life. In the next life, verdad, but not in this one."

"She will be in your heart. You can take comfort in the thought that Brad will be brought to justice. He will be punished." Jacob squeezed her hand.

"Yes, Brad will pay for this *mal*, this evil." There was new resolve in her voice.

"You're right. The courts will see to that. I promise."

Rosita rested her chin on folded hands. Jacob sensed she wanted to say something. He waited. Reaching into her purse, Rosita withdrew a piece of heavy twine. She looked at Jacob as she began toying with the string, tying and retying a slipknot and pulling sharply to make each knot disappear.

"No, not the courts. I have prayed to the spirits. My request to JuJu will be honored. I have called on the spirits; they have heard me, they will answer. Maria's death will be avenged. There has been a juju put on Brad. He will not escape," Rosita said. She jerked the twine again, almost breaking it; her eyes never blinked. Rosita then smiled, staring at the twine.

Jacob turned off the recorder. He didn't want to hear about voodoo. He believed the legal system would convict a murderer; he had no faith in magic and the supernatural. If Rosita sought religious comfort in a cult, that was fine. He would just have to be careful about summoning her as a witness. He hoped there was enough circumstantial evidence to convict Brad. Surely a jury could be convinced.

As they left the café, Jacob pressed a business card into her palm. He held her hand for a long moment.

"You'll be hearing from me soon," he said.

Outside, he flagged another taxi and dropped Rosita off at her hotel.

"Take care...cuidado. I'll be in touch very soon."

As he drove back to Willow Creek, he thought quietly about cut rope and twisted twine.

* * *

Jacob recognized the red glow in the night sky; as an insurance investigator, he had seen night fires. It was coming from the direction of Willow Creek, the waterfront homes, those nice people he had just met.

"God, I hope those folks are safe!" he thought as he followed a fire truck racing toward the glow.

The truck continued around the bend of Willow Creek to the undeveloped side of the river. Jacob saw a fire and rescue vehicle with EMT medics standing near what he assumed was a sheet-covered body.

The boat was fully engulfed. The ferocious flames seemed to mock the efforts of the newly-arrived firemen futilely linking hose sections. The boat would obviously burn to the waterline.

"What happened? How did it start?" Jacob shouted over the roar and commotion.

"We don't know. The boat was already totally engulfed when we got here. We couldn't tell what it was, but one of the medics said it looked like a big Catamaran. The guy must have missed the channel. You'd think a local would know the channel markers."

"Any ID?" Jacob shouted back.

"I don't know. Ask the EMT's, they were first on the scene. They're over by the body." The fireman pointed to the medics.

Jacob introduced himself and flashed his West Coast Life ID saying he had reason to believe he was the insurance rep for the deceased. He asked if anyone else might have been aboard.

"Naw, not likely. Someone called about a boat running aground, thinking people might need help. When we got here the fire was still small. One guy was on the forward deck, I guess trying to see what the problem was. We didn't see anybody else. We yelled for him to get into the water as we tried to launch our Whaler and we called in our pumper. Guy wouldn't listen. All of a sudden BOOM! Huge explosion blew the guy right off the deck and right onto that cable."

The EMT pointed at a thick steel guy-wire attached to a marsh-surrounded telephone pole. "He must have died instantly; hell, he was almost cut in half. We couldn't do a thing. By then the fire was so intense, all we could do is watch it burn and get the guy off the cable. The medics are waiting for the coroner now. God, I hope I never see anything like that again." The man shook his head as if trying to lose the memory.

Jacob waited several minutes before asking.

"Tentative ID?"

"Yeah...Harper. Pulled his wallet out of the...." The EMT held a bloody lump in his gloved hand.

He lived right across the river. See those two houses with the lights on the decks? His place would be the one between them, the house that's dark."

Jacob walked slowly back to his car thinking about that twine...that twine and the peculiar snap the slipknot made.

186
SO MUCH, SO LITTLE

by Carla J. Wiederholt

Crawl back into your shell.
Not a word then you will tell.

Back up far against the wall.
Leave no space for you to fall.

Look to the ground, not in my eyes.
Dare you see a knowing surprise?

Sit in darkness; no light is shed.
What sadness has your soul been fed?

To open your world, what might I do?
There is so much I could learn from you.

So much you could offer, so little you expose.
So much wants to escape you, so much no one knows.

STOP

by Joel Furches

"Stop!" said the voice in the mind of every human being, simultaneously, all across the world. And stop they did. Noisy restaurants were hushed in silence as people ceased their talking. Busy highways filled with vehicles rushing from one place to another were now suddenly still as the traffic slowed then halted in obedience to the voice. Babies quit their crying. Factories, the very engines of industry, ground to a halt. Somewhere in the Middle East rioters were hurling curses and burning bottles at a band of police armed with semi-automatics and riot clubs. Both parties froze. One young man dropped a ceremonial sword in mid-swing, as both the police and the rioters followed the dictates of that inner voice. Two nations' leaders stopped mid-signature on a peace treaty. Two political candidates hushed mid-sentence at a presidential debate. A mugger lowered the hand holding the switchblade. His intended victim, a woman, who moments ago had been screaming hysterically, was now silent, her fear forgotten. Somewhere in the deep jungle, two warring tribes dropped their spears. A doctor paused mid-surgery. A patient paused his dying breath. The guards at the city gates paused in their patrol.

The world was engulfed in silence, broken only by the sounds made by oblivious animals. For one moment all of humanity held its breath, waiting for the inner voice to continue, to finish its statement. And, after a moment, it did.

"You're doing everything all wrong." the voice completed.

"Oh." said humanity, and everyone continued as they had been.

Ted M. Zurinsky, "Ghost Ship"

THE WOODEN PONY AND AN OLD MAN

by Ann Cook

Today I saw a little boy
  barely past the age of five.
He rode a broomstick pony
  with princely ease and pride.

It brought to mind those long-gone times
  when I, too, rode wooden horses.
Does he dream those dreams I often dreamed
  of cheering crowds and winner's purses?

I've seen my mount through finish line
  his nose a bit ahead.
This boy's so filled with hope and fire
  an old man has to smile.

IRIE AND ME

by Lois Gilbert

As I opened the front door, the cold January wind swept across my face. I pulled my scarf a little closer. We stepped out onto the driveway and I watched in horror as his hind legs flew apart. He went down in a spread eagle position. As I reached for him, I went down. Was anyone looking? I felt shaken. Was anyone even awake at this time of morning? I attempted to crawl to my knees; I slipped again.

I felt the icy cold under the palms of my hands. Irie and I had both slipped on a sheet of ice. What a way to begin our morning hike. Irie is my youngest daughter's eleven-year-old dog, an Australian Shepherd, and we were having a visit.

This time I made sure that we walked around the glossy spots. Irie has a hip problem and I have a knee that I can't trust completely. As we walked up the road I glanced toward the river. Geese were everywhere. I could feel the tug on the leash. Irie had spotted them. His ears were pointed straight towards the heavens.

My heart began to beat a little faster as I remembered my first canoe trip across this river. The leash tugged. Was Irie's heart beating a little faster because he was remembering his dashes to the river...*before* his hips began to weaken? We turned back towards the icy driveway. I would be careful this time.

I unhooked Irie's leash and hung my coat in the closet. I filled his water dish and looked out at the river through the sliding glass doors. A neighbor was walking her dog on the crushed oyster-shell path that followed the river. A year ago, Irie would have been aware of their presence, but this year his hearing has begun to fail. I reached up and felt for one of my hearing aids. I had just had my seventy-sixth birthday. Irie is seventy-seven in dog years.

Irie raced past me toward the slider—he had spotted the dog on the path. He began to bark. I didn't need my hearing aids to hear his excitement. I went into the kitchen and poured another cup of coffee. Irie followed and licked my toes as I took my first sip. Was it a reminder that I hadn't yet given him his breakfast? I reached for his bag of dog food and scantily filled the little dish. Lois, my daughter, had reminded me that we must not let him get too heavy because of his hips. What little food he now requires! I could feel myself smiling as I thought of *my* efforts to use smaller bowls. My hips also required smaller portions.

Lois would be coming to take him home tomorrow. I could feel a lump forming in my throat as I remembered one of our nights together. I had a terrible cold with a horrible cough. When the coughing began, Irie would circle the bed and, at about one foot intervals, he would hit the bed with his paw. I would get up, take my cough medicine, and Irie would give me a lick. I could hear him again flop heavily onto the floor as I crawled back into bed.

*   *   *

My anticipation of tomorrow has come and gone. Tomorrow has become yesterday and on this day I sit here with my pad and pen, remembering.

Lois stood at the door patiently waiting as I ran my hands through the thick grey and white fur. Irie licked my face as I looked into his silver blue eyes.

It was time to leave. Lois didn't want to be caught in traffic. I felt the tears begin as they pulled out of the driveway. They drove over the spot that had been icy. I went back into the kitchen and emptied his water dish.

I turned on the TV. I must have dozed. The telephone rang. "Mom, we're home. Irie wants to hear your voice. He seems to be looking for you."

"Hold it up close to his ear," I said. I took out my hearing aid. Sometimes it squeals when I place the receiver tight against my ear. I settled back in the chair to "listen" and then I spoke....I heard him bark. I thought of his silver blue eyes. I thought of God's wonderful creation of animals.

*   *   *

Months later, I climbed up into the jeep and watched in silence as Irie was placed in the small wagon that was attached. Lois had covered the rough boards with a soft blanket. She crawled in beside him. Andy slipped in behind the wheel and we moved slowly down the dirt farm road.

It was the day after Thanksgiving. The preceding months had been a challenge to all as Irie's mobility lessened. Lois bought him a doggie wheelchair. The neighbors cheered as he strolled by. But then his whole body became weary.

Lois found him a playmate, hoping it would lessen his frustration while she was at work. She named him Webster. He was a small black dachshund. Lois had grown up on Webster Road and Webster was born there. He was a gift from the present owners of the house in which Lois had spent her youth. Irie trained Webster well. Sometimes they curled up together.

Andy drove slowly. I looked at the rolling hills and felt a tear roll down my cheek. Out of the corner of my eye I could see Lois gently stroking Irie. We had all watched as the vet gave him his final shot. We buried him on a hilltop in Darlington. Andy had prepared the place and he and Lois gently laid him in. We bowed our heads and began, "The Lord is my shepherd."

I will always remember Irie…and me.

LOVE, LUCK, AND LUCIANO

by Sarah Shilko-Mohr

Charity shuffled into the kitchen hugging her thick robe around her, the ears of her bunny slippers wiggling with each step. Lowering his newspaper, Mitch smiled warmly and chimed, "Good morning, beautiful."

One eye closed, Charity tried smiling a cheery hello in return but it came out as a grimace and a grunt. She was not a morning person.

Mitch was a carpe diem kind of guy, an early riser and had probably already ordered the mulch for the beds, checked his stocks via the Internet, read three or four newspapers and, for all she knew, scaled a mountain and planted a flag. But as long as his special blend of coffee awaited her, she could forgive him his morning perkiness.

Rich and strong and filling the kitchen with an aroma, that coffee drew her as surely as Pavlov's dogs responded to a bell. Charity made her way to the counter. Maxwell House had always been good enough when Charity's first husband had been alive but, she had to admit, Kenyan beans from Africa created a brew fit for the Gods. This was one of the nicer routines that had developed in her and Mitch's first year of marriage.

Cradling her mug and two pieces of dry toast, Charity sat down at the kitchen table and began nibbling her breakfast. She could feel Mitch's surreptitious glances as he waited patiently for her to come fully awake. His patience warmed her as much as the coffee. A smile curved her lips, whether from the delicious Kenya Gold or Mitch's respect, the true origin would remain unspoken. Or "ungrunted," if the truth be told.

It was Lucky, the resident Rottweiler, who determined Charity was awake enough to be addressed. Laying his enormous head in her lap, he shifted his gaze toward the vanishing toast in a plea for a tidbit.

There was a special place in Charity's heart for this horse of a hound. It was Lucky who had brought Mitch and her together. It had been one morning, when Charity had looked out her kitchen window and spied a strange brown mound just beyond a hummock in her backyard. Curious—and wearing the same floppy bunny slippers she wore right now—she'd scampered out to investigate.

She was brought to a dead standstill when the mound lifted a gigantic head then proceeded to heave itself up to a height that looked her straight in the eye. A stare-down contest proceeded while Charity's mind raced through scenarios of escaping alive. A huge tongue languished from the beast's mouth. Charity heard herself asking, "Are you thirsty Big Boy?" When the monster lumbered over to where Charity stood rigidly, she laughed at the sheer absurdity of his size. In spite of the fact this humongous dog could snap her neck without effort, it couldn't turn on a faucet and fill a bowl, or as it turned out, a bucket with water.

Lucky followed Charity into the house and fell asleep on the kitchen floor but not before she was able to read his tag telling her the Rottweiler's name was Luciano and his owner's name and phone number. Charity had to leave a message about finding this dog belonging to someone named "Mitch" and said she would call back. She didn't leave her own number. Being widowed and alone at fifty-three had made her especially cautious.

It had taken two days to reach the owner at home—the same amount of time it took Charity to fall head-over-heels in love with Luciano. When she finally spoke with Mitch, the conversation was not at all what she'd expected. What should have been a five minute call turned in to a lively two hour conversation in which she learned that Mitch was also a widower and Luciano had been a gift to help him through the worst of his grieving. She understood entirely. It felt so good to talk anonymously to someone who had also been happily married then lost a partner to death and not an ugly divorce. When Mitch said he would come right over to pick up Luciano, Charity choked. He'd hesitated. He suggested he send his driver instead.

"No, no, that won't be necessary," Charity spit out, inwardly surprised at her sudden reluctance to give Luciano back to his owner. Perhaps she was still protecting her own privacy as well, she thought. "I'll bring Luciano to you."

"Okay," Mitch replied a bit brighter. "When you reach the gate, the guard will have your name."

Charity felt silly at possibly hurting Mitch's feelings with her need of not letting a stranger know where she lived.

Especially after their conversation had touched her in ways that left her giddy.

It seemed especially stupid now that Luciano and Mitch had lived in her house for the last year and a half.

Charity turned and looked into the big brown eyes of Luciano's huge head resting on her shoulder.

"Do you want your favorite breakfast, pretty boy?"

"Ah! You're awake."

Mitch took the question posed to the dog as the demarcation line between Charity being a walking zombie and a flesh and blood person capable of conversation.

Charity poured cornflakes and milk into the trough that served as Lucky's food dish. At first, cornflakes had been all she'd had to feed Lucky during his stay with her. The cornflakes had become an occasional treat reminding them both of the happy, life-twisting event that led to her and Mitch meeting.

"What would you like to do today?"

Mitch had to almost shout over the slobbering noise of Lucky wolfing down the cereal.

"I was thinking we could go to the nursery and pick out some bedding plants."

"Why don't you just let the landscaper do that?" Mitch folded the last of his newspapers.

"And let him have all the fun?" Charity smiled and minced over to her hunk of a husband. Mitch was fit and good-looking, despite his seventy-four years. "What's the matter, old man, is planting some impatiens too much work for you?"

Their friends had given them a million reasons why the nineteen years difference in their ages would doom their marriage. It wasn't as though she hadn't thought of those very reasons too. To be fair, she'd screamed in surprise the day she discovered Mitch's upper teeth in a Polident bath. Suffering a moment of panic, she'd wondered what other nasty discoveries were around the corner.

"So off to the nursery it is," Mitch responded flexing his well-exercised biceps. "Then how about lunch at the club?"

Charity gave Mitch a closed lip smile, raising her eyebrows. Getting ready would take a bit longer if they were going to the club directly from the nursery. Curled hair, makeup, something other than jeans. Mitch was retired and Charity had given up working over a decade ago, but still liked her jeans and sneakers on the weekends. There would be plenty of people in jeans at the country club with most of the men in golfing attire, but Charity always felt better when she took extra care in her appearance for stops at Mitch's favorite hang-out. She wondered what her new friends would say if they knew she haunted thrift stores, discount warehouses, and end-of-year clearance sales to acquire her wardrobe. Would they celebrate a fabulous bargain as much as she did? Charity's philosophy about life in general—and money especially—was waste not, want not. It was Mitch who taught her she could even apply this philosophy to exotic coffee beans.

Charity picked up Lucky's trough and, while putting it in the sink, suggested, "How about we take the van to the nursery, bring the plants home, change and take the Jag to the club."

A Cheshire grin spread over Mitch's face as he stood and then wrapped his arms around Charity.

"Yeah, honey...let's drive the Jag!"

"I swear you sound just like a teenager," Charity teased as Mitch stared into her eyes making her feel like the most beautiful creature on Earth despite her uncombed hair, thick robe, and bunny slippers.

"And what a deal you got on it!" Charity added as she and Mitch began a slow waltz, Lucky begging to make it a threesome.

"I knew you'd love that part." Mitch gave Charity a quick kiss on the forehead. "Now go get dressed while I take our lucky charm for a walk."

"Have fun," was her reply but it was overridden by Lucky barking. He whomped his huge feet in approval of a walk and slammed the doorframe with his big butt in exuberance to be on the way.

Laughing, Charity floated toward the bedroom on a cloud of contentment. A blissful marriage was karma; it was all about being in the right place and time with the uniquely right person. And sometimes, love was really about how a person made you feel about yourself and your worth than your ages or how much or how little money you had.

Susan C. Buttimer, "Skipjack on the Bay"

A BIG LIE

by Lee Bruce

The scent of spring was in the air. Neighborhood children played together in front of the houses. Mothers peeked out of the windows of the newly constructed homes as the preschoolers met after the older children had gone off to the neighborhood grade school. It was a safe environment filled with young families of stay-at-home Moms and young Dads trying to support the families housed in these structures.

We were all house poor, furniture deprived, lawn ignorant, and frightened that we had made too big a step but proud as peacocks at being able to call ourselves "homeowners."

The children at play were all bundled with hooded ski jackets, scarves, mittens and heavy corduroy slacks or snow pants. It took considerable time just to get a child ready to go out to play. I was surprised when my daughter in her red jacket and ski pants burst through the door. Her blond curls framed her rosy face and she was angry. I had seldom seen that because she was a very even-tempered child.

"You lied to me, Momma."

"Susan, honey, Momma would never lie to you or your sister."

"Oh, yes you did," she said, becoming more annoyed.

"What did I say?"

"You said that spring was just around the corner. I rode my bike clear down to Steinmann's and I looked around the corner. It is still cold down there and I could not find spring."

It took a while to sort out "my big lie."

A DRAGONFLY

by Joyce M. Shepherd

What is life?
It is birth, death, joy, and sorrow.
It is seasons, sunrises, and sunsets.
It is wind, thunder, and rainbow-hued skies.
It is the hope of mankind.

>What is life?
>It is seeing a child's smile,
>Or hearing the music of laughter.
>It is the touch of a wrinkled hand,
>And the scent of familiarity.

>>What is life?
>>It is the first act
>>Of a beautiful play.
>>It is the stepping stone
>>To the promise of eternity.

>>>What is life?
>>>It is faith and wishing on a star.
>>>It is to love and be loved.
>>>It is a gift, a moment in time
>>>To be cherished forever.

In memory of Janice
1959-2005

Something's wrong, thought Jessica, as she and Nick walked into Dr. Morgan's office.

"Have a seat Jessica...Nick," Dr. Morgan said as he shuffled the papers lying on his desk. "We're canceling the lumpectomy scheduled for today, Jessica. Your pre-surgical blood work came back showing you're pregnant."

Jessica's eyes welled. She was as stunned as when the doctor first told her the lump was alarmingly large and extremely suspicious. How was it possible to have the miracle of life in one hand and, possibly, have death clutching at the fingertips of the other? It had to be a cruel joke.

*   *   *

Jessica, blonde, blue-eyed, and bubbly; and Nicholas, an Alec Baldwin look-alike, met in 1995. Nick, a mechanic, was not the three-piece suit type to which she was usually drawn. One of Jessica's best friends, Marcie—a tall, attractive professional with lush, dark hair—reminded her it was the good man inside that was important, not the image.

"It's far more important, Jess, to find a man who'll take care of you and be around for the long haul," Marcie said. "We've both learned that lesson the hard way if you remember correctly."

Love blossomed and Jessica and Nick were married in a private ceremony on a chartered boat out of Chincoteague, Maryland in May, 1998. The bride was radiant—love glistened in her eyes as she looked up at her groom dressed in a gray morning suit. Their bright and happy faces were the sunshine on an otherwise ominously dark and threatening day.

Settling into married life and a new job on the eastern shore of Maryland, Jessica felt she had finally found the happiness that had eluded her most of her life. She had been born to alcoholic parents and two much older siblings. Her mother died when she was six and her older siblings quickly went out on their own leaving Jessica to cope with a series of stepmothers—eight, in fact. Only two formed any kind of bond with her. Her brother eventually became an inmate of Jessup prison. He was still in the penal system…somewhere. A lost soul, lost especially to her. Her sister she knew to be just plain evil.

Nick became the steadfast, loving force Jessica had been searching for all of her life.

Both Jessica and Nick were excited at the thought of children and, because of their ages (teetering on forty), they were hoping for sooner rather than later. She dreamed of a normal home with a mother, father, and the classic two children; a home where kids could grow up in a happy and secure environment. When Jessica's friend Marcie, forty-three, delivered a bouncing baby girl, Jessica was thrilled for her best friend but frustrated.

She still wasn't pregnant. She was a doer and go, go, go person, and the conception process was not moving fast enough for her.

Three years passed and, although Jessica loved being a doting aunt to Marcie's little Emily, she was coming to the realization that, after almost six years of trying, she might never become a mother herself.

"Why don't we find a nice B and B in the Virginia countryside this weekend," Jessica asked Nick. "We need a change of scenery for a few days."

Nick looked up from his paper.

"Sounds great! We could use a fun weekend and a little relaxation. Too much baby stress. We need to loosen up and just let nature take its course."

Jessica laughed. "I thought basically that's what we *were* doing!"

"More or less, but there *is* the theory you can try too hard—not that I'm complaining."

The weekend was perfect with an abundance of sunshine, a cooling breeze wafting through leaves, and the fresh scent of forget-me-nots, pink lady's slippers, and loblolly pines. At least it *was* perfect until Jessica discovered the lump on her breast.

After their return home she saw a specialist who determined the lump to be "extremely suspicious." It was an alarmingly large lump that had appeared quite suddenly. The oncologist agreed with the surgeon—a lumpectomy.

* * *

Clutching Nick's callused hand, Jessica managed to gather her thoughts.

"Pregnant! After all this time, I can hardly believe it, Dr. Morgan. But why now? What will we do? What's going to happen?"

"A decision doesn't have to be made today," Dr. Morgan said. "You and Nick go home and talk. I'll consult with some colleagues about the best course of action. We'll figure it out."

Arriving home, Jessica called Marcie.

"I don't want to talk, just listen to me," she said. "They didn't do the lumpectomy because they discovered I'm pregnant. Nick and I are stunned." She hung up.

Dazed, Marcie sat down slowly. Marcie watched her little Emily playing happily. The phone sat uselessly in Marcie's hand.

What a weekend Jessica and Nick had. Bittersweet. Jessica sat out on her patio hoping the sultry summer day would warm her chilled soul. She watched her beloved dragonflies darting over and under the smiling sun-kissed flowers. Her mouth turned upward and her eyes sparkled as she thought of their carefree, uncomplicated existence.

Rubbing her stomach, she thought about the little life beginning to form inside her. "I can't believe you're inside me, a little peanut just beginning to grow," she thought. "What are you, my little peanut: a boy, a girl…maybe one of each? One thing for sure, you're my special miracle."

Jessica went inside and curled up next to Nick.

"I want this baby so much Nick. There has to be a way. Maybe the doctor is wrong about the seriousness of the lump."

Nick pulled Jessica closer to him.

"Jess, I want the baby as much as you do, but if continuing with the pregnancy would jeopardize your life, keep you from having the tests you need or the treatment you might need if the lump is malignant, I want to terminate it."

"Hopefully the doctors will figure out a way for us to keep our baby." Jessica closed her eyes and sighed.

The doctors worked quickly to diagnose and plan an attack on the cancer. Within a week an MRI was done. The test confirmed the worst.

"Jessica, I'm so sorry," Dr. Morgan said. "The test shows an invasive form of Infiltrating Ductal Carcinoma which means the cancerous breast tumor has broken through the wall of the ducts or lobules and spread into the lymph nodes. I'm referring you to another specialist at Johns Hopkins. You need more extensive testing to determine exactly where it's spread and what stage it's in."

Dr. Morgan stood up and came around in front of Jessica and Nick. He did a deep knee-bend to be at eye level and took Jessica's hand.

"Because the treatments are so rigorous and system-altering, they could be harmful to the baby while you're in your first trimester. The cancer seems to be very aggressive and I would urge you not to delay treatment to await further tests. I can only recommend you not continue the pregnancy."

Life had dealt Jessica and Nick a cruel double blow. Jessica's body trembled as a sob erupted from her mouth. Nick held her and wiped the streaming tears off her cheeks.

"Oh Jess! I am so sorry. I want the baby as much as you do, but I want you even more. Let's get you well. That has to come first."

"It's not fair Nick. It's just not fair."

A sonogram validated the pregnancy test. One week later, however, the baby was aborted. The little peanut that Nick and Jessica had so wanted and had waited so long to have would have been a girl.

Over the next few days Jessica languished in silence as she shuffled around the house. Her sorrow became a viper, poisoning the simplest activities; a vampire, draining her physically and emotionally. Jessica thought about what Nick had said. She paced, pounded her fists on the kitchen counters, shook from head to toe, and at one point, while alone, screamed in anguish. Finally one afternoon, she suddenly sank into her sofa. She picked up a photo sitting on the end table. She looked at Nick's handsome face and he looked back at her in his calm and comforting way. She clutched the photo to herself. *I have to pull myself together, not just for me, but for Nick, for our future.* In that moment, Jessica decided it was time to be as aggressive in finding a cure for the cancer as the cancer was aggressive in trying to kill her.

She made an appointment with a cancer specialist at Johns Hopkins in Baltimore. More testing was done. Days later, Nick, Jessica, and Marcie returned for the test results. The doctor, a fatherly type, gently told Jessica he concurred with Dr. Morgan's diagnosis. She had an aggressive form of Invasive Ductal Carcinoma. He showed her the new test visuals; the cancerous mass of spikes radiated throughout her breasts, lymph nodes and beyond.

"Jessica, the cancer is in an advanced stage III, metastatic at presentation, which means the cancer has spread beyond the breast and nearby lymph nodes. It's even more extensive than at the time of the first diagnosis."

Jessica's voice quivered. "What do you mean beyond the breast and lymph nodes?"

"In your case, Jessica, the cancer has already spread to your lungs."

Marcie put her arm around Jessica. Nick dropped his face into his hands.

"How much time, doctor?" Jessica whispered.

"We cannot say exactly why your last mammogram did not show the primary breast cancer," the doctor said, "but with the cancer at this stage...I feel, at the most, you have six months. I am so sorry."

Jessica fisted her hands and pursed her lips as Nick pulled her firmly against his side.

"It's not fair. It's not acceptable. I'll fight this with every last breath I have." She needed to start chemotherapy right away.

Before she began chemo, Jessica decided she would take control of her life and not let the cancer take control of her. She went to her hairdresser. "Hi, Tracey. We won't be doing the usual 'do' on my hair today. Shave it all off. Let's go for the Yul Brenner look. Since I'm going to lose my hair anyway, let's just get it over with." An hour later she left the salon with a straw hat on her head and a black marker tucked in her purse.

Nick was somewhat shocked when he walked into the house that evening.

"You said you were getting your hair done today, Jess. You should have prepared me for your new look."

Jessica went up to Nick, gave him a kiss and turned around. Nick's shock turned to a smirk which turned quickly into guffaws. "Please, *please* tell me you didn't have that happy face *tattooed* on the back of your head!"

"Well, it *is* permanent marker, but I'm sure with time it will wear off."

Next came shopping for wigs. Jessica decided she would go for the flamboyant, hip, even off-the-wall look.

"Just think, Nick, it'll be like having a new woman every night."

"You're all I need Jess and all I want, but go for the gusto. You might as well have some fun and be outrageous while you're at it."

A long blonde wig, a shag, and a brunette wig with chunky caramel highlights became part of Jessica's collection. She also ordered turban-type soft hats and fashionable scarves in every color. She wanted to be as colorful, full of life and whimsical as the dragonflies she loved so much.

Then a year of weekly chemotherapy began, starting off like an appalling horror story. The port that had been put into Jessica's chest was rejected. When they removed the port, a tube was accidentally left in and Jessica developed sepsis, poisoning of the blood. She almost died.

After Jessica was stabilized, another port was inserted. This one, at least, was not rejected. Drug regimens combining Taxotere and Doxorubicin were administered in an attempt to shrink the tumors and improve Jessica's quality of life. There remained a slim possibility of slowing down the cancer. She suffered the dreadful side-effects experienced by many cancer patients: vomiting, diarrhea, fatigue and burning, shooting pain. One week was especially bad. She felt like her insides had turned inside out, felt like the treatment would kill her before the cancer did.

Nick held Jessica as she lay on the bathroom floor.

"This has to be worse than dying Nick. Tell me all this agony is worth it. I'm going to make it, right?"

Nick felt like he had a man-eating shark gnawing at his gut as he watched Jessica suffer.

"You're going to make it Jess. You have to. You deserve to."

Finally Nick made the decision to quit his job and spend all his time with Jessica. He had taken his vow for better or worse seriously. He had also become the man Marcie had said every woman needed—a man who would take care of his wife and be with her for the long haul. Nick was that and more.

Radiation came next. Thankfully, it was not as bad as the chemo. When Jessica wasn't going on the endless doctor appointments, recovering from surgeries, visiting a holistic doctor who Marcie called the "witch doctor," or searching the internet for other treatments to try, she was also preparing for the worst. No one else wanted to think or talk about the worst, but Jessica made them do so.

Becoming an advocate for other cancer patients, Jessica allowed doctors to use her as a live patient at seminars. She was a frequent speaker at her wellness group and was an inspiration to many people.

Still wishing to have some control over her life, Jessica spent many hours with Marcie telling her she especially wanted Nick to be okay.

"I've changed the magazine subscriptions to Nick's name because I don't want him to be morbidly reminded of me if I should die."

"Don't say that Jess. You have to beat this."

"Well, *if* I don't, I want everything to be in order. I've made detailed lists of funeral arrangements and special requests for loved ones."

Marcie, and Jessica's other two best friends, Carrie and Dawn, were designated to be Nick's "surrogate wives" after she was gone. Their immediate duties were to be to keep Nick busy, keep him fed (she supplied a list of his favorite foods and certificates to his favorite restaurants), and try to help him see she would be all right in heaven and he would be all right here. She also advised them if Nick ever took another wife to make sure she was "worthy."

Jessica was not a believer in any organized religion, but she was very spiritual. On one of the weekends Marcie came to visit, she shared some of her thoughts.

"I've been thinking a lot about my life. Remember the day we met? Living in the same condo complex, we were both coming home from work and ran into each other in the hall. I remember we both burst out laughing when we realized we were wearing the exact same business suits. You're a great friend, Marcie, and we've had wonderful times together."

"Yes, we really have, Jess."

Jessica sighed. "Then I met Nick. He is so wonderful and has made me very happy. I've also been thinking about what will happen, if I don't beat this. I've decided I will come back, Marcie. I believe I'll be reincarnated."

Marcie was somewhat skeptical. "I guess if it's possible, you *would* come back, Jess. You have more determination and spunk than anyone I've ever known. So if you are coming back, you'd better tell me in advance what you'll be coming back *as*—and please don't sneak up on me."

Jessica had put a lot of thought and research into re-embodiment. "I can tell you right now," Jessica replied. "I'll be returning as a dragonfly, and believe me, you'll know my reintroduction when you see it."

Marcie wasn't exactly sure what made Jessica pick a dragonfly, and others she spoke with said the same thing. Thinking about it though, she decided it was a combination of inferences drawn from her life—not just one inspiration. There were many dragonflies around Jessica's home and she loved to sit out on her patio watching them do aerobatics as they flitted around her black-eyed susans, peonies, daisies, roses, and her many birdfeeders. They provided her with hours of entertainment with their daredevil stunts. Jessica thought they were beautiful and free. They liked to travel and go, go, go—just like her.

Nick knew one of Jessica's wishes while she was struggling for her life: to go on a trip. A few weeks later he decided to make that happen.

"We're going on a vacation where the winter is warm and sunny," Nick announced. "I've booked us for a Caribbean cruise!"

"A Caribbean cruise? That sounds like a gift from heaven," Jessica whispered. "I can be packed in a flash. When do we leave?"

Nick smiled and put his arms around Jessica. "How does next week sound?"

Jessica squeezed Nick tightly. "It sounds perfect, just like you, Nick. Thanks. I love you so much."

"Ditto," Nick said as his eyes welled with tears.

The cruise went well. Jessica had only one bad day. They tried to enjoy themselves and forget about the cancer. While renewing their wedding vows in a ceremony conducted by the ship's captain, both Jessica and Nick shed a few silent tears of joy and sadness. They both knew deep down their life together was on borrowed time.

Jessica's forty-sixth birthday approached and she decided to have a party. She planned all the details—minute, exacting, but crucial to Jessica—details. She taste-tested cakes and selected the perfect napkins, plates and tablecloths. It was a perfect day and, although Jessica was weak and tired, a rosy glow reflected her tranquility.

Marcie stayed and slept next to Jessica that night to give Nick a break from caregiving. Jessica was restless and shared one of her greatest fears about dying.

"I don't want to suffocate, Marcie," Jessica murmured. "That's what the doctor said I would die from because the lung tumors are going to take away my ability to breathe."

Marcie couldn't say anything. She had a lump in her throat and her own breathing felt restricted as she held her friend's hand.

After the birthday party, Jessica faded quickly. She was still on radiation. The tumors grew bigger and, though the radiologist kept zapping them, her body felt like the battle zone in some science fiction/horror movie. One night as Jessica lay in bed next to Nick, she turned to him.

"I'm done Nick. No more radiation."

Nick's eyes widened as he gripped Jessica's shoulders. "You can't give up Jess. I need you."

Jessica rasped, "You'll be okay Nick. You know one good thing *did* come from all the treatments..."

"Yeah, I know Jess. We had a little more time together—some good, *quality* time. But I know how hard it's been for you."

"I'm tired Nick. I'm weary of all the pain and I'm ready now."

Nick quivered and sighed with resignation.

Jessica took off her oxygen mask, wrapped herself around Nick, and peacefully died in his arms, two terrible and wonderful years after her initial diagnosis.

*   *   *

Held at a waterfowl museum on a river on the Eastern Shore, the funeral was beautiful. There was a video of her life and there were posters filled with photos of Jessica with her family and friends. Her friends from work came accessorized with colorful boas around their necks. That would have made Jessica smile as she favored the bright and even outrageous. There was a brief ceremony with readings she had selected. White doves and pink balloons were released and soared toward the heavens. Marcie,

Carrie and Dawn tearfully exchanged gifts they had gotten each other—angels, dragonfly necklaces, and dragonfly lanterns. They would forever be members of the Dragonfly Club.

*   *   *

On the day of the funeral Nick felt as rigid and cold as a piece of dry ice and his world was surrounded by a foggy vapor. He was in a daze, grief-stricken, but thankful Jess was finally at peace. He would not have to see his Jess suffer any longer, but oh, he was going to miss her so much. Where do I go from here, Jess? How will I make it without you? Time, it would just take time, maybe an eon or two.

Jessica's post-funeral plans soon kicked in. One week after the funeral Marcie sent a bouquet of flowers to both Carrie and Dawn, each with a card enclosed: "All my love, Jess."

Marcie should have known what was coming, but she didn't. That same day a florist deliveryman arrived at her doorstep. There were two bouquets of flowers, one for Marcie and one for her five-year-old daughter, Emily. The cards read: "All my love, Jess, All my love, Aunt Jessica." Jessica's plans forgot no one—Carrie had placed the order.

A couple of months after Jessica's death, Marcie and her daughter were at their community pool on a muggy September afternoon. Emily was playing in the kiddy pool as Marcie sat in a lounge chair chatting with a dad of one of the other children. James seemed a serious, even dour, father. As they were talking, a dragonfly, which seemed to have come out of nowhere, landed on Marcie's knee and faced her squarely. It had two eyes that touched at the top of its head and four translucent silvery wings it proudly held out from its electric blue body. She pretended it wasn't there. But it continued to stay, not making any sounds, just cocking its head and moving its mouth.

After five minutes or so, James looked at Marcie. "Did you know there's a dragonfly sitting on your knee?"

"Yup," Marcie said nonchalantly.

"Do you realize the dragonfly is trying to talk to you?"

Marcie grinned. "Yup. I even know who she is!"

The dragonfly flew away.

The next day while watching Emily going down the slide at the playground, Marcie stood by a fence. An electric blue dragonfly lit right next to her and, again, began to move its mouth. This time Marcie spoke to it, not caring what others around her might think.

"I know it's you Jess," she whispered. "Thanks for letting me know you're okay, and for helping me believe angels come in many forms, even on the wings of a dragonfly."

Marcie and Emily often go to that playground. While in the past dragonflies were seldom around, many young and a number of adults are now constant visitors. Always free, always on the go, go, go.

TWISTED FATE

by Karin Harrison

"Open the door or I'll kick it in!"

Steven hammers the heavy apartment door with both fists. His brown eyes are lit up from within by a raging fire; the unruly, thick chestnut hair spills across his brow.

"What is your problem?" Kurt opens the door a tiny crack and he's slammed against the wall. Steven storms into the room.

"Where is she?"

"Who?"

Kurt has been Steven's best friend since childhood and feels what's coming. He has never seen Steven so angry.

"Don't play games with me." Steven stumbles across a handbag and a pair of high heel shoes carelessly discarded near the sofa. Steven's straight right catches Kurt on the nose. Blood spurts and he lands on the floor somewhat dazed. Steven storms forward and readies another right.

"Steven! Stop it!" Sally pleads from the bedroom doorway. She's hastily donned Kurt's white dress shirt.

Kurt attempts to staunch the blood with his handkerchief and rises on wobbly feet.

"I'm through...*you* can have her!" Steven steps aside. He looks at his wife; his face is twisted in pain, anger and loathing. He loads an opened backhand. He stops, pauses and applies his anger to the door on his way out of the apartment. Outside, Steven braces himself against the brick wall. He feels as if *he* were the one hit by a fist. He also knows from this day forward, trust will never again be easy.

*   *   *

Months later, Steven is back at work on his novel. For the longest time, betrayal crowded out any creative thought he had. Now, finally, Steven finds the ideas, characters, and plot flow have returned. He even finds the monotone tapping of the keyboard comforting. The arrhythmic muted "pud, pud, pud" melts into the silence of the late afternoon at this Hawaiian beachhouse borrowed from his editor and friend, Sam Petterson. More "pud, pud, pud" of useful writing.

He pauses momentarily to look out to sea and sees billows of black smoke. Steven jumps out of his chair and rushes out on the patio. Three hundred feet from shore a small cabin cruiser with a sputtering inboard rocks helplessly on clear blue waves. Two figures move frantically to the stern when an explosion instantly changes the trim white boat into nothing more than a shower of shrapnel and then an empty burning hull. Steven races down the beach, dives into the sea and swims determinedly toward the wreckage. A young woman wearing a life preserver sways like a buoy in the restless waves. She appears to be unconscious. Not far behind her, the head of a man pops out of the water.

"Are you all right? Can you swim to shore?" Steven shouts as he pulls the woman toward the beach.

"She can't swim." The man yells. "I can make it."

On reaching the surf, Steven gathers her up into his arms and lays her gently on the warm sand of the upper beach. He peels off the life preserver. She opens her eyes and struggles to sit up. A coughing spell wracks her body and she spews a gush of seawater.

"Where is Joe?"

At that moment, the man staggers out of the water. He wears only a pair of denim shorts with a bloody rip on the upper right thigh. He's still bleeding through the tear from what seems a fair-sized laceration.

"Let's get you inside the bungalow and call the ambulance."

"No ambulance." The man says firmly. "I'll be all right once I get the wound cleaned and bandaged."

Steven checks the leg, frowns, then wraps his arm around the man's waist as he helps him limp up the dune toward the house. The woman looks forlornly at the wreckage, then follows. Behind her, screeching seagulls attack bits of something edible spilled from the guts of the small craft still bobbing and burning on its way out to sea on the tide.

They enter through the kitchen slider and the man slowly lowers himself on a chair. Steven fetches the first aid kit. His lips tightly pressed together, the man pours hydrogen peroxide over the open wound and bandages the leg expertly.

"You should have that stitched up." Steven hands him a glass with two fingers of bourbon.

"Thanks, this is all I need." The man gulps down the drink. "I'll be fine. I could do with some rest. By the way, my name is Joe and this is my wife Irina." He could pass for the sunny side of fifty. Joe is short and stocky but with muscle of a former athlete. He's balding at the top; his head is fringed sparsely with fine white hair. His small gray eyes are deepset and penetrating as they roam across the room in cold speculation. "A cunning and cold Friar Tuck," thinks Steven.

"Hello." Irina flashes a big smile. Her teeth are small. Only the incisors are somewhat prominent. A deep cleft dominates her square chin. Fringed with long lashes that curl up, her eyes are an unusual muddy green. "Mmmm, Cameron Diaz meets Bram Stoker's vampire seductress," muses Steven to himself.

"You've saved our lives."

"You're just lucky I was around. This is an isolated area and the bungalow is only occupied for a few weeks out of the year. There are no neighbors for miles."

Steven offers Irina a mixed drink. She declines and asks for coffee instead.

"Steven's the name," he says, reaching for the jar of instant coffee. "There's plenty of room here. You're welcome to stay to rest that leg. When you feel up to it, I'll drive you into Lihue where you can catch the commuter plane to the Big Island."

His eyes on Irina, Joe nods decisively. "Thanks for your hospitality. We're gonna take you up on it."

"Sorry about your boat. We can check the beach to see if any of your belongings wash ashore."

Steve hands Irina the steaming cup. "I hope you didn't have anything of value aboard."

"Nothing in particular." Joe looks down at his hands.

Steven shows Irina to the bedroom. She finishes the coffee, drops on the bed, curls up into a fetal position and falls asleep immediately.

"I've got an idea that may help. I'm heading for the beach to search for a piece of driftwood." Steven leaves the bungalow. Joe watches him disappear.

The steady breeze moderates the effects of the hot sun. Steven deeply inhales the salty air as if it will free him of the unwanted intrusion of guests. He walks along the upper surf line where flotsam has created a line of broken shells, sand-smoothed branches, pieces of boards, and trash humankind has given the Pacific and the Pacific has given back. He sees a four-foot, wrist-thick remnant of a sapling. Steven braces the ball end on a lava rock and, with a downward strike of his foot, snaps off an excess ten inches of the thin end. He uses the surface of the rock like a rasp to give a semblance of flatness to the broken end. He returns to the bungalow with his makeshift cane.

"Try this. Let's see if it will support your weight."

Joe grimaces in pain as he stands up. "It'll do." He quickly sits back down, with an audible sigh.

"What happened out there? What caused the explosion?"

"I had engine trouble almost right after we left Honolulu. There must have been an oil leak that started the fire...Irina was afraid to jump and I had to push her. We hit the water only seconds before the explosion."

"Where were you headed?"

"One of the small islands off Kauai. We've got friends there and planned a surprise visit." He rises gingerly from the chair. "I wanna rest my leg. Do you mind if I stretch out on your sofa?" He's already shuffling into the living room with the help of the driftwood cane.

Steven's nod goes unnoticed. Something's just not right. Or maybe he's just not ready to believe *anybody* anymore.

"I'm going back to the study to work on my writing. Your wife's asleep in the guest bedroom."

The monitor of the laptop, rising above the chaos of his desk, shows an accusatory blank screen. Sally and Kurt, Sally and Kurt. If it weren't for the catharsis of writing and the solitude of Sam's bungalow, he'd have no way to escape the image of his wife and his best friend. Now, though, the image returns less often and the novel helps.

Since his arrival, Steven has filled pages with some of his best work yet. The interruption of unexpected visitors has spurred a renewed effort and his fingers fly across the keyboard. He finishes a whole chapter and is pleased with the result.

"So you're a writer." Irina stands in the doorway. It is almost dusk and Steven flips on the desk lamp.

"I woke up and heard the tapping."

"I'm trying to finish my novel. It's behind schedule." He turns around. She wears one of his teeshirts which caresses her breasts and extends down to her slender thighs. She exudes an innate sensuality that reminds him unpleasantly of Sally in Kurt's shirt.

"How're you feeling?"

"I'm fine...I'm getting ready for a walk. Hope you don't mind that I borrowed one of your shirts. My clothes are still wet." She gives him a slight wave and slips out the door.

Steven sits motionless as he realizes that it's been two months since he left Sally. His heart runs a maze of conflicting emotions. He steps out on the patio for a smoke and some release. The sun has transformed into a golden sphere on an orange canvas and the evening breeze brings salt, seaweed and clarity. In the distance, Irina strolls the beach stopping repeatedly to pick up shells and shards, only to discard them disinterestedly.

A taxi approaches and comes to a sudden stop in a puff of light sand. Kurt exits and pays the driver. He smiles crookedly as he walks toward Steven and throws up his hands. "Before you say anything...or hit me again, please hear me out."

"You're taking a big chance coming here." Steven turns and walks away.

"Look," Kurt swallows hard and follows. "I am truly sorry. I've made a colossal mistake. We both did and we both know it. Can you forgive us? Can you forgive *me*?"

Kurt's face is flushed. His slightly pugged nose makes him look like a young Rocky. Steven stares at his longtime friend. After a long silence, he laughs. "At least I improved your looks. When I think about it, it was my fault too. I find a great girl like Sally and what do I do? I bury myself in work and ignore her."

"That you did. However, I took advantage of the situation and I feel really rotten. So does Sally. It's *you* she loves. She wants to talk to you." Kurt stretches out his hand. "Will you forgive me?"

"Let's drop it for now. Come in the house; I want you to meet the crew of the Minnow."

Steven ignores Kurt's "Huh?" and walks up the steps.

They enter the living room and find Joe reading an old copy of *GQ*.

"Joe meet Kurt, Kurt...Joe."

Joe drops the magazine and looks at Kurt. "Hey," he mumbles.

"Joe and his wife have crashed my solitude. Their boat got ran into trouble, exploded and sank. They're staying for a few days while Joe recovers from his injury. Listen, how about some pizza tonight?" He removes a cheese pizza from the small freezer.

"Fine." Joe says. "We're not picky. Has Irina come back?"

"Here she comes now."

Irina approaches the dune. Steven watches her through the slider as she trudges through the sand. The intense setting sun illuminates her long sandy hair. A Venus on the half shell he doesn't entirely trust. The damp teeshirt clings to her tanned body.

"What a magnificent sunset!" Irina shakes the sand off her feet. "I'm Irina." She smiles engagingly at Kurt.

"Irina, how was your walk?" Joe yells from the living room as he lets the *GQ* slide to the floor and studies her face with unusual interest.

"Uneventful...but beautiful. The beach is gorgeous."

"I believe I've got a bottle of Chianti here somewhere." Steven hunts for a corkscrew. Irina joins Joe on the sofa. Their whispered conversation is brief but animated.

*   *   *

The next day Steven and Kurt go for a swim. The waters of the Pacific are warm and relaxing. Bougainvilleas in breathtaking colors vie with the ubiquitous hibiscus in a kaleidoscopic spread beneath the palm trees lining the beach. The friends return to the shore and sit.

Steven begins. "There's something peculiar about these two. The guy is absolutely tight-lipped. I can't get a thing out of him. Each day Irina spends hours searching the beach. She won't say what she expects to find and I don't press her."

Kurt digs his bare feet deep into the sand. "Joe looks familiar somehow. I've seen him somewhere."

"Really? Where?"

"I can't remember."

"Keep trying. By the way, are you staying for a while?"

"If that's okay with you. I need a break." Kurt hesitates. "Steven...how about Sally? She wants to see you."

Steven looks out to sea as if the answer could come from the deep blue. "I don't know. I miss her. But no amount of apologizing—hers or mine—would ever make things the same."

* * *

The next morning Steven asks Kurt, "I'm driving into town to pick up the mail and get some supplies. Do you want to join me?"

"No thanks. I'm going to stretch out on the beach and get a suntan. If I'm lucky, Irina may join me."

"Fat chance. And don't get your nose broken again."

Steven always enjoys the spectacular drive along the coastline with its crescent lagoons protected by the coral reefs. The ocean laps aquamarine blue at the white-sand beaches and the waves whisper against the shore. Tall coconut palms stand as sentinels to the sea while shoreline ironwoods bow and search the surf.

He arrives at the Island Trading Post where he makes his purchases, then walks across the street to the tiny post office. He's back at the bungalow before noon.

The beach is deserted. There is no sign of Kurt, Irina or Joe.

Relaxing at his laptop, he glances briefly at the mail and pulls out the island newspaper. His eyes are drawn to the headline: THIEVES STRIKE HIGH END JEWELRY STORE. A male and a female robbed the Cartier Jewelry Store in Honolulu and got away with loose diamonds valued in the millions. When the clerk pushed the alarm button, she was shot and killed by the man.

Steven exhales slowly and carefully. The date of the robbery is the day of the boat accident.

He suddenly hears voices from the kitchen. Joe and Irina are arguing. Steven catches "waiting..., sand,...not so smart,...the attaché case." He quickly hides the newspaper in the desk drawer, makes some noise as if finishing work, and joins them.

"Have you seen Kurt?" He asks casually.

Irina stares silently out the window. Ignoring Steven's question, Joe helps himself to two fingers of bourbon, downs them in one gulp, and gets a refill.

"There's no sign of Kurt," Steven says more emphatically.

Joe glares, helps himself to more bourbon and stumbles toward him. He thrusts his chin toward Steven's face.

"I'm not his babysitter. Maybe he didn't like the company."

"Joe, why don't you lie down?" Irina grabs Joe's arm and pulls him into the living room. "He's in a lot of pain and doesn't know what he's saying."

"It seems to me that his leg is healed enough that you can be on your way. After I find Kurt, I'll drive you into town. I'm sure you want to join your friends, wherever they are.

Irina gasps as Joe pushes her aside. She stumbles into the kitchen cabinet knocking a glass into the sink and breaking it into several pieces. Joe laughs angrily, reaches for the bottle of bourbon, and limps out onto the patio. Irina quickly follows him.

Steven picks up the glass shards carefully from the sink and discards them. He watches the couple through the window; their heads are close together, their conversation heated. Joe's twisted face glowers at the kitchen slider.

Irina enters the kitchen, followed by Joe. She throws her hands up in exasperation. "We're truly sorry about this, Steven. Let me help you clean up." Her tone lacks conviction and she is strangely calm. Joe, standing behind her, quickly reaches for one of the large kitchen knives on the counter and pushes it against Steven's back, just piercing his skin. Steven flinches.

"You're a nuisance and you ask too many questions. There's a dune buggy in the shed. Where's the key? Come on, where is it?" Steven winces as Joe puts more pressure on the knife. Steven can feel his own warm blood trickling down his back.

"I don't know where Sam keeps the key. He didn't tell me."

"You're a liar." Irina's beautiful mouth curves into a sadistic smile.

"We'll just have to search the house." Joe pushes Steven on a kitchen chair and orders Irina to find some rope. She returns with an electrical cord. They tie Steven's hands behind his back.

"You watch him Joe. I'll search for the key." Irina ransacks the house, pulling out drawers, scattering their contents on the floor. She moves from living room to the bedrooms and then into the study.

She returns with a set of keys.

"Let's try these. Guess what else I found?" She hands Joe the newspaper.

"So you know." Joe scans the headline. "You want to know where Kurt is? We'll show you in just a minute."

Irina dashes outside to test the keys. One of them opens the lock, another fits in the ignition. She drives the dune buggy out of the shed. When she returns, Joe orders Steven out of the chair and pushes him toward the door. Joe hands the knife to Irina while he reaches for the driftwood cane. Steven swiftly kicks the knife from her hand and, bull-like, buries his head into Joe's midsection. They go down in a roll with Joe gasping for breath. Steven twists the electrical cord freeing his hands just as Irina races toward him swinging the knife. He sidesteps most of the slash, but feels raw lightning sear through his side. Irina stabs at him again but misses. They struggle for the knife. Steven suddenly abandons the fight for the knife and thrusts his left palm blow directly into her temple. She collapses and remains motionless on the kitchen floor. Steven turns toward Joe who is fumbling to pull himself up. He hits Joe full force across the head with the driftwood cane. Snatching a kitchen towel for his wound, he rushes outside, pulls the keys from the dune buggy and tosses them into the brush. The pain almost doubles him over. He climbs into the jeep and peels off. His side is pulsating with pain as the vehicle speeds down the road. He checks the kitchen towel stuffed against the wound inside his shirt. It's soaked with blood.

The minutes to town seem like hours. Ten more miles. Steven starts to lose consciousness. He shakes his head violently—once, twice. He must make it into town before he passes out. Five more miles. Would Sally be sorry if he died? Her face appears in front of him. She smiles, then fades away. The road bends, twists and even spins before him.

Off the edge of the road, the surf breaks on the beach in little foamy crests that coil back like iridescent sirens in endless but inviting patterns.

The jeep comes to a screeching halt in front of the squat police station. Steven faints. His head hits the steering wheel and the horn screams in protest.

*   *   *

"How is my favorite author?"

Steven opens his eyes. Sam—wavy white hair, lined face, and Hal-Holbrook good looks—grins at him.

"I can't believe the kind of trouble you can get yourself into."

"Hi, Sam." He sheepishly returns the grin. "They've stitched me up. I've got no internal injuries and will be out of here in a couple of days."

"I brought the paper. Your picture is plastered all over the front page. Great publicity." Sam chuckles.

"Joe Piccaci woke up with a lump on his head and handcuffs already on his wrists. Irina had even worse luck, however. She was pronounced dead at the scene. In the fight you had with the two of them she must have fallen on the knife she had apparently already used on you."

"I've got no sympathy for either one. They were going to kill me."

"No doubt."

"Where is Kurt? Why isn't he here?"

Sam shakes his head. "Kurt is dead."

"What?" Steven abruptly sits up in bed. He winces with the pain.

"Joe and Irina killed him. The police think it happened when you drove into town. They rolled his body in an old rug I had on the porch and shoved it under the deck. By the way, Sally will be here shortly. She phoned me and said if you send her away, that's okay. She'll take that chance."

Sam knits his brow and waits for Steven to reply. Steven says nothing but his thoughts run to lost friends and lost chances to forgive.

"Did they recover the jewels?"

"Not yet though the search is still on. I doubt they'll be found. Did you know the boat was stolen as well?" Sam shakes his head. "They're quite a pair. Both are married, apparently not to each other. Talk about crime and betrayal...." Sam quickly realizes the irony and stops.

*   *   *

The mild surf hugs his legs as Steven reclines in the warm sand. The novel is finished and he feels marvelous. His side is almost healed. Sally has been with him for two weeks. Right now, it's a truce and daily minefield negotiation but a treaty could be reached in the weeks or months ahead. Sam is to pick up the manuscript today and Steven will soon return to their apartment.

"Steven!" Sam's standing on the deck pointing at the shoreline. He scrambles down the dune. Steven turns his head in the direction of Sam's gesturing and spots a dark lump draped in slimy seaweed resting in the sand some forty yards down the beach. Sam has reached his side and together they run toward it. Steven gets there first. It appears to be an attaché case; although badly dented, it's still intact.

"Is this what I think it is?" Sam is breathing hard. "Open it, my boy, open it."

Steven gets down on his knees and examines the lock and latches. The lock reads "000" and the latches, though slightly deformed and reluctant, finally give with a snap. He pries the lid open. Blinding brilliance of dozens of the most exquisitely cut diamonds reflect the afternoon sun.

"All right, hand them over." Steven looks up at the business end of what appears to be a small caliber automatic. Sam's no longer smiling. "I'm sorry, my boy, but these beauties are mine."

Steven slowly raises his hands in surrender; his face is a study in anger and surprise.

"I didn't think they would show up." Sam smirks. "Imagine, they washed up on *my* beach. Not as surprising as you might think, though. Joe and Irina were to hide the case beneath my little hideaway without your being the wiser. My lifestyle demands a bit more income than your books can produce. You see, I met Joe when he came to me about an autobiographical work. Not much writing ability, I'm afraid, but he had other skills. With some unsavory contacts I have, I found I could provide the fence needed to unload the diamonds at a decent return for both of us.

"And now you'll have to kill me?" Steven can see Sally approaching warily beyond Sam's shoulder. She has the driftwood cane and she is slowly assuming a baseballer's swing pose.

"Nothing personal, my boy. No one was supposed to get hurt, you see. Even now, had the diamonds been lost, I wouldn't have to do this. However, great wealth seems to attract desperate means to retain it, don't you think? I'm going to suggest to the authorities that Joe must have an accomplice who confronted you and Sally and killed both of you in an attempt to discover the diamonds or merely for revenge. I just won't mention it's me. And now, regrettably...."

Steven's eyes must have given away Sally's approach. She's still outside her swing range. Sam pivots quickly and the sand unbalances his aim. He fires but misses high left. Steven grabs the opened attaché case and swings at Sam's head. He delivers a glancing blow but the hit is enough to topple Sam and send the gun flying. The diamonds scatter in the white sand. Sally snatches the gun. Steven leaps onto Sam, pins his would-be killer, and begins to strangle him with both hands.

"You're supposed to be my friend! You'd have murdered me and then murdered...." Enraged, he squeezes tighter and tighter until Sam's eyes roll back into his head.

"Steven, let go!" Sally cries. "You don't want to kill him!" Pointing the gun at Sam, she pulls her cell phone out of her pocket and starts dialing. Steven releases his grip. Sam has passed out.

*   *   *

Steven and Sally celebrate the store's modest recovery reward with dinner at The Ship's Tavern, a Honolulu in-spot. The light is low, the wine perfect, and the peace has finally been declared.

"What do you think will happen to Sam?" Sally asks.
"He'll be locked up for a long time."

They pause to look at each other and remember. Steven suddenly laughs. "I'll never forget the picture of the cops crawling in the sand, searching for the diamonds in a desperate attempt to beat the incoming tide."

"Poor Kurt. He must have seen Joe's picture on TV at the airport in Honolulu. That must be why he told you Joe looked familiar. He didn't pay attention because he was a man on a mission." Sally sighs. "At least his mission was partially successful."

Steven stares out the window. Funny how having your life saved by the woman who had betrayed you goes a long way to restoring trust.

*   *   *

Joe meanders through the prison yard. He has no friends and his anger and meanness have earned him more than his share of enemies. His time is spent in plotting how to get out, get rich, and then achieve retribution against the man who killed his Irina and ruined his life. He's thinking about a cut brake line when the shiv punctures his lower back and the twist produces excruciating pain. Joe's last living thought is of the irony of knives, well-used and accidental.

224
Dianna J. Zurinsky,
"On the Edge of the Infinite"

SHOOTING MARBLES

by Frank Soul

The other day I was looking through a box of V.I.S. (very important stuff) that I had stored away in my garage. I came across a small cloth bag that had about twenty marbles in it. Way back (more than a *few* years ago) when I was about nine or ten, marbles were a very important part of your V.I.S. that you took to school in the springtime. The boys got together during recess outside and played marbles.

It would be very interesting today to see how many ten-year-old kids that you would have to ask before you found one that even knew what a marble is, let alone how to play marbles.

We would always look through our marbles at home to sort them out. We had them in cans or a cigar boxes and we would pick out our favorite ones to take to school and hope they would be *lucky* ones so we could win the other guys' favorite ones when we played.

And here I was, decades later looking at those very same magic marbles. I sat down in my garage and dumped the marbles out of the little cloth bag onto my bench and picked them up one by one and got a smile on my face thinking about the great times we use to have. Some of them had little chips in them or had a chunk of glass missing where they got hit by a kid's marble trying to win yours or you trying to win theirs. We had some beauties too. We had named some of them like "cat eye," "sky blue," "greenie," "orange crush," "red fireball" and so forth, and we hoped that no bully sixth grader would bring a "steelie" (a steel ball bearing) to the game. These steelies, when they would hit a glass marble, would most often shatter it. However, if you told the mean bully not to use his steelie, you might as well plan on getting your pants dirty or a black eye—unless you got in a lucky punch!

The way the game was played was that one would draw a circle in the dirt about two or three feet around and two to six guys would each drop so many marbles in the ring and each guy, in turn, would try to use his shooter marble from the outside line of the circle to hit the other guys' marbles. If you hit one out of the circle, it was yours to keep. If you didn't hit it out, the next guy around the circle would take his shot. At the end of recess you would pick up your marbles that were left and go back in school until the next time you had recess. Hopefully, you still had your favorites and maybe some of the other guys' marbles too.

As I looked at the little cloth bag, I had another wonderful memory. When I was a kid, we raised chickens as did a lot of other people who lived in the country. My grandmother lived with us and she would take care of the chickens: feeding them, watering them and gathering the eggs from their nests every day. We had a little country general store near us that we shopped at for the chicken feed, and we would get our feed in fifty-pound cloth bags. After we got the chicken feed home, we would dump it into a big metal container and my grandmother would use these feed bags to make a lot of different things. They had designs or patterns or neat looking things on them just like material in a clothing shop. My grandmom would make some of her clothes like aprons, some dresses, dusting caps, tablecloths, potholders and neat things for me like my marble bag.

As I put the marbles back in the bag, I think about how good it was growing up at a time when you could walk up the street without worrying about getting abducted or just have fun being a kid with a big imagination. You could have fun playing with things that you built or repaired with your own hands, or you could go anyplace in the world, or be anybody that you wanted to be just by reading a book. What a time! *And*, you could go to bed at night with your doors unlocked.

Well, I put the marbles back in the box of V.I.S. and maybe next time I get them out I'll remember who I won some of them from.

227
GRAY AND THREADBARE

by Leslie B. Picker

It was hot, very hot. There's no air conditioning in the old city school where I teach. I was notified at the beginning of August that I had to move into another classroom, and I had just spent four days packing up all my paraphernalia. This was no easy task. I am a "seasoned" teacher; I have accumulated a large assortment of books, bulletin board materials and teaching guides. This was going to be my third move in five years. It just seems that special education teachers are always being moved. And this move was to the basement.

With keys in hand I was on my way down the stairs to see if all of my boxes had made it to the new classroom. The one clear window left in the bank of frosted Plexiglas on the landing permitted sunrays to zigzag across the stairs. I stopped for a moment. The pattern of startling bright sunlight and dark leaf patterns cast by the tree just outside caught my attention. I tiptoed to look out and saw an old woman standing in the shade next to the bus stop. She was a "bag lady," judging by her appearance. I noticed she was wearing an old winter coat which was at one time probably a dark gray but now seemed unevenly faded and threadbare. Strange, in this heat.

It had to be close to ninety degrees, but there she stood, scarved head bowed, clutching a stuffed, oversized purse. Two bulging vinyl-type bags were at her feet. It was hot where I was standing; sun streaming across my chest and the humidity like it gets after a summer rain; I continued on, wondering why the woman was so bundled up on such a hot and humid day.

*   *   *

It was October and I was slowly and carefully negotiating my way down the stairs to my classroom. My arms were piled with stacks of graded and ungraded papers, my gradebook, and my lunch bag. Rain was pounding on the window; it was a typical late October stormy day: cold, windy, dismal and dreary. Preoccupied with my students since their behavior mirrored the weather, I was dreading the coming afternoon. I came down the last two steps onto the landing, and glanced out the window to see that old woman again waiting at the bus stop.

She was huddled under the stark branches of the oak tree. A few stubborn leaves, curled and dark, clung tenaciously to the branches. Wet leaves were scuttling in the wind which was whipping the rain around her dark mottled coat. Almost blending into the surroundings like a camouflaged sentry, she held onto her purse as before, with her two other bags at her feet. Rivulets were streaming down the window making her appear blurred and ethereal. I felt instant pity and concern for this poor soul. She had to be soaked to the skin as her coat appeared to cling to her stick-like figure. At that moment the doors flew open above me with the clumping of many feet and a group of very boisterous students entered the stairwell. I quickly moved on, not wanting to get caught in the hubbub, the vision of the old woman lingering.

The next time I saw her, it was December 23. Christmas decorations adorned the building, holiday parties were taking place in classrooms, and children squealed and giggled happily walking down hallways with plates of cookies for the principal. It was the last day before break and, while I was descending the steps to the basement, my mind was filled with the thoughts of vegging out over the next ten days, catching up on much needed sleep, going to see my parents and siblings on Christmas, and being with friends on New Year's Eve.

It had been flurrying and snowing all day, so I stopped and tiptoed to look out of the one clear pane, curious to see how much had fallen. I peered out of the now partially-frosted window. I saw her again. The frozen branches of the oak tree clattered and moaned in protest of the strong gusts of wind and swirling snow in the twilight of that stormy mid-afternoon. She stood there, huddled in her old gray coat into which she seemed to disappear, scarf on her head, white wisps of stringy hair blowing from underneath. Her purse in hand and bags at her feet, she looked utterly forlorn. I decided this time to try to find out more about her. The least I could do was to give her my old winter coat, the one I kept at school for playground duty.

Her appearance this time reminded me of old Mrs. Schlegal, a neighbor of mine when I was a child. Kids used to taunt and tease her and call her names whenever she appeared on the street. She talked to herself, wore inappropriate clothing, and screamed at the neighbors. She terrified me. One day, I guess I was about seven years old, I ran back inside the house to avoid her, and my mother kindly explained to me that poor Mrs. Schlegal was "eccentric" and "senile." She also said that sometimes people became peculiar as they aged. Little did we know then of Alzheimer's or senile dementia. I thought about the similarity between Mrs. Schlegal and that old woman over the holidays. She probably worked at the Opportunity Center, a business across the street that hired the mentally challenged. I decided to stop over there after the school break to drop off my coat.

*   *   *

It was early January when I arranged with the teacher in the classroom next to the side door to watch for me so he could let me back in. The doors were always locked, and I didn't want to have to walk around the building. During my lunchtime, I took the coat and left the building. It had lightly snowed that morning, but now the sun was shining. Clumps had dropped off the old oak, leaving miniature sparkling disco-like balls on the ground. It was so beautiful—it literally took my breath away.

The memory of that day is so clear. When any momentous event occurs in life, we find ourselves reliving it over and over again. Like the day my youngest sister was killed. I can still recall in vivid detail the last time I was with her, what she was wearing, what we talked about, and how I wished I'd told her how much I loved her. We usually hugged in greeting, but for some reason, we didn't that one time. It still gives me pangs of regret even though it's been five years. But one learns that even the "awful" passes and it gets to the point where one stops reliving it.

I ran towards the street, passing the bus stop on my way, and suddenly felt chilled. The absurdity struck me; I wasn't wearing a coat but I *was* carrying one! I crossed the street and entered the Opportunity Center.

The sudden plunge into darkness from the bright snow-reflected sunshine took me several seconds to adjust. Sitting at a reception desk was a well-coifed and manicured young lady cracking her chewing gum. I heard her before I could actually see her. I asked her about the elderly woman I had seen on several occasions at the bus stop. I described her as well as I could and, at first, the young woman looked puzzled, then a look of bafflement and surprise flickered across her face. She said that she thought she knew who I was referring to and excused herself. She said she needed speak with her supervisor.

Mr. Belter, "Charlie," he insisted I call him, asked me into his office. The look on his face was both consternation and dismay—a furrowed brow and pursed mouth. His bald head reflected the bleak overhead lighting, and there were stacks of papers covering his desk. He asked me to describe this woman to him. I explained that I had seen her several times, but admittedly never very clearly. After describing her, I added that I always saw her waiting at the bus stop across the street.

Charlie cleared his throat several times. A slight whimper came from the doorway, and I turned to see the gum-smacking receptionist standing there with her arms tightly wrapped around her chest. She was trembling. I was confused and apprehensive. I just couldn't figure out what could be wrong.

He kept clearing his throat, and hoarsely explained that the old woman I had seen several times was the exact description of a former employee. I extended the coat in my arms and explained that I wanted to give it to her, and would there be a way of contacting her?

Charlie looked even more startled and confused. And with his reaction, I felt the hackles rise on the back of my neck; something was definitely horribly wrong. I stuttered an apology, told him I was sorry if I had caused a problem, and turned to leave.

"Can I leave this?" I remember asking, desperate to bolt back into the sunlight. Charlie quietly informed me that the woman I had clearly described to him had been hit and killed by a bus at that very stop during the previous winter. I dropped the coat and ran out the door towards the school.

It wasn't until April that I had garnered enough nerve to approach the dreaded stairwell. It frightened me. I didn't want to see anything out of that window. When I approached the staircase, a custodian with a mop and bucket stopped me. He explained that there had been a fight on the landing, and that I would need to use another stairway. "Whew, a reprieve!" I thought ruefully.

The next day I debated whether or not I should try that stairway again but I bravely steered myself in that direction. I reasoned that there had to be an explanation. Maybe the old glass pane was so distorted it had made a some natural object appear like an old woman. Maybe it happened because I had to tiptoe to see out or I was looking through it from the second step from the landing. Maybe the way the light hit the tree made it appear that there was someone standing there. It would forever haunt me, and I just couldn't avoid that landing the rest of my life. That stairway was so convenient to my classroom. I also didn't want to be afraid. It was ridiculous, avoiding that area of the building.

    With heart pounding and sweaty palms, I slowly descended, carefully looking down at my feet. I got to the landing, took a deep breath, and slowly lifted my face towards the window. It had been replaced with frosted Plexiglas.

MYSTICAL HANDS

by Joyce M. Shepherd

They are gentle as a caressing hand,
Or as aggressive as a charging bull.
Their spirit entices with boldness,
Welcomes with glittering sun specks.

They carry mysteries from the depths
Of seas and oceans far and wide.
They casually toss forth lost treasures
Once captured in violent storms.

With impatience, they form and roll
Bringing forth living creatures.
With agitation, they toss and turn.
Savagely, they take away.

They enchant with tender gracefulness,
Persuade with alluring strength.
As they brazenly do a merry dance,
They tease the churning sand.

They are the restless spraying waves
Coming with the ebb and flow.
Reaching for earth's endless shores,
They are grasping mystical hands.

Joel Furches, "Windmill"

PAYMENT

by David A. Stelzig

Bastard. For twenty years and more, Spumelli has sent his thugs to steal from me. Protection he calls it. Protection? I have no need. *Stealing* is what it is.

Now he is here, in my shop, expecting to be treated with respect.

He looks up at me with cold, dead eyes. His face is a tangled patchwork of thin, purple, spiderweb veins. His skin, a pasty-white parchment. The complete lack of wrinkles belies his eighty-four years. So does his full head of long black hair he has center-parted and plastered to the sides in flat, oily mats. When I bend forward though, I see, near his scalp, snow-white roots.

Spumelli continues to look at me. Expressionless. Unblinking. He mocks me with his serenity.

I stare back. Seething. Powerless. And yet...I *am* in control. I furtively glance over my shoulder. We are alone. Before anyone can stop me, before I change my mind, I pull a scalpel from under the table and, with two quick slashes, emasculate my old enemy.

I step into the bathroom and flush the evidence and then, humming softly, return to work. Speed is important now. Viewing of the body begins in three short hours.

The extortion? I'll continue to pay; a younger brother, Joseph, has taken over the business. But Joseph is not that young. Soon he too will visit my shop. And then I will again extract my small revenge, dispatching another eunuch to hell.

235
BUTTERFLIES AND CHILDREN

by Peter Raimondi

This past summer, as I was sitting on my patio deck, a beautiful butterfly visited my flowers. I watched in amazement how this tiny creature of God did its turns and twists and visited each flower. I couldn't help noting a parallel in nature—a little girl, about two, was doing the same thing, in essence. She hopped, skipped and pirouetted on the sidewalk just across the way.

Yesterday, as I stood in line waiting for the light to turn on Main Street in Bel Air, I noticed a little girl walking with her mother and father. With near desperation, she clung to the hands of her mother and father as she crossed from the sidewalk and onto the grass. Then her right shoe came off. They all stopped and her father bent down and put the shoe back on her tiny foot. She quickly took hold of her parents' hands and proceeded to skip and hop across the parking lot.

Like the butterfly, this little girl was full of life. She was enjoying every moment with her parents and investigating how far she could jump and skip while grasping the hands of her parents for safety and assurance.

It is amazing how much little children look to their parents for confidence. Like the butterfly, this little girl, for example, was taking in the sweet things of life as her little eyes saw them. Unlike the butterfly, she was innocent and free from all worries because of the grasp of her parents' hands.

I noticed more children. The similarity of the children with the butterflies was remarkable. Flitting, alighting, hovering—they had no agenda, no timetable, no motivation except their own curiosity. The middle of a flower, a gray rock, a passing cloud; everything was interesting, everything worthwhile. The next time you see a small child see if you don't see a butterfly.

The thought came to me that we adults should grasp the hand of a friend or loved one so we can also feel safe and secure. We can then take time to touch the flower for its sweet nectar as the butterfly does or skip and hop without a care as the young child does. We can really enjoy life and not let the troubles of the world keep us down. We will be secure in knowing we are loved.

Today—right now—grasp the hand of a friend or loved

one and tell them how much they mean to you. Friend, grasp *my* hand.

TAKING A NAP

by Frank Soul

I have read over the years how important it is to get enough sleep every day. Lack of sleep, authorities tell us, leads to all different kinds of ailments from heart disease to premature ageing and additional minor ailments as well. Some companies even provide nap times and areas designated for nap time. However, somebody (maybe, a supervisor) once told me that the place where I work wasn't one of them.

However, I would venture to say that the powerful in business and government get their naps in sometime during their busy schedules. Decades ago, when I and my friends were kids, I can remember in school when we were listening to the teacher talking to us about something that was really boring the Automatic Boring Device in our brains would kick in and we would take a nap—I'm sure it occurred to save us for more important activities. Finally, the teacher would notice us nodding off and would kick our chairs, drop a book, or ask us some kind of dumb question about what he or she was talking about just to verify our napping and embarrass us.

As I got older and wiser, I learned how important it is to try to get a nap, but if I am driving a car or truck I make sure I pull off in a safe place before I nod off. I want to make sure I can see another sunrise.

When we are up at our cabin during deer hunting season, a very, very important part of our day is when we come in for lunch. We make sure after we eat and get our chores done that we get our naps. And it seems like the older we get the more important it is. Even our young guys who hunt with us now realize how important taking a *timely* nap is. If a guy is late getting back to our bunk room, it's full. It sounds like a sleep test center contest to see who snores the loudest.

Sometimes I will hunt with my buddy, Leo. We'll take his truck up on the hill on his farm and we'll sit there and talk about anything and everything until he lays the seat back to get a nap. He always tells me that, if I see a buck, be sure I wake him up before I get out of the truck to hunt him so he doesn't have a heart attack when I shoot. He also says that he doesn't want to freeze to death if I'm too long getting back to the truck.

Even our babies, our puppies, and our kittens take naps. It must be part of God's plan to help us reach a contented old age because I have never heard of anybody dying from *taking* a nap. And usually when we wake up from our nap we have a whole different and more positive outlook and we feel so much better too! One more thing to consider—if we don't wake up, we can't ask for a better way to pass on.

It's a shame that in today's world people can't relax a little more. It seems they think that if they can make something a little easier or more efficient, *that* will make their lives less hectic. Instead, they find more to do and get even further stressed out. They get burned out to the point where they need a power nap just to make it through the day. So much for the good life.

Wow! It looks like I have been writing right up to my naptime, so I guess I'll put down my pencil and take a little trip down to dreamland and I hope that you will join me. Just think! It might help us to live a little longer. Nighty night till later.

ABSOLUTION

by Joyce Shepherd

I knew something was wrong. Two weeks earlier at the family reunion, at my aunt's home in Pennsylvania, I could see the evidence with my own eyes. Mom's complexion, pale and yellow-hued, along with the significant weight loss, said it all (but she had told me nothing). I had not seen her for over a year, since we lived 3,000 miles apart. I was shocked by the changes, even more stunned when I received the phone call upon her return home. She had been taken to the hospital immediately after her plane landed. Her liver was the size of a quarter. She was dying. I was on the next plane headed west.

As my Dad and I stood on either side of Mom's bed, I rubbed her ice cold hand with my warm hand. Her nails were ice-blue. My other hand gently wiped the single tear straggling down her face. Her eyes told me she did not want to leave as she quietly took a final shuddering breath.

*   *   *

Dad was lonely, but finally worked through his grief; a few visits and many phone calls may have helped. About a year after Mom's death I received a cheerful, almost giddy, call from Dad.

"When I was in Vegas visiting your sister, I met a classy lady with legs like Betty Grable."

"Are you going to see her again?"

"She's flying down to LA next month." I imagined the smile on his face.

Time, in its unrelenting way, marched forward. Nine months later I was flying to Las Vegas for a wedding. I had misgivings about the nuptials, but having yet to meet the woman face to face, I wisely held back judgment. How bad could she be?

Well, life is full of surprises—many of them unpleasant. Dad introduced Grace. In shock, I gazed upon an aged floozy: an over-made-up, gaudy-wigged, hot-pants-wearing senior citizen. The midriff top, backless stilettos, and varicose-veined "Betty Grable" legs completed the eye-opening package. Dad was definitely not thinking with the most intelligent part of his anatomy.

The wedding was the beginning of many surprise-filled years. Apparently, I should have expected a Cinderella stepmother scenario.

With slow determination, Grace chiseled at the walls of our family structure. And like a master conductor, she orchestrated the music, told Dad when and how to perform. He became another victim of this Cinderella stepmother.

One evening my sister called. "You're not going to believe this one. Do you remember the heart with Mom's name tattooed on Dad's arm?"

"Yeah, I remember it," I answered.

"Dad had a pattern tattooed over Mom's name."

"Why would he do that?"

My sister sighed. "Grace didn't think it was fitting for her husband to have another woman's name tattooed on his arm."

The tattoo incident was just the start. The yard sale came next. Grace decided the extra baggage had to go. Everything Dad possessed that even smelled of "former wife" sat on the grass with a tag on it. The remainder was hauled away.

The next fiasco was Mom's headstone. Dad and Grace decided they should be buried next to each other. They purchased side by side wall crypts. If that was what Dad wanted, it didn't affect me one way or the other. The phone call I received was a different matter.

"Hello. This is Grace. *We* wanted to let you know you, your sister, and your brother need to buy your mother a new headstone."

I could not have heard correctly. "What do you mean a new headstone? What happened to the old one?"

"Since your father and I are now going to be buried beside one another, we felt it was inappropriate for your mother to have a double headstone with your father's name on it," Grace replied. "We sold the extra plot, removed the headstone, and gave it to your brother, since his name is the same as your father's. It's stored in his closet."

I tried to imagine my brother opening his closet door each morning to my mother's headstone.

"I've got news for you lady. I'm not buying any headstone," I bellowed. "You took the headstone off. You buy my mother a new one."

Dad refused to speak to me. Not surprising. What could he have possibly said at that point?

Given the fact there was no money forthcoming from the daughters, the cost for a new headstone was squeezed from my mentally-challenged brother. From his *disability* check.

Dad called me soon after the incident.

"I'm sorry, but I won't be keeping in touch with you anymore. You upset Grace, and since *I have to live with her*, it's for the best."

My Dad never spoke to me again.

A few years later, I received a call at work. My boss said, "Your sister's on the phone."

I picked up the phone. "Dad's dead isn't he?"

There was a gasping sob. "How did you know?"

"I just knew."

My sister received the news in the worst way. She had called Dad to tell him Buddy, Mom's dog, had died.

Grace answered the phone. "You can't speak to your father. He died two weeks ago."

In shock, my sister replied, "What do you mean he died?"

"He had cancer," Grace explained. "I dropped him off at the hospital. Two weeks later he died. He was buried the next day."

No call to his children. No funeral. Nothing!

The next day I left for Las Vegas. A death certificate was acquired and a memorial service was planned. I called the physician noted on the death certificate. That conversation began my healing process.

"Your father was dropped off by his wife. He signed himself into the hospital and claimed no living relatives. In his final days he called out the same names over and over again."

The doctor told us the names, *our names*.

My father died, alone, calling out for the ones who loved him the most in his life. What a high price to pay for a pair of Betty Grable legs. Five of us attended Dad's memorial service. After everyone walked away, I sat down on a bench in front of his crypt. There was unfinished business.

Clasping my hands and bowing my head, I prayed silently, "Dear God! Why did it end this way? I never stopped loving Dad. I should have been with him."

There was no sense of time in those moments. Tears rolled down my cheeks yet I wasn't really crying. My anguished soul was expressing itself for the words I had not yet spoken.

At first I thought, I don't want to say those words. I want to bang my fists on Dad's crypt and yell, "You hurt me so much. Then you had the nerve to die!" There were years of anger and pain. It was as if a panther had its fangs gripping my throat, slowly crushing my wind pipe. I could let it smother the life out of me, or I could search my soul for forgiveness.

Looking up at the spot where Dad was discreetly tucked away, I stood. I breathed a quivering sigh. "Dad, I'm sorry you were alone. You shouldn't have been. Not having you in my life has been so hard." I drew in a shuddering breath. "I forgive you for hurting me. But most of all, I want you to know *I still love you so much.*"

All of a sudden I felt light-headed, as if everything was awhirl around me. With wobbly legs, my body folded down onto the bench. A surreal heat began to surge through me, flowing through every limb. Then a glowing inner peace cooled the surging heat. It was an all-encompassing sensation, a peace I could touch, taste—even smell.

My inner spirit smiled as I heard a whispering voice, "Thank you. I love you too."

With forgiveness came peace, *for both of us.*

243
Ted M. Zurinsky, "Winter Frosting"

Authors, Poets, and Photographers

Lee I. Bruce. My writing reflects my "people person" attitude. This facet of my character results from my roles as a mother, grandmother, therapeutic dietitian, health care worker with the elderly, and church and prison volunteer. While raising a family and working, I hadn't much time for writing. However, as my family grew, so did my involvement in editing and reviewing for food service magazines and family cookbooks. Later, my interest in writing led to membership in the Harford Writers Group.

Susan C. Buttimer. I have always had a fascination with both the creative and the performance arts. I have both published my poetry and shown my photography. In addition, it has been my pleasure and privilege to be a performer and vocal soloist with the Baltimore Symphony Orchestra, the Philadelphia Orchestra, and the Concert Artist of Baltimore. I created *In Harmony*, a program of original music and musings consisting of my photography, poetry, and piano compositions. Hopefully, both product and performance will continue to be hallmarks of my artistic efforts.

Ann M. Cook. After thirty years working in the field of computers, I began writing in earnest. It had been a hobby I always enjoyed. When I retired in 1990, I spent more time than ever before writing fiction, traveling, and gardening.

I completed four semesters of creative writing courses at Harford Community College. I've also been a member of the Harford Writers Group for a number of years. I enjoy the writing efforts of the young and old, the published and the yet-to-be published.

My stories are gathered from my many life experiences, particularly vivid dreams (and, sometimes, nightmares!), and an always active imagination.

Mary Beth Creighton. I am an aspiring novelist who has completed both a romance and a suspense manuscript. I am an Occupational Therapist and adjunct faculty member for the Department of Occupational Therapy at Towson University. I've had much experience writing reports, proposals, and presentations. Writing short stories is a recent and enjoyable interest for me. My three sons inspire me daily. My husband, soulmate and best friend, Jerry, helps me balance all these commitments and interests. My family, work, the outdoors, reading a variety of genres, and—of course—writing satisfies and fulfills my life.

Marie Edmeades. I came to writing late in life. At the age of fifty, I enrolled in graduate classes at Towson State University. My concentration was in the area of art education. A part of this program allowed me to take several art history courses which required that I write papers on artists and their works.

Initially I was overwhelmed with the scope of the assignments, but I gradually found it very satisfying. Since then I have continued to write short essays on a wide range of subjects from Baltimore's City Hall dome to surviving breast cancer. While visiting my son and his wife in Chile a couple of years ago, I was inspired to write *Kume and the Volcano*, an original legend about an indigenous Chilean girl and a special hummingbird.

A decade ago I began work on a historical novel for young people. The story takes place in Baltimore during the late 1870s. I hope to finish it before I am in my late seventies.

Joel Furches. I'm an amateur author who lives in Jarrettsville, Maryland, and currently write a column for examiner.com. I have completed a novel and I'm looking for publication. I've been writing short stories, poetry, and comics my entire life.

I began to write because I was an enthusiastic reader, but was constantly frustrated because I could think of all these great stories that no one was writing. Finally, I began to write the stories *I* was interested in reading.

Joanne Galantino. I am constantly watching people and things around me, and I am endlessly surprised and amused by what I see. Mental notes of these observations, along with my own life experiences, comprise my stories.

I relate very well to children, and remember all too well my struggles growing up. If my stories help a child solve a problem, feel less alone, teach a valuable lesson, build self-esteem, or give him or her courage and hope, then I am fulfilled. I work for and with children, and while I am not their parent, they are looking to me, as an adult, for the answers.

Lois Gilbert. I grew up in Greenville, North Carolina. I attended Duke University where I met Joe Gilbert from Havre de Grace, Maryland. We married and moved to Maryland in 1953. I am the mother of five, grandmother of fourteen, great grandmother of five, and mother-figure to three grand dogs. I write for *The Methodist Visitor,* a monthly publication of the Havre de Grace United Methodist Church and have been published in *Plus* and *Mature Living.*

I will never know what I could have been; I just know I've been what I loved. Every now and then when I'm sitting alone, my mind gives my heart a little shove and I begin to write. I suppose it's just another way for me to talk to God about the many things that have been said or done and the many roads I have trod. Once put down on paper, I knew these heart-thoughts were safe and sound, for the moment just between God and me were but tucked away, later to be found. Now they are all together, these God-talks about your life and mine, and I give them to you my precious ones. You did, indeed, make my heart shine. Shiny with tears sometimes, most times shiny with joy; nevertheless, I praise the Lord above, because I've been able to do what I love!

Karin Harrison. I've nurtured a dream of writing all my life, but did not avidly pursue that objective until my retirement in 2003. I've been writing ever since. All of my stories take place at locations I've personally visited. German is my native tongue; however, I write in English. Mastering the English language remains one of the greatest challenges in my life.

Nancy Heath. The poem *His Way* shows that our choices are not always those of God but He has a better path for us. I am looking forward to writing more poems and am considering a short story based on my most recent experiences. God has inspired my writing with the events of my life and has inspired my photography. I try to capture God's work in nature and that makes me look more deeply into what he has created for us. I have recently attended Harford Community College and hope to continue my studies there. Some of my hobbies are walking, swimming, exercising, and creating a website. My poetry has been inspired by God and his plans for each of us. How much he loves us is amazing to me. I hope to write more and publish more photographs in the near future.

JoAnn M. Macdonald. I began writing in earnest in the late 1980's. My focus was on fiction and short stories. However, when I began researching women in early American history, those of the 1800's particularly, I found that writing biographies was my calling. Through the Unitarian Universalist Association of Congregations' (www.uua.org) Dictionary of Unitarian Universalist Biography (DUUB), in 2001 I answered the offer to contribute a biography of Antoinette Brown Blackwell, the first American woman to become a minister (1853). After Antoinette's bio, I contributed a biography on Maria (Mah RYE-ah) Mitchell—the first American woman to discover a comet, Comet Mitchell IV, (1847). These two women did more for my self-confidence in writing, publishing, and speaking in public than I could ever imagine.

Continuing my interest in American women, I began giving sermons at my church. Unitarian Universalists ordain women, and so I began with Antoinette Brown Blackwell's contribution to American history and Unitarianism.

As a member of the Harford Writers Group I submitted a biographical sketch of Antoinette Brown Blackwell to the group's first anthology, *Voices from the Susquehanna*.

Also, through the Harford Writers Group, I was introduced to the Havre de Grace Decoy Museum in Havre de Grace, Maryland. I wrote three biographies of decoy carvers and decoy collectors as a Contributing Writer for the Museum's quarterly publication *The Canvasback*.

Enjoy reading everything you can get your eyes on!

Leslie B. Picker. While artists paint and sketch to express their creativity, I find that writing enables me to shade, tint and color with words. Finding the right word or phrase to fit a thought is both a challenge and a delight. I have a love affair with words and phrases—especially adjectives. Writing gives me the platform to express myself without self-censorship. I can develop stories that include things I would never say aloud, such as musings and observations. There is nothing more rewarding than expressing oneself through language, music and art.

Peter Raimondi. When I was eight years old, I came down with polio. For the last seventy-five years I have walked with a leg brace on my paralyzed left leg.

I started a scrap drive during WWII because I could not join the armed forces like all of my friends did. This was my first adventure in advocating for a worthwhile cause. I have always been interested in advocating just causes. My first letter was to Congressman Wilber Mills, speaking for the disabled.

In the last several years I have spent much time getting restaurants to furnish chairs with arms so that the disabled and elderly can easily sit and rise. Several years ago I joined the Harford County Writer's group and have enjoyed writing and sharing my writing experiences. For approximately two years I wrote a monthly column for *Prime Time Magazine* called, *This Is How I See Things.*

All of my writing efforts now are focused on getting a level playing field for the disabled and elderly.

Joyce M. Shepherd. I create because my mind overflows with expressions of life. Recently, I completed a project, Constellation Cancer, which follows my journey with metastasized breast cancer and multiple myeloma. My hope, through my writing, is for others to see goodness and gain strength, insight, and hope amidst the chaos.

There are moments when I feel
No contribution is forthcoming. Flashes of
Sadness and 'why' prevail.

I move through those moments,
Those impressions of melancholy,
For they are frosted with miracles
From family, friends, and faith.

    So let my heart-song manifest beauty,
    And share the spirit of joy
    Which I have carried throughout life,
    And strive to share with
    Those who pass through my days.

Sarah Shilko-Mohr. I used to make up stories to entertain myself, pleasant distractions while doing housework. After years of this exercise, the related stories took on their own life and kept jolting me awake at night. After lamenting to a friend about my lack-of-sleep dilemma, she gave me the best advice ever by responding, "Why don't you just write them down!" By the end of the subsequent 550-page novel, a love of writing had been born.

Frank Soul. I started writing in 2004 and I wrote a book and had it published in 2005. The book, *Deep Creek Rod and Gun Club: The Beginning of a Dream* is about two brothers dreaming about starting a hunting and fishing club. A natural consequence was their construction of a cabin in the mountains of Garrett County in western Maryland. Some of this true tale is about the actual hunting and fishing experiences and the firm friendships created. Some of the story is about the lives of the individuals who built the cabin.

    My mom passed away in 2004 and there were many things about our lives and our family she didn't get the chance to tell me. I wrote my first book to help keep our legacy alive, both for my own descendants and for our friends' families. Now they'll always know about our lives and our love of the outdoors. Our lives are preserved—you could say I put my heart and Soul into this book.

David A. Stelzig. Some authors claim to write because they have to. It's who they are. Not me. I don't even particularly enjoy it. I write because I can. And once in a while when I rewrite my rewrites, I come up with a phrase or sentence—on a good day, a whole scene—that truly pleases me. That's not much, but for me it's enough.

Ryan Twentey. I am an Art Educator finishing my tenth year of teaching photography and computer graphics courses at Parkville High School in Baltimore County. I've won several awards for teaching including the Three Arts Club of Homeland Art Education Award and the Maryland Art Education Association's (MAEA) New Art Teacher of the Year Award and am currently nominated for the MAEA Art Educator of the Year Award. My artwork is often only completed in what little spare time I have and spans a wide range of subject matter as many pieces become examples for students. I photograph in both traditional film and digital formats ultimately editing and printing digitally. Aside from teaching, I do freelance design and I've also worked as a Senior Art Education Consultant on the textbook *Communicating through Graphic Design*. My life is complete with my wife Mary Lynn and puppy Golden Retriever, Bodhi.

Carla J. Wiederholt. During my Kansas childhood when threatening weather approached, my Father would stand out on the front porch. He'd look out across the sky, monitor the situation and listen to the weather reports on the portable radio. Mother would watch over my three sisters and me making sure everyone was within reach. We all anticipated what came to be a familiar shout from the porch: "Mother, you and the girls get down to the basement!" Items sure to be in my hands would be my little red diary, my notebook full of poems, and my pillow and blanket. No tornado was going to take my treasures. To this day, I still keep my poetry tucked safely away, guarding my poems as if they were members of my family.

Poetry has been and continues to be a great comfort to me. As I look back through my growing collection, I see that they are the story of my life. They are snapshots of my feelings and thoughts captured with pen and paper. Oftentimes, with my earliest writing, I preferred not to be forthcoming. Hidden deep within what is written are ghosts of words I had not yet mustered up the courage to speak. Later poems find me shouting out those once-hidden words for all to see and hear. My words reflect my life evolving, simply being me, nothing more or less than just who I've become.

Dianna J. Zurinsky. I suppose my interest in photography evolved from the simple practice of capturing cherished moments in the family I love. My interest must have been contagious: both our daughters became prize-winning amateur photographers as teens.

As time passed and I retired from my thirty-six year career in psychiatric nurse management in the Sheppard Health System, I found time to enlarge the scope of my photography to include the fascinating places we visited.

As long as I have a steady hand, a fascination with the unusual and unique, and time to take it all in, I expect to put my Pentax to work.

Ted M. Zurinsky. Over the thirty-two years of teaching English, managing a high school English program as department chair, and nine years of additional part-time work in educational consulting, I've probably read or written tens of thousands of pages. Now, my reading and writing is more of a treat than work. The individuals represented in this volume are practiced, careful creators of new ideas, stories, and photographs. Reading these pages is a pleasure and working with individuals who are dedicated to improving their expressions and presenting fresh scenes and characters is very rewarding.

I suspect you'll see these new voices publishing additional excellent pieces in the years to come. I'm pleased to help bring them to you for what may be your first taste of them.

CPSIA information can be obtained at www.ICGtesting.com
Printed in the USA
BVOW060040160512

290167BV00001B/1/P